LIES
They
Tell You

Jennifer Dennis

Are you the new person drawn toward me?
To begin with take warning, I am surely far different from what
    you suppose;
Do you suppose you will find in me your ideal?
Do you think it so easy to have me become your lover?
Do you think the friendship of me would be unalloy'd satisfaction?
Do you think I am trusty and faithful?
Do you see no further than this façade, this smooth and tolerant manner
    of me?
Do you suppose yourself advancing on real ground toward a real
    heroic man?
Have you no thought, O dreamer, that it may be all maya, illusion?

-Walt Whitman
Are You the New Person Drawn Towards Me?

You ever been in love?

-Harley Quinn
Suicide Squad

PART ONE

Something Borrowed

Madhouse Sonata in the Key of F.U. All
AKA: None of this is any of your business, but what do you care? We all
have to punch a clock.

So I turned in my first journal entry, but my doctor didn't like it. He told me that I was too esoteric and that I should probably try to stick to how I actually feel about things. My concrete feelings. So how's this? I feel like I've been lied to. Not everyone finds love in the world. Sometimes you find the person you're supposed to be with and they die. Not everyone will find happiness or contentment or satisfaction in life despite their constant, endless struggle. We all know that. We do. It's the dark underbelly beneath all of our frantic life strategies and endless self-examination. It's the monster under the bed of our society's pathetic collective id. But here's the thing. That's not the lie I'm talking about. I'm talking about the other lie. The one that says that it's worth it. I want to storm the White House and tear it down brick by brick. I want to blow up the world and then give a big double-fisted kiss to the audience Elvis-style before I collapse back into the abyss like a pile of leaves. But mostly, what I want is to get out of here. And as my father once told me, since I'm no longer interested in getting busy living, what I want to do is to get busy dying. Too esoteric for you? Then try this one on for size—fuck you. Fuck you very much.

CHAPTER ONE

Ophelia

I COULD TELL YOU THE EXACT DAY IT ALL STARTED TO GO wrong, but that isn't really what it's about for you, is it? I've been here for six weeks now ringing the bells at Bedlam, and taking my pills and doing everything I'm told—but somewhere, someone above you has decided that it isn't enough and now it's up to you to "reinvigorate" my progress. Yeah, I heard that word. And let me tell you something else—the reason they've sent me to you isn't nearly the opportunity you think it is. Trust me. I used to work for the kind of company that likes to measure progress with a ruler too, and all I can tell you is that I'm not so much a test for you as a guaranteed black mark on what I can only imagine has been a pretty average, conventional career.

Believe me when I say that that doctor who signs your checks—the one who paces around this floor like a captain, trying to figure out what dead weight he can toss overboard in a storm—I worked for someone like him. I'm not your big chance to prove your therapeutic prowess, I'm a dead end he's looking to write off in someone else's account—someone he doesn't like very much. Someone he doesn't think will be missed.

For some reason, he can't quite get his mind around, no matter how much you people try to reach me—I just can't seem to Get with the Program. So, in the spirit of living drone comradery, I'm going to do something I promised myself I wouldn't. I'm going to give you some of what happened and you can tell him whatever the fuck you want. It won't be the whole story, but trust me, he won't know the difference. Job security in the nuthatch—that's my gift to you. Raise the pages to God and you shall be healed.

So, I got to work late—this was sometime in late September. And it wasn't unusual that I was late, just so you understand that up front. The chronic inability to manage how much time it actually takes me to drive somewhere has been a long running theme in my life. I've tried all sorts of things to train myself out of it. Nothing works. Beneath it, I suspect there is some deep philosophical aversion to leaving my house for any reason whatsoever, but that'll figure in later, so no need to borrow trouble. Anyway, like I said—late.

Most mornings it wasn't about anything at all, but that particular morning it was about finding a quick way to pull together just enough gas money to get me to all the basic city appointments I had to keep the Northville ink flowing. On a weekly paper like ours, our pages of copy were always running neck and neck with the amount of advertisements our sales staff had managed to hustle that week. Maybe hustle is the wrong word for it, but to be honest, it certainly was starting to feel like a hustle for over a year—the time I had been writing there. At that point, our newspaper had basically become a grocery store circular with pretentions. And almost no one read anything at all that we wrote.

As long as we submitted enough pages to round out the advertisements, the Powers That Be swooped through the room like the Pope granting absolution, off to do god knows what on the mysterious second floor. Some people claimed they were going to be our brand-new offices. My co-worker David and I joked that they were probably just some wormhole to another dimension where the owners would flit Doctor Who style back to the seventies when print journalism was all the rage, and then live it up at all-night drug and orgy parties banging their own grandmothers. Who knows? We might've been right. None of us were ever invited up there.

So that morning was about making some quick cash—which for me, meant a humiliating call to my then ex-boyfriend, or a trip to the blood bank to sell some plasma. I chose the plasma. That morning, it took longer than usual because the only girl working was someone who didn't like me and kept me waiting at the front desk—mostly as a point of honor. By the time she got me seated it was already almost eight-thirty, and when I asked if I could move closer to the window, she told me it was impossible even though there were at least three open chairs within eyeshot.

That's the kind of dislike I'm talking about, and we settled into our roles and our comfortable disregard of each other, blood giver and blood letter, as if we sensed a larger social context at play—one which we could never acknowledge but which made us instant, natural enemies. I'm sure, in her mind, there are lots of reasons for it, but the truth is that the kind of people who sell blood for money are uncomfortably easy to spot. I don't look like any of them. I'm clean, wear new clothes, drive a decent running car. This tells her that I am simply Not with the Program. And I have found in my strange and weary travels that there is simply nothing the whole world hates more.

By the time I got in, it was already rounding the corner to twelve o'clock, which was incredibly late—even by my standards. I walked through the room as inconspicuously as I could—dark glasses, coffee in hand—like some half-shamed celebrity that had just been released on bail. I sat down at my desk as David looked up and gave me a wave—strangely and solemnly amused—like he always was, about everything. I pulled off my glasses, turning my head as my editor, Noah, walked past with the determined look of a man of industry and was honestly relieved when he didn't glance in my direction. It was something he had been making a point of doing more and more often, without ever mentioning my unofficial slowdown in any way I could point to. A strange omission that even I could sense wasn't a good thing.

"Have you had a chance to read it yet?"

I glanced up as David took a seat beside me, shuffling some papers onto my desk as if we were deeply involved in some important work discussion and . . . look, the thing about David is that he's hard for me to talk about. I know that you'll say that's exactly why I should talk about him because Christ, that's your line and god bless you, you all say it—but he's just a really good guy who got dragged into this for no reason. Actually, for some reason. My fault. Pure and simple. And I'm not going to get into that right now either, but what I *will* say is that he was just one of those people I really liked to see every day, no matter what. I grew up with brothers and in a lot of ways he kind of reminded me of them—each with that same brand of amused stoicism as if perpetually entertained by my inability to get my life together in any real way. The only difference was that there was no judgement in his empathy.

David never looked at me with pity the way my oldest and only real friend Madge sometimes did. When he found out how cash poor I was following a needlessly messy break-up with my last live-in boyfriend, he simply accepted this new information and adjusted his perceptions accordingly and then went about solving the problem in the kindest and least obtrusive way possible. At the time, I didn't realize how much I leaned on that. That pleasant crutch of someone who was simply always on my side and therefore, saw everything I did through a kinder lens.

David pushed his Kindle across the desk and I flipped through a couple of pages of the comic he had pulled up, drawing my legs up into my chair as I scrolled back to the beginning.

"No. Not yet. When did you get this? Is this the new one?" I asked him.

He gave me a small grin, his dark eyes dancing behind his glasses and pressed his knuckles against his lips as he shook his head. *I know you,* that look said. *Whatever else you're going through, this shit is going to make your day.*

"You have to. Seriously. Take mine. Do it at lunch."

"That good?"

"Excellent. I think the Joker is coming back."

"Seriously?"

"They keep hinting."

"How?" I asked, scrolling through the pages quickly as David raised a hand to the screen and pushed it down toward the desk, nodding in Noah's direction. "When? No. Don't tell me . . ."

"Aww," Madge said, poking her head between us. "Sorry to interrupt this nerd-a-thon mating ritual, but there are important things happening this morning. Oh. I'm sorry. Were you in deep conversation? What is that, like second base for you two? What's next? Do you slide your Kindles together until they're almost touching?"

"Madge" was what she liked to be called. Her full name, and I swear to god I'm not making this up, is Magdalene Lacey McGhee—an unintentionally hilarious porn moniker coined by her crime-show obsessed mother. Madge always wore an armful of colorful enamel bracelets which jingled when she moved, giving even her most caustic comments a slightly festive air, like a sleigh of tiny reindeer jingling all the way.

"They're bringing in a fresh round of temps today—just for festival season." She looked at me significantly. "Or so they say."

I glanced between her and David for a moment, reaching for my coffee and Madge looked down at my arm and seized it like a vulture, picking up my wrist as she turned it around to see the bandage.

"Oh god, not again," she said, rolling her wide green eyes at me in a mixture of alarm and actual anger. "Christ, Lea, I told you I would lend you a few hundred dollars if you needed it. No need to sell off your blood to the highest bidder."

I cringed a little as David leaned closer, yanking my sweater down over my bandage. Then he turned his calm eyes in Madge's direction, wedging his body between us a little as he raised his hands.

"Is that really any of your business?" he asked her mildly.

I pressed my fingers against my forehead as Madge cut her eyes in his direction, shaking her head at him until her glossy bobbed hair bounced.

"I'm not being a bitch. I'm offering because I can. And because she needs it. And by the way, that white-knight act is only endearing when you're actually sleeping with her, you know. Tell me, David, do they even allow that on the planet you come from?"

"Shut up, Madge," I said, brushing my fingers in her direction as Noah led a group of girls down the hallway. "I'm fine. I told you that."

I watched him abandon his new recruits importantly when they reached the outer cubicles that separated the sales department from our sad little collection of desks along the far wall, thinking that if ever we needed a reminder about what kind of talent the paper really valued, that argument wouldn't go much farther than those two rooms. Madge glanced in the girls' direction, bringing herself up to her full height as they fluttered together like a collection of restless racehorses and looked them over as her expression darkened, nodding to the men from the breakroom who came wandering out to gawk at them as if entranced.

"Fucking Noah and his cheerleader fetish," she said, rolling her jaw as David glanced in my direction. "Seriously, Lea, has he even offered to hire you on since last quarter?"

I felt my stomach tighten as Noah reemerged from the IT office, all smiles and graciousness to his newest round of bright-eyed alpha females eager to take my job, and ducked a little lower behind my cubicle wall as Madge walked over to introduce herself, admiring her determination to establish a pecking order as if it were her birthright.

I had honestly never seen Madge get intimidated by anyone. She was beautiful in a way that thin, fashionable girls could never quite get their minds around. She had a twin brother, Thomas, who was just about the most beautiful, gracious person I had ever met and when he was in town, every party would always end the same way—with the two of them in some corner somewhere, cackling like maniacs, those two royal heads pressed together as if trying to decide how to divide the world between them.

My eyes turned from one girl to the next, each a variation on the blonde, play to kill theme, and decided that out of the three, the one hanging back next to the wall seemed to be the only non-sequitur—a sweet, unassuming audience to her friends' aggressive friendliness. I cleared my throat as I noticed David was staring, his brow furrowing a little at my expression, and sat back in his chair as he reached for his Kindle, tucking it into my purse.

"Don't worry about Madge," he said. "She doesn't know what she's talking about. She shoves her anxiety off on other people."

"He really hasn't though, David. I can't remember the last time he brought it up."

"If he hires one of them instead of you, I'll quit in protest."

I smiled at how serious he sounded and felt it freeze on my face as Noah cleared his throat, extending his arm behind the quiet girl's back as he catapulted her in my direction. The entire room turned as the two of them passed down the aisle into our collection of cubicles—Noah calmly leading as if courting her through some kind of old-world promenade.

"Ophelia, this is Abbie," he said, with just enough petty enjoyment to make me grit my teeth. "She handles the Northville area."

The girl raised her brows, smiling gently as she started to extend her hand and then pulled it back at the last second as if embarrassed.

"Ophelia?" she asked, her voice a sweet half-whisper that floated through the air as if it were in italics. "I love that. Is that your real name?"

"My dad was a lit major. Hazard of the trade. Everyone just calls me Lea."

And then she smiled and all my worst fears came true, because her smile absolutely transformed her. No longer the cute sidekick to a gang of ambitious alpha females, one who you suspected only rose to the level of other girls around her by being so perfectly and obviously blonde. There is something about that particular shade of pale blonde, the kind you have to be born with and can never quite be imitated, which has a way of inching cute, delicate features into that strange nether region of the eternally coveted. When she smiled, it was worse. She became an absolute fluttering blonde froth of femininity, so heartbreakingly lovely that I hated her instantly and irrationally.

"That's nice too. Unusual."

I sat there in my unwashed brown hair and my overly made-up eyes in the face of this timid, doe-eyed temp, wondering how thin of an excuse I would need to bolt out of the room, and raised my brows as Noah turned to me with an expression just short of triumphant before nudging her in my direction.

"Thought you two could kind of work the beat together for a while. You know, take her downtown, show her the lay of the land."

I started to laugh before I realized he was serious and then smiled a little too brightly.

Ah, fuck, I thought. *Not really.*

"Oh sure," I said as she looked around for a chair. "Absolutely. Yeah, you know. Absolutely."

"Not a lot of stuff," he insisted, with just enough emphasis for me to realize that he meant exactly the opposite. "Maybe just the town hall meeting. Some of the festival stuff. I know there's a lot of it this time of year."

"There is," I choked as I caught Madge's face out of the corner of my eye, her expression frozen somewhere between horror and delight. "It'll be nice to have some help."

Noah ushered Abbie into his office as she turned and thanked me in that shy voice of hers and I did my best not to snap my pen in half, realizing as he closed the door that I had underestimated Noah's hatred of me by leaps and bounds. He didn't just hate me, he hated that anyone liked me. And he was hoping to correct the issue with my strongest supporter there by drawing the most direct comparison he could between everything she was and everything I wasn't. *My god*, I thought. *I finally understand Lilith Fair.*

I shook my half-full coffee cup around as Abbie's friends rounded the corner to the sales department. I grabbed my pack of cigarettes out of my purse, pocketing them quickly before heading for the breakroom. Madge glanced up as I entered, shaking her head a little as she held up her hand and rested her back against the counter as she picked up her coffee mug.

"What did I tell you?" she said, rolling her big, judgemental green eyes at me as I cracked the plastic top off of my cup. I refilled it with the last of the lukewarm sludge at the bottom of the coffee pot.

"It's just for a few months. And we do need the help. Fall festival? Fire and Ice? Chili cook-off?"

"My god, *listen* to yourself. You could write that crap in your sleep."

I turned as one of the newest IT guys stepped into the breakroom and glanced at both of us as he plucked one of his earbuds out and moved his hand around in a circle.

"Copies?"

Madge glanced at him over the top of her cup.

"Yes. Very good. Now try using it in a sentence."

The kid glanced at me as I pointed him toward the hall, and left looking crestfallen as Madge followed him with her eyes.

"Goddamn that kid's depressing."

"He's actually all right. You don't always have to be so rude to him."

"Don't I, Lea? Don't I? Look, don't be nice to that girl."

"Abbie?"

"Right. Whatever. The siren sitting at your desk. That's what gives them their power you know."

I patted around in my other pocket for my lighter and pulled it out, glancing at the back door.

"I'm not going to be rude to her."

"I didn't say not to be polite. I said not to be *nice*. That's what these girls do. They sidle up to someone like you, someone just as pretty but a little less . . . polished, and start complimenting them on their hair and their work and their bags. And pretty soon, you're out of a job. Haven't you ever seen *All About Eve*? *Single White Female*? Girls like that are the enemy, Lea. Never forget that."

"It's funny that you call her that because D.C. has this whole Sirens thing . . ."

"Yeah," she said picking up her cup. "Good. Keep talking like that. That's perfect. Oops. Gotta run. I have three full pages of copy this week and I want to make damn sure they run every bit of it."

I headed for the backdoor as she swept around the corner, tapping a cigarette out of my pack, and paused as Abbie looked up at the end of the storage room, smiling a little as she noticed me.

"Lost?"

"Noah sent me back here for supplies but . . ."

I tipped my finger toward the closet along the far wall.

"Through there. The time clock is right around the corner."

"That's right. I should've remembered. He was just kind of walking us through so quickly . . ."

She laughed as if this was a joke between us and I found myself hating her a little more without meaning to—and also without apology. After all, she was the one that biology had decided—in all of its elegant, random brutality—to back from one generation to the next. I watched her walk past, thinking that all her life people would see that fluffy little shock of white blonde hair and men would smile and doors would swing wide open. She would be one of those girls who would become some sort of actress or news anchor and the whole time, she would just flutter shyly in front of the cameras that everyone pushed into her delicate, fine-boned face and say that she really didn't know how it all happened. She would go to her grave thinking that people were just naturally generous and open and kind and would be so grateful for it all—a living unicorn—so eternally humbled by everyone's support and their willingness to try so hard to make all of her dreams come true.

I headed out the back door, glancing at the clock as I tucked my cigarette into my mouth and reached for my lighter as I headed out into the parking lot behind the building, squinting at the sun as I lit up. I turned my eyes toward the road, the dark sign in front of the bar I rented an apartment over just visible from my angle and found myself thinking about Jacob—a strange irrational rush of homesickness for the comfortable emptiness of our relationship passing through me as I paced along the blacktop. After all, Jacob and I had always been better friends than lovers, and life had been easy with him. Simple, efficient.

Both writers and solitary creatures on our best days, we organized our time together in lazy two- to three-hour spurts before retreating off into our separate offices five nights out of seven. When Jacob finally realized that I was actually serious about leaving him and not having, what he liked to refer to as one of my "fits", he became very calm and simply started asking all of the pertinent questions. Who would move out? When? Where would I go? Would there be a reconciliation period? No passion, no tears—just straightforward problem-solving.

I had once joked that if Jacob had been in charge of bringing our troops back from the Middle East, it would've been organized like the invasion of Normandy in reverse. Everybody in, everybody out—planes in the air, ships at sea and everyone home in time for Sunday dinner. Jacob never had seen the point of investing in anything that appeared, on the surface, to be an enterprise of more loss than gain. What was the point, he wondered, once you were really losing? Why let the house win it all?

I wondered what he was working on, pondering if I had ever really given, the kind of technical writing he did, the attention it deserved and crushed my cigarette beneath my heel as I forced myself to do a quick merciless rundown of all the reasons we weren't together—beginning with the big ugly fight that had started it all. I pulled my hair out of the low ponytail it was in and headed back inside, brushing my fingers through the ends as I headed for the bathroom.

"It's not what I expected."

"It's just a temp job."

I paused in the hall as I saw Abbie speak to someone along the outer wall of the breakroom and took a step backward as the guy she was talking to circled her casually, glancing around at the chipped tile and coffee mug littered counter as he shrugged.

"I know. But what do you plan to do with it? Give me your best endgame here. I'm sure you don't want them to actually hire you."

"I might want to be a reporter."

"You're a poet, not a reporter."

I watched her smile and stiffen from the doorway, the look on her face telling me that this had become a strange fight between them. One that looked something like his desire to see her as unconventional and her desire to become someone he admired. He paused when he noticed me, his eyes sweeping over my face as Abbie raised a hand, and I panicked as I got my first good look at him, his face so strikingly handsome, I blinked.

"Jordan, this is Ophelia. Sorry, Lea. She's the girl I'm going to be shadowing for a little while."

I stepped into the breakroom, making a conscious effort not to stare as I raised a hand, and reached for my coffee cup, suddenly aware of every movement I made as if the simple magnetism of his attention had knocked my equilibrium out of whack.

"Hi. Nice to meet you."

"Ophelia, huh?"

"Yeah. My dad had a Shakespeare thing."

Jordan tilted his head a little to meet my eyes and I held my breath as I noticed how blue they were, watching him brush his long dark hair away from his face.

"She's the one who goes nuts and then drowns herself, right?"

"That's the one. Died of a broken heart. Hard to top a death like that, but you know. Fingers crossed."

He looked me over curiously for a moment, not arrogantly—not exactly. More like he was sending out feelings underground, like some kind of in-born seismic wave detector. When he was through, he made a decision. He smiled.

I don't believe in love at first sight. In truth, I'm not really sure that love exists at all—not for long anyway. But I do believe in belonging. In belonging to something larger than yourself and recognizing it. And his smile was like a flood of dawn in a dark room. A room I didn't know existed until he stepped right in without invitation and flipped on a switch. I shifted my coffee from one hand to the other, suddenly feeling like there was too much space everywhere around me, and his expression softened a little, as if he was quite used to the way women reacted to his movie-star good looks and it merely amused him.

"How long have you been working here, Lea?"

"I think a little over a year now. I started as an intern. Well, technically I'm still an intern . . . just a paid one."

He raised his brows as he glanced around the breakroom, glancing up at the flickering fluorescent light that sputtered strobe-like above the exit and then swung his attention back to me as I tapped my fingernails against my cup, barely able to bring myself to meet his gaze.

"And do you like it? Being a reporter?"

His voice made it worse. Voices are important to me. He had a good one.

"It's not terrible. I've had worse jobs. At least you're getting paid to write, you know?"

"See?" Abbie said, stepping forward to slide her hand down his arm. "That's what I said. At least you're getting paid to do something you love."

I felt a quick jolt of irrational jealousy as she coiled her hand into his and gave him one of those shy, half smiles. We were friends for now—two against one. Jordan glanced at her as Abbie pressed her lips together at his expression, and I looked at him quickly as I noticed the diamond band around her finger.

"Engaged?" I blurted out before I could stop myself and Jordan glanced back at me, the humor in his eyes darkening a little as he brought his ringed left hand against his chest for a moment.

"Nope," Abbie said, squeezing him a little tighter. "Everyone thinks that. Married. Five years in May."

"Wow," I said. "That's really great. Five years. That's something."

Abbie leaned a little closer to him and Jordan's expression changed as he held my eyes.

Aren't you going to ask me if I like it?

I set my cup down as I heard his voice in my head so distinctly, I blinked and glanced up as another one of the sirens rounded the corner, dragging my eyes away from him as he gave me a sudden brilliant smile. Abbie disengaged instantly, all of her attention turning to a girl she had been separated from for less than an hour and watched them chatter together excitedly before they pulled Jordan into the fold, the circle closing in front of me as Abbie turned in my direction.

"I'm sorry?" she said, the apology in her voice turning everything into a question. "I actually have to meet with my recruiter downtown? Noah said it would be all right if I started officially tomorrow . . ."

"Sure," I said. "Why not? Tomorrow's fine."

"Around ten?"

I raised my brows, picking up my cup as I tried not to let my irritation show and finished what was left of it. Ten thirty was better for me. Less hard edges.

"Ten's great," I muttered, heading for the door. "I'll be here right around then."

"Nice meeting you, Ophelia," Jordan said, his expression once more relaxed and disengaged.

I glanced up at him as I walked past, my nails digging into my cup as he turned to watch me go.

"You too," I said, all my frantic nervous energy wilting under his stare. "Nice meeting you."

I took a deep breath as I bolted down the hall, pressing my hand against my face and headed for the bathroom as I saw David glance up from his desk, letting the door slam shut behind me as I set my coffee cup down on the counter. I flipped on the overhead lights, turning on the water as I heard Abbie's soft, lilting voice pass down the front hall and ran my hand through my unwashed dark hair, leaning a little closer as the fluorescent glare seemed to magnify every wrong turn my life had taken lately.

I hadn't been sleeping well. I blushed at how dark my eyeliner seemed against my pale, washed-out skin, and ran a finger beneath my lower lids, trying to will it back from all-night fuck fest into unassuming bohemianism. I gave up as my mind conjured up the clear dark tenor of his voice, running over the question I'd heard in my mind and shut the faucet off as Abbie's angelic face seemed to float next to mine in the mirror—evolution's sweetheart versus the grunge era's last stand.

Jesus, I thought, pulling my hair back with both hands and tucking it into a slightly more presentable bun at the bottom of my neck. *Get a grip already. He's just some guy. Some insanely beautiful guy who happens to be married to the perfect girl one cubicle over from you that's just dying to take your job. Game faces, sweets. Time to start thinking strategically. Eventually, it's going to come down to her or you. Natural selection can be a bitch.*

I tossed my cup into the garbage, flicking the lights off as I stepped out into the hall and paused as Madge glanced at me from the front doorway, looking up and down the sidewalk for a moment before noticing my expression. She laughed a little, striding over as she popped her nicotine chewing gum loudly, tilting her head at me. She had been off of cigarettes for about three months at that point and refused to vape to ease the cravings. According to Madge, addictions were supposed to hurt a little when they went. Otherwise, what was the point?

"Aww. You took your hair down for him."

"You saw him too?"

"Sweet, sweet Lea. Everyone saw him. The whole sales department is in an uproar."

"He seemed nice."

"You talked to him?"

"Just for a few seconds. She's married to him, you know. Abbie."

"Siren number . . ."

"The blonde one. The blonde blonde one."

Madge rolled her eyes and smiled around her gum.

"Typical. If it's any consolation to you, he doesn't seem like the type that will stay married for long."

"Five years?"

"That long? Really? The girl must have skills."

"Or maybe they just love each other?"

"Wouldn't that be nice? And don't get hung up on him. Trust me, right now, a guy like that is the last thing you need. Best admired from a distance."

"Get hung up on him?"

"Me. Remember? He's in a band, you know. Local one. They play around here sometimes."

Her expression softened a little as I looked up quickly.

"Really? What's the name?"

"See? That's the look. Poor Lea. Already a goner. Think summer thunderstorm. Think category five tornado. Let's go out tonight. Some place terrible. That little dive bar below your apartment. You need a night out. I'll get the scoop on what's-his-face for you and you can tell me all about staring into those blue, blue eyes of his."

"His name is Jordan."

Her wide eyes danced as her red lips pulled into a too-wide smile. Her Cheshire-cat smile—all devilish enjoyment at someone else's expense.

"Of course, it is."

"I have that zoning thing."

"That'll have you home by eight-thirty. What's on the agenda then? Quilting bee until nine? Late-night prayer circle? Live a little, Lea. You have to come back to the land of the living sometime. Just text me when you're out."

She turned as the Noah rushed past, her attention pivoting on him like a hungry predator and held up her phone as she flagged him down.

"When you're out," she said, glancing over her shoulder. "Don't forget."

I started to argue and then shrugged and headed back to my desk, sinking in front of my desk as David stepped into the IT office, his face uncharacteristically worried as he threw a glance in my direction. I was barely paying attention. I pulled up the two stories I was churning out one paragraph at a time on my computer, shifting between them for a moment without a flicker of interest and felt all the butterflies in my stomach burst into flight as I thought of the way he had smiled before I left, one that was not quite an invitation. More like a dare.

Aren't you going to ask me if I like it?

Tornado, Lea, I reminded myself as I flipped through my notes. *Beautiful, utter devastation. Lives left in ruin.*

Would it be that bad?

I brushed my long bangs behind my ear as I shook my head, typing quickly as I reached for my earbuds. Because here's the other thing about me. The one you've probably figured out by now unless you're the least perceptive therapist that ever rolled out of Michigan State on the wings of your seventy-thousand-dollar degree. I also didn't care. Consequences aren't really the stop-gap you think they are—not to an addict. That's why I told you going into this that I'm not going to be the patient who does you any professional favors. Because what non-addicts never get, is that it doesn't matter what you're addicted to—it's the passion you're after. And until you can find a cure for that, until you can find a way to replace passion in someone's life—until you can offer me something that makes me feel like he did the first time I saw him smile—it's all just one long desert rain. That's the trick, you know. Sell us something better.

CHAPTER TWO

AS IT TURNED OUT, THE ZONING MEETING RAN LONG AND I ended up texting Madge from my apartment, just so I could change out of my work clothes and shake off the day a little. She was right though. I didn't get out enough, and the place I rented after the break-up was a colossally bad apartment. And I mean really bad. The kind of apartment Sartre would've had a lot of fun imagining. Dark rooms, stained wallpaper, weird, low, exposed wood beams lining the ceiling. The bedroom was the only real bright spot in the place, kind of a little pocket of warmth tucked away at the back of the house, but for the most part, it was essentially uninhabitable. It's the kind of place that when the door swings shut behind you, you actually feel the weight of a thousand wrong turns in life flying through your mind like some kind of terrible, cosmic blooper reel and you think, *Wow. I have made some really bad choices in my life.*

I headed for the bathroom as she sent a flurry of texts in response and glanced at them briefly before setting my phone face down on the dresser outside my postage-stamp-sized bathroom, shrugging off my long gray sweater. There wasn't any room in that place for superfluous items. There was a tub I never used, butted up against the lip of a toilet that had gone out of date in the seventies and a tiny pedestal sink with about three inches of counter space all the way around. All business, no nonsense. I did my best to scrub off the thick cake of make-up that I always applied when a good night's sleep was about three nights over the horizon and took down my hair, turning my head from one side to the other as I considered the color.

During the last few months with Jacob—when it was obvious that we weren't so much navigating our relationship through some kind of year-long storm, but literally turning it into the rocks just as quickly as we could—I had cheered myself up briefly by dying it auburn, and it still hovered somewhere in the nexus of not-quite brown, washed out around the edges, darker underneath. I twisted it up with one hand, letting my long bangs slide into my eyes like a full-on sex kitten and then let it drop as my phone let out another frantic yelp, shaking my head at it as I headed for the bedroom. I grabbed the first t-shirt dress I laid eyes on, pulling up a pair of black tights as I stood on one foot and reached for my only pair of boots, swiping on a thick coat of eyeliner before shrugging and grabbing my jacket.

I picked up my phone as it pinged again, rolling my eyes as I pulled up Madge's long stream of messages and started to write back before I realized they were a collection of photos, most of them color, one black and white. I scrolled through them quickly, pausing on my way to the door, and pulled my camera closer as I saw they were all professional studio shots—one shot after another of Jordan with his band. I pulled up the first close-up I found, running my fingers over the screen without quite touching it. He looked serious in the photo—serious and relaxed. I felt a strange jolt of recognition as I looked over his too-perfect face, his eyes so blue they seemed to jump off the page and shook my head as I tucked my phone into my pocket, grabbing my purse on the way out the door.

When I got downstairs, Madge was already in deep conversation with the bartender, her eyes cheerful and glazed over as she laughed a little too loudly at whatever he had said. She waved as she noticed me, resting her chin in her hand as I cut through the mid-week crowd and sat down on the stool next to her as she gave my outfit a quick swipe of her eyes.

"I love the nineties. Promise me you won't ever grow up, Lea."

I pulled my phone out and turned the face toward her as her smile became a little brighter.

"Did you like that? I thought you would."

"Should I even try to keep up?"

Madge wiggled her fingers at the bartender, exchanging a meaningful glance with him as she ordered two more drinks. He poured out a cloudy looking gray mix into two tumblers, giving her a smile as he walked away and

Madge turned the full force of her attention on me as I shrugged my coat off, scrolling through my phone casually before pulling the close-up of Jordan up.

"He really is ridiculously good-looking," she mused. "What was that girl thinking, marrying a guy like that?"

"How long have you been down here?"

"Since around eight? Can't really remember. So? Tell me the story. I've been dying to know. You have no idea how much money I would've paid to watch you two meet."

"There wasn't anything to it, Madge. He's just a nice guy. That's all."

"Hmm. Magnetic. He's a nice, magnetic guy. Voodoo eyes. You should tell him that. I bet he'd like it."

She sat up a little straighter as I tucked my phone away and rolled her drink around a little as she laughed quietly.

"Don't get jealous. I was just saying. He's your type, not mine, Lea. I don't get the kind of philosophical thrill you do chasing after all the wrong men. There's very little upside, you know. Once the sex dries up."

She pointed to me lightly, her gesture just uncoordinated enough for me to notice that she was drunk.

"Frankly, I'd rather have you chase him than David, to be honest."

"Oh, really? Why's that?"

"You know why."

I rolled my eyes as I scanned the crowd quickly, taking a long drink as I ran my fingers through the back of my hair.

"He's not gay, Madge."

"That's what you say."

Madge's mom was gay, which she felt gave her a unique perspective on homosexuality. She would lay out her judgements on other people's sex lives like the worst game of I Spy ever conceived.

"I really don't think he is. And anyway, who cares? Why should it matter?"

"Please. You know I don't care. And I'm not against straight people sleeping with gay people either, Lea. I wouldn't exist if they didn't. I just think you should know what you're getting into. That's all."

"Is Tom coming to town for Thanksgiving?"

"Maybe. You know how he is. You can never get a real answer out of him and then he'll just show up on my doorstep at three in the morning. He doesn't even bother making excuses anymore."

"The acting thing?"

"The acting thing. The artist thing. The model thing. It's always something new. The funny thing is, he's brilliant at everything. He's always been that way. Since we were kids. But that just seems to make it worse. It's like he can't force himself to focus, you know. I didn't used to worry about that. Lately though . . ."

She raised her hand as a woman called to her from across the room and then grabbed my shoulder as she turned me toward the door.

"And look at that."

I glanced over my shoulder as David spotted us from across the room and smiled automatically as he raised a hand, wearing the same clothes he'd had on at work with a slightly darker shirt.

"Did you invite him?"

"I just mentioned it," Madge said, emptying her glass. "He must really like you. Out on a school night and all. David! You came."

She gave him an awkward one-shouldered hug that seemed to mystify and flatter him and then took a step back and glanced around, nodding a little at the ramshackle look of the place.

"Nice place."

I nodded back as he grinned.

"It's really not."

"No. I guess not."

"Cheap beer though."

"That's good."

He leaned over the counter as the bartender made the rounds and handed him a five for a Budweiser in the bottle.

"So?" he asked, taking a drink. "What's going on? Did you read it?"

"Actually, we were just talking about whether or not you were gay."

I rolled my eyes as Madge laughed at his expression and then slid off of her bar stool as she patted me lightly on the shoulder.

"You kiddies have fun now."

I sighed as she swept across the room, her long black skirt swishing around her ankles like an incantation and smiled a little as I pushed my bangs away from my eyes.

"Please ignore her. She was shit-faced when I got here."

"Were you really asking that?"

"No. I mean, she was, but she kind of asks about everyone. Her mom is gay. I think she grew up feeling weird about it. So now she makes it a point to be some kind of neutral ambassador of goodwill."

He looked at me curiously for a moment.

"What do you think?"

"No. I never thought so. I mean, I wouldn't care if you were. That would be cool. Whatever."

"You wouldn't care? Not even a little?"

I glanced up at him as he tilted his head at me, leaning against the counter he brushed a smile away from his lips.

"I don't know," I said, finishing my drink. "Maybe a little."

David smiled, glancing toward the doors as another group of patrons bustled through the door and glanced toward my jacket.

"Are you still smoking?"

"Yeah. Here and there. Can't quite make the crossover to vaping. It's just so—"

"Sanitized?"

"That's a good word for it. Sanitized. It's like our bad habits aren't even allowed to be bad anymore. As if vaping isn't just the new health-conscious way to kill yourself. Which, you know, no one seems to mind."

"I can't make the switch either," he said, shoving his hands in his pockets before shrugging at me. "Want to go outside and kill ourselves the old-fashioned way?"

I grabbed my coat as he dropped a tip on the counter, covering it with his bottle and followed him through the crowd, ducking under his arm as he swung the door open for me. We stepped out onto the sidewalk, the long row of streetlamps lining the factory across the road giving us a wide stretch of spotlight. We shunned it as naturally as vampires, heading for the dark corner of the road under the overhang, and avoided the annoyed glances of the people vaping around us, as always—a party of two. I had a cigarette out before he did, which David lit automatically and then took a long drag as he looked up at the moon, the ghost of its yellow half-full body visible for a scattershot of seconds before disappearing behind a cluster of clouds.

"I really didn't want to come out tonight," I said, huddling a little closer to him as a cluster of people crossed the parking lot behind us, heading for the entrance. He raised his brows and then glanced up at the windows above the bar, pointing to it with his cigarette.

"Don't you live right there?"

I glanced overhead as he gave me a look and laughed as I shrugged into my jacket, tilting my head at him as his eyes ticked from one window to the next.

"Yeah. Your point?"

He held up his hands.

"No judgement. Just an observation. I get it. Trust me."

"I'm not really big on going out in general."

"Me neither. I guess that's why I decided to become a reporter."

"Same here. I don't really like other people that much."

"Tell me about it. And I'm not really interested in their lives or how they feel about things."

"I think we picked the right paper for it."

"Yes. Indeed, we did."

He glanced up at my windows again and I watched the shadows play over his expression as he wandered into the light, the sharp contrast emphasizing the handsome angles of his face.

"Is that your bedroom?"

"No. It's in the back. Why?"

"No reason. Just curious."

"Because you're a stalker?"

He grinned as my phone went off and I glanced at it and then raised my brows—turning the screen to face him as he walked back over.

"Who is it?"

"Who do you think?" I asked, flicking my cigarette to the ground as I typed back a message to Madge quickly.

"Madge is . . . something."

"She's a mom with no kids, that's what she is. You should see how she acts with her brother. Her twin brother."

"Oh, I believe it. That guy I saw you with earlier."

"What guy?"

"In the breakroom. One of the temps was there . . ."

"Oh. Him. That's Abbie's husband."

"The short blonde one? She's married?"

"I know, right? Five years. Isn't that nuts?"

"How old is she?"

"Twenty-three, maybe? Twenty-four?"

"I would've guessed younger. Jesus. Right out of high school, huh? That's kind of retro."

He glanced up at me curiously as the streetlights turned his glasses into a smooth, reflective pool.

"What's he like?"

"Her husband? I don't know. Normal. Confident. I guess."

"Confident?"

I looked back toward the door as I tapped my ashes onto the sidewalk.

"I don't know. I overheard them arguing about her temping there. As if he thought she was too good for the place or something."

"Well, we're all too good for the place."

"True. Still, I don't know. I guess he's in a band or something. That's what Madge said."

"I heard actor."

"You heard he was an actor? From who?"

"Just one of the other temps. The red-blonde one."

"In what? Movies?"

David tilted his head at me and then let out a long stream of smoke, the light turning it into a dark cloud around his head.

"Don't know. Didn't care enough to ask."

I took another drag of my cigarette as my mind reeled and brushed my hair from my face and then tucked it behind my ear, as a clear, perfect image of Jordan's face burned through my thoughts like a nuclear blast. When I glanced up, David had stepped out of the light and was watching me carefully, the frown of annoyance on his face so rare, I had to scramble to place it.

"He sounds like kind of a dick, if you ask me."

"No. I wouldn't say that. Maybe . . . reserved? He was friendly enough once Abbie introduced us."

I watched his expression become a polite blank as his phone rang in his pocket and he raised his hand to me, turning away quickly.

"Give me a minute," he said, his voice clipped and even.

I lit another cigarette, happy and anonymous on our little patch of sidewalk and watched him speak quietly and emphatically to someone on the other line, the crowd shifting around like a school of fish. I sighed as my screen lit up with a sudden avalanche of texts and scrolled through them without much interest, tucking my phone into my pocket as David hung up.

"Who was that?" I asked as he lit another cigarette, glancing over his shoulder as a small crowd vaping in front of the door rolled their eyes in our direction. He held up his hand as one of the younger guys nodded in our direction and then shook his head as they all turned their backs on us at once.

"See that?" he said, smiling a little as he walked back over. "Cultural cold war. Our kind are dying hard, Lea."

"Who was that?"

"Oh. Just my mom. My little brother moved out a few months ago and she's not really used to being in the house alone. So when I go out, I just try to check in. That's all."

"I understand. That's cool."

"It is definitely not cool. I really should be going though. I have that interview tomorrow morning with the city planner at 8:30."

"In the morning?"

"That's exactly what I said. If Noah didn't want to run it with the pavilion thing this week, I would've rescheduled. Is that really still her?"

He looked down at my jacket as my phone rumbled in my pocket like an angry hummingbird. I pulled it out and turned it in his direction, scrolling through the mountain of three-word texts and emojis like I was spinning the wheel on *The Price is Right*.

"See what I mean? She kind of goes into hyper social mode when she's drinking."

David rolled his jaw at me and then held out his hand.

"Here. Give me that."

He tossed his cigarette as he typed something into my phone quickly and then held up his finger as I reached for it back, shaking his head. He raised his brows as the phone went off and then laughed as he turned it around for me to read it.

Can't right now. Upstairs with David. Talk tomorrow.

What?????

David shut the phone off mid-chime and then handed it back to me, reaching for his lighter.

"Easy enough."

"For you. Eventually I have to turn the phone back on, David."

"Didn't you say you wanted to leave? There's your excuse."

"That's really not the point."

"Look, Madge just needs some boundaries. She doesn't actually want to know everything that's going on in your life the moment it happens. She's just lonely."

"I think she just wants to feel like she's part of everything."

"What do you think being lonely is?"

I paused as he turned toward the parking lot, reaching for his cigarettes before dropping his hand.

"When I get lonely, I just kind of shut down. Draw the curtains, head under the covers. Watch old movies."

"Yeah, that's the normal, human response.

He held up his hand and then tapped his curled fingers like a claw over his other palm.

"Sarcophagus, Lea," he said. "The art of containment. Trust me. I'm a master."

He raised his eyes toward the windows of my apartment pointedly for a moment before grinning.

"Still. What are you going to tell her tomorrow?"

"What should I tell her?"

His eyes ran over me slowly for a moment as his grin widened and gave me a shrug, glancing at me over his shoulder as he turned around.

"Tell her whatever you want. Good night, Lea."

"Stalker."

I watched him walk across the parking lot, raising my hand as he reached his car. I waited until he pulled out of the lot, some ancient superstition holding me in place until his taillights where a little red blip on the horizon and shook my head as I headed back to the door. I waited politely while a gang of college kids burst through the door at once and caught a quick glimpse of Madge talking animatedly to a table of admirers, her enamel bracelets jangling so cheerfully I could practically hear them from the street. I took a step back quickly as the door slammed shut, knowing I should go back inside—and not quite able to make myself do it, I walked down the length of the building before disappearing around the back, the noise dulling a little as I reached the wooden stairwell leading up to my apartment.

I took the steps quickly, a thousand brutal winters making the wood quake under my feet, and paused when I got to the small balcony outside my bedroom, the brand-new guardrail very white in the darkness. I opened the screen door, shoving the backdoor hard above the knob and stepped inside as it creaked and then swung wide, catching it with one hand as I stepped inside. The truth was, the lock to my door had never worked properly. After a few frustrated calls to my landlord, who seemed to file my complaint under Other Things Women Bitch About, I gave up and started shoving my dresser in front of the door at night, the idea that I had very little a motivated thief might want to steal, beating a comforting refrain in my mind.

I had taken very little in the break-up, like a passenger lowering herself onto a lifeboat off of a sinking ship—all useless items, precious only to me. I had gone back for my computer and desk, and then replaced the rest of my furniture in fits and spurts, a garage sale coffee table here, a cheap mattress there. I splurged on comforters and pillows, the last expensive purchase I had made since moving out and reasoned that I spent most of my days off in bed anyway, books scattered everywhere, laptop within reach. As I shrugged off my jacket, I pulled out my phone and tossed it onto the bed, pulling my hair up into a ponytail as I headed for the kitchen. I grabbed a can of pop out of the door, noting that aside from that there was exactly one half-gallon of milk and a jar of spaghetti sauce in the fridge and kicked the door shut as I padded across the living room floor—the music from the bar downstairs thumping mildly under my feet.

I set my pop down as I slid into bed like a teenager, pulling my plush gray and white comforter over my head and reached for my phone as I tapped at the screen impatiently, scrolling through Madge's fresh wave of texts as I glanced at the clock. It was after eleven. I thought idly about texting her back, choking back my guilt as I scrolled to her earlier messages and pulled up the first shot of Jordan with his band as I studied it carefully, passing to the next one with a quick swipe of my fingers. I paused as I came to the one of him alone again, reading the short bio below the pic and danced my fingers over his face again as I tugged the blanket a little farther over my head, thinking of his smile as his blue eyes burned through the screen.

Madge's right, I thought, searching for a link to their website as I blushed, his face so beautiful I could barely bring myself to look at him. *Trouble, trouble, trouble. The guy's too good-looking. How could she marry a guy like that? I would be looking over my shoulder my whole life.*

Maybe. The question is, how would you say no?

"Good point," I muttered as the website popped up under my fingers, all black and white—very artsy. I started to scroll through the pictures again—some crowd shots, some professionally done—and tapped the first video I found as I reached for my can of pop, sitting up to take a drink while I waited for it to load. I felt a quick, vicious desire for their music to be terrible, the idea that I was standing at the edge of a dark sea and that the sand was shifting too quickly below my feet filling me with dread, and set the phone down as if it would burn me as I took a deep breath.

Not even bad, I thought. *Just not good. Not my style. Whatever. Just so this all can stop. And he can just be some other beautiful guy that I don't connect with and in a few weeks, I won't even really think about him anymore. And his face will fade from my mind and he'll just be Abbie's husband . . .*

And then I heard his voice. I looked at the phone out of the corner of my eye as the first song on the list began to play and picked it up like a sleepwalker as I set my pop down, cradling the phone in my hands as my eyes darted over the screen. I turned up the volume, my mind drawing up a perfect memory of his speaking voice and looked back down, as Jordan paced restlessly in front of the crowd, some dark shadow of people reaching toward him at the front of the stage. His voice was clear and dark and beautiful. Powerful. Moving. I listened as I pressed my lips together, watching the camera shift to his face and felt the sand shift more violently as his band raged around him, my fingers quaking a little as I listened to the next song and the next.

By the fourth song, I had set the phone down again and ran my hands against my temples as they launched into another track, the melody so achingly beautiful I got out of bed and paced around it as I fished through my coat for my cigarettes.

Oh no, I thought, lighting up on the fourth try as I watched my fingers dancing in front of my lips. *Oh no, oh no, oh no...*

AFTER A WHILE, YOU START TO TELL YOUR THERAPIST ABOUT your dreams—little things, the kind that won't give anything away. You tell her that you have been having the same dream for as long as you can remember. You wake up and your whole family is dead and so you go into the kitchen and make yourself a bowl of cereal and watch cartoons. She will be interested. Happy that you're finally Opening Up. "Do you ever think that's why you read comics?" She'll say. And you'll say, "I never really thought about it." But of course, you have. You have already thought about everything she's thought about, only a long time ago. You read comics because they placate you and make you happier. And the one thing you can never ever tell her is that the dream isn't really a dream, but a fantasy.

At the bottom of it all, down deep where your sickness started to take root and grow, you secretly wonder what it would've been like not to have parents who hate you and who trained your siblings to hate you. And then the world. And it doesn't matter how pretty you are or how smart you are. It doesn't matter that teachers are always impressed by you and encouraging you in the way that good adults will, because in the end, they will find a way to dismiss you. And then the world will understand, the way a pack of hungry jackals comes to understand, that you have no home-court advantage. They can treat you any way that they want because no one will ever defend you. In the end, their long game isn't even about teaching you to hate yourself, although that's what happens. Their long game is about making themselves feel better about hating their own kid—and how better to do that than to convince everyone around you how fundamentally unlovable you actually are.

They will take your voice from you, so you will learn to write. And when the jackals take that, you will learn to kill.

Eventually, you will begin to change. One day, you will get tired of being the only person around who doesn't see yourself as easy prey. And you will be certain that they will all understand that too. The way everyone understands everything. Once it's far too late.

I've already decided that you're not going to get this page of things. I told you I'd tell you some of what happened, not all of it. When I leave, I will take these pages with me and bury them in some metal container like a time capsule and scroll a big hazmat insignia on the side. Sarcophagus, baby. Toxic contents. Half-life of a thousand years. If the human race survives that long, maybe someone will dig them up someday and puzzle them out—put them on tour like the Egyptian hieroglyphics. And then, as every generation has ever done since the dawn of time, they will find a way to misinterpret everything and turn me into a god. Or the devil. No telling which.

CHAPTER THREE

I DIDN'T SEE HIM AGAIN FOR TWENTY-NINE DAYS. IT WAS SIX days before Halloween and the moon had the same waxing half-moon shape that it had when I first met him, as if the lunar cycles where suddenly pivoting to the magnetic weight of my obsession. October had always been my favorite month. And not just because Michigan blooms with color everywhere you look—whole swaths of trees going red orange at once as if caught in the crossfire of some primeval fire. There was an edge to fall, a subtle quickening. People seemed more animated, stores leapt to life and every conversation seemed to hum with the soft thrill of anticipation, gently at first and then growing stronger. What can I say? The ancient rhythms of farm country are very hard to shake. And beneath it all, I suspect it's merely an echo of that collective memory running through the bloodline of everything we do. *Harvest time*, it whispers. *Work hard now and survive the winter. Food and plenty. Mate, mate, mate.*

To that end, I had essentially taken Abbie completely under my wing at that point—dragging her to meetings, introducing her around. On a professional level, I had to admit that she took to the art of reporting, which essentially just boils down to being a sympathetic ear for residents to open up to, much more naturally than I did. People bloomed around her. They took one look at that shy half-smile of hers and stumbled all over themselves to be accommodating. *How can I help?* their expressions said. *Ask me anything.*

As someone who had worked the beat for over a year and felt that they had cultivated certain city relationships slowly and painstakingly, her instant acceptance was almost an insult—one that I would've been more worried about if my mind hadn't been absolutely fixated on bleeding her for as much information about Jordan as I could. It wasn't as difficult as it sounded. Abbie was an easy person to work with—shy, quick to trust, and once she considered me an ally, she opened up like a high schooler about their whirlwind courtship and marriage, gushing over photos in her phone while I scrolled through them like a sleepwalker and then looked up my favorites online, saving them shamelessly, utterly helpless.

There was one in particular that I returned to over and over again. It had been taken at a festival when he and Abbie had just been dating. She was nineteen then, she told me. He was twenty-eight. They were sitting on a pink-and-red striped blanket in the middle of the crowd, several people behind them in a vast, green, sunny field. Abbie was wearing some loose bohemian dress, a colorful flower crown woven through her white-blonde hair. Jordan was sitting next to her, smiling at her gently as she leaned against him and there were a handful of white daisies in his long, dark hair—a latter day Jim Morrison, the exiled king. I loved that photo. Loved it and hated it. Eventually, I cropped Abbie out of it completely and made copies in black and white, tucking them all into a secret folder on my desktop—photos that I would go over at night before I slept until his face burned behind my eyelids like a magic spell.

David hadn't been wrong either. He was an actor too, Abbie told me. Just starting out. He had starred in some small independent film that one of his friends had made and though it hadn't made any money, Abbie assured me he was brilliant in it. A total natural. I listened attentively, like I always did, and then managed to hunt down a used copy of it online and watched it on my computer with my face three feet from the screen, eating up every moment, every turn of his eyes. In it, Jordan played the brother of young addict who was gradually descending into madness and the camera lingered on him like a lover, following him around when he walked until the two seemed to become shadow images of each other—a man desperate to save himself from his own worse fate.

I watched it over and over again—listened to his music, let my obsession grow. It filled up my mind like a lush garden, and by the time the Halloween party Madge insisted David and I accompany her to had rolled around, it was in full, twisted bloom, keeping me awake at night with strange, lucid dreams. I made a point of inviting Abbie, who seemed flattered and promised she would try and then made sure to mention it in front of the other sirens later, hoping that the idea would take root and spread.

When we arrived at the Emerald Room it was already after ten, and the main lot was packed bumper to bumper with cars. Madge threw up her hand as a slutty coven of witches blocked our turn into the grassy back lot and flashed her lights at them as they laughed and scattered.

"Really?" she said, adjusting the gilded shoulder of her long white dress as I pulled my visor down, giving my long Harley Quinn pigtails a quick fluff. "I hate driving in this shit. We should've just ridden with David."

I glanced in the rearview mirror, tightening the lace ties of my red and black corset as she pulled into one of the last open spots.

"What time is it?"

"Ten after. He said he was just a few minutes behind us."

Madge gave me a look, her heavily lined eyes rolling over my outfit as she shook her head a little and bit back a smile.

"You're obsessed. You know that, right?"

"Excuse me?"

"You know what I mean. I heard you invite her, Lea. And then her friends. What are you hoping is going to happen here?"

"I was just being friendly."

"Look, I kind of left this alone at first because I thought you just wanted to fuck him. And frankly, I thought it would just burn itself out. But it hasn't. I haven't seen you this far gone since college. If I thought it was just about that, I mean, whatever, you're both adults. A little heartbreak never hurt anyone . . ."

"Are you finished?"

"Are you?"

"It's just a stupid crush. I'll get over it. I always do."

"The way you got over Logan?"

I glanced at her quickly, surprised by how concerned she looked and took a long drag of my cigarette as I glanced out the window, trying not to get angry as I saw David turn into the lot.

"I'm not going to dignify that. It was ten years ago. Let it go."

Madge flashed her lights twice as David drove up and down the lot and I cracked my door open as he made the turn into the makeshift parking area around us.

"Lea, I'm just worried about you . . ."

"I told you I'm fine," I said, cracking the door open with my boot as I stamped my cigarette out in the ashtray. "Seriously, Madge. Stupid crush. It's no big deal."

I slammed the door shut as David parked behind us, ran over to his side of the car and gave him a quick hug as he got out, laughing at the look on his face as he locked the door behind him.

"You're not wearing your glasses."

David grinned and then pulled a thick black pair out of his pocket, putting them on as he opened the front of his dark button-down shirt enough to reveal the Superman insignia inside it.

"Clark Kent!"

David raised a hand as he looked over the low front of my corset, his smile becoming a little broader as he tucked the glasses back in his pocket.

"That's Superman to you, Harley."

He glanced at Madge as she brushed her hair out of her eyes and squinted at her costume for a minute before nodding.

"Diana. Goddess of the hunt."

"Jesus. No. Just a goddess. You two aren't going to torture me with this Comic Con shit all night, are you?"

David shrugged.

"No promises."

We headed for the back entrance as a group after deciding that the front door had too many people coming and going at once and I felt David take my hand as the crowd started to close in around us, maneuvering through it deftly as I felt a dozen different bodies slide past me at once. He let it go instantly once we were inside, the dark vestibule so dark we had to force our way into the light and I reached for Madge's arm as I caught my first glimpse of the floor—the walls decorated with a thousand different neon slogans and symbols.

A harassed-looking bouncer with dead eyes checked our IDs at the door and we followed the crowd into the bar just as the house band finished its set, a large crowd in the front bursting into applause. David looked around at the mayhem, glancing around to look for a booth and then leaned over and pointed to a small round table in the middle of the back wall, meeting Madge's eyes over the crowd.

"This place is nuts," he said. "That table. Over there. Go."

I bolted before he did, dodging around the crowd as I saw Madge raise her hands and stopped dead as the crowd parted and I noticed another couple huddled in the corner, whispering together as they stirred their drinks mildly. I stopped in front of them, my heart leaping into my throat as Jordan raised his brows in my direction and felt a thousand rehearsed lines die on my lips as Abbie gave me a sudden smile—completely without undercurrent, simply excited to see me.

"I didn't think you were coming," Abbie said, raising her voice over the crowd as she waved to David behind me. "We almost didn't come in. This place is insane! Emma and Kayla said they were on their way but . . ."

"They're always late," Jordan said mildly, looking my costume over slowly as some emotion a little too convoluted to be humor shifted behind his polite expression. "For everything."

"This is David," Abbie said, scooting over in her seat. "He works at the paper too."

I looked between them for a moment, the sight of them huddled together giving me a quick pang of irrational bitterness, and blushed as Jordan caught the look and bit back a smile, pressing his fingers against his brow for a moment as David stepped forward and extended his hand.

"Nice to meet you," he said as Jordan leaned forward to shake it.

"Jordan. Same here."

He picked up his drink, looking over my costume again and then grinned as if he had figured something out.

"Are you Harley Quinn?"

I rolled my jaw a little at his expression, which only seemed to amuse him more and shrugged as David pulled out the chair next to Abbie, gesturing to the booth next to her.

"Kind of a fan," I said.

Jordan tilted his head at me and then glanced at Abbie as she grinned, her eyes a little bloodshot as she pushed her hair away from her eyes.

"Who isn't?" he asked, coiling one of the blonde tendrils around his fingers before tucking it behind her ear, smiling down at her gently for a moment as she lowered her eyes.

"Come sit down," she said, patting the booth next to her. "I love Harley Quinn. She's my favorite."

I hesitated—the dark, pleasant garden in my head recoiling slightly in the face of reality—and felt my ego propel me forward as the entire table turned to stare, sliding in beside her as she picked up her drink.

"I don't even know what this is," she said, sloshing it in my direction a little recklessly as she giggled. "I told him to bring me anything."

"Do you want something to drink?" David asked, leaning over me and I shook my head, nodding to the bar.

"I think Madge is getting it. She said the first round was on her."

David leaned back, looking over Jordan's costume thoughtfully for a moment and then pointed between them as he rested his elbows on the table.

"Are you Jack the Ripper?"

Abbie laughed at Jordan's expression and he gave her a cool smile as he leaned back against the booth, resting his arm behind her shoulders until his fingers were almost touching my skin.

"Everyone always guesses that first," she said, taking another drink. "I told you no one would get it."

Jordan turned his eyes in my direction, smiling a little as he pulled something out of his pocket and snapped it open with a quick turn of his wrist, the old-fashioned razor blade catching the light as one of the tables closest to us turned to watch.

"Is that real?"

Jordan eyes narrowed as I glanced between him and his wife and then smiled, raising my brows in Jordan's direction.

"He's Sweeny Todd," I said, and felt that other world quake closer again as he gave me a sudden smile, snapping the blade around in one hand like a magic trick as he pointed it in my direction.

"You're the first one who's gotten that on the first try," he said, snapping the blade closed as he set it down on the table and picked up his drink.

"You really are," Abbie said, her eyes bright and vacant as she leaned her head in her palm and tilted her head in David's direction. "You're . . . don't tell me."

David pulled his glasses out of his pocket and popped them on, making a quick gesture to his t-shirt as he gave me a wink.

"Oh my god! Clark Kent! That's so funny. I was just wondering what was different about you. You look so different without your glasses. Doesn't he?"

David glanced at me as he pulled them off and I grinned as Abbie held out her hand.

"You really do."

"People are always saying that," he said as he passed them over. "Is that a good thing?"

"I actually thought you might come as Ophelia," Jordan said, meeting my eyes behind Abbie's back as she leaned forward to chatter aimlessly in David's direction, the dark, square frames inching her angelic good looks into something almost artsy. He smiled a little at my expression and then finished what was left in his glass.

"I just reread it," he said, shrugging. "After what you said."

"It is one of my favorites. I think my dad first read it to me when I was six. Romantic, right?"

Jordan glanced at me curiously as Abbie scooted a little closer to the table, his eyes shifting over my face slowly as he ducked his head closer.

"You thought their relationship was romantic?"

"How they felt about each other was."

"Hamlet strung her along, left her alone to go crazy and then she killed herself. I'm sorry. Am I missing something? What's so romantic about unrequited love?"

"But he did love her. He was just too fucked up to know it. Until it was too late."

"Or maybe he was just a selfish asshole who didn't give a damn if she loved him or not."

"I don't think so. Fatal flaw, remember? All great Shakespearian characters have them. His was procrastination. He just waited too long. Too long to kill his uncle. Too long to tell Ophelia he loved her. Too long for everything."

I brushed my hair away from my face as I noticed his gaze following it, his eyes running from my lips to my neck and back again.

"He was his own worst enemy," I said, tearing my eyes away from him as I noticed David staring. "It's kind of sad, really. When you think about it."

"Who was?" David asked, his eyes running between us for a moment as Abbie pulled his glasses off and set them on the table, picking up her drink as she shook the ice in Jordan's direction.

"*Hamlet*," I said as Abbie turned her phone over and began to type into it quickly. "We were talking about *Hamlet*."

"They're outside," Abbie said, glancing back at the entrance, the floor so packed with bodies I could barely make out the dark hallway. "Looking for a place to park."

"Tell them to try the back lot," I said, my eyes shifting to Jordan's face as he looked restlessly around the dance floor. "I think everything else is full."

"What do you do at the paper, David?" Jordan asked glancing up as the crowd burst into scattered applause, his eyes darting across the stage as another band began to set up quickly.

"Mostly the sports stuff. Political coverage. That sort of thing."

"I don't really follow sports that much."

"Not everyone does," he said, his voice clipped and ironic. "You're a musician, right?"

"Yeah. That's why I never really followed sports. Lots of moving around, different towns. It's hard to keep up."

"Hard to know who to root for."

"Sure. That too."

"Ares Rising, right?" I asked, turning in his direction as Jordan glanced in my direction. "I listened to some of your stuff online. It's really good."

"I'm sorry. What was the name?" David asked, leaning closer.

"Ares Rising."

Jordan's smile cooled a little and he looked over my face carefully for a minute as he raised his brows.

"It's actually pronounced like the zodiac sign," he said, glancing away. "Ares Rising."

David turned his head in my direction as I felt my heart stop and brushed away an amused smile as Jordan shifted his empty glass around on the table, throwing a look in my direction that was more annoyed than wounded.

"I'm sorry," I stammered. "I didn't know . . ."

"It's no big deal," he said, shrugging. "Lots of people make that mistake."

I blushed as he stood up, looking at the bar and gestured to it as he glanced in Abbie's direction, his expression once more a polite blank.

"I'm going up. You two want anything? David? Lea?"

I felt my body curl forward as he swept his eyes in my direction and David pulled out a ten, holding it up to him as Jordan waved it off.

"Seriously? Drinks are high here."

"It's honestly not a problem."

"Beer? Lea?"

David glanced at me as I looked down at my phone and then pointed to Abbie's glass and shrugged.

"One of those?"

"I'll be back."

I turned my head slightly as he passed in front of the table and sunk a little lower in my chair as David leaned over, lowering his voice as he spoke into my ear.

"It's Ares Rising," he said as I bit my lip, looking so amused I felt a sudden irrational rush of hatred pivot in his direction. "Christ. Can you believe that guy? What a prima donna."

He pulled away as I looked up at him, his brow furrowing slightly as he searched my face, and then glanced toward the bar, his expression souring.

"Is Madge even still here? It's been almost half an hour."

"She'll be gone a while," Abbie said. "That bar is nuts. The only reason we got drinks so fast is because Jordan knows the bartender."

"So," David said, raising his voice a little as the band up front tested their amps loudly for a moment before going silent. "You and Jordan. How long have you two been married?"

"It was five years in May."

"Five years. Wow. That's . . . something. Did you two meet in high school?"

Abbie laughed and gave him one of her shy half-smiles, her heart always an open book when it came to her favorite subject.

"Oh no," she said, shaking her head. "Jordan's older than me. He just looks really young."

"Oh. So no 'hot for teacher' situation? I won't tell. I promise."

"No. No! Nothing like that. It was pretty boring really—how we met. I was working in this ice cream parlor . . ."

"An ice cream parlor?" David choked. "Not really."

"Yeah. I know. But he came in late one night with the band and I think they were all really stoned. His friend Paul was just being rude, almost belligerent, and I was by myself, and it was late . . ."

"And he came to your rescue," David said, raising his brows.

"Kind of. I guess. Jordan kind of just—took control. He told the others to take Paul outside and then apologized for the whole thing. And I forgave him, you know. He seemed so genuine, like honestly embarrassed. And then about a week later, he came back. Alone."

She shrugged and held up her hands.

"And that was that."

David glanced at me and gave me a strange smile.

"And that was that," he said.

David turned his phone over as it let out a low chime and read it quickly before glancing over his shoulder, raising his brows before typing back.

"Is that Madge?" I asked.

He opened his mouth as if to say something, his eyes rolling to my phone and then tucked his into his pocket, his expression becoming a perfect blank as he stood up.

"Yeah. Give me a minute. I'll be right back."

"Hold on," Abbie said, holding her phone up as she slid closer to me on the booth. "Let's get a picture."

I turned my head as David disappeared into the crowd and then tilted it next to Abbie's as she put on a bright smile, the neon graffiti behind our head a shock of green and orange slogans. I turned my eyes as she took it—a few shots in a row, gushing over them before zooming in on her favorite one and then passed the phone to me, draining the ice-diluted vodka in the bottom of her glass.

"God, we really do look alike," she said. "Emma said it the first day, but I really didn't see it until now. I think it's your hair. I always wanted to go red, but Jordan's so weird about stuff like that . . ."

I looked over the photo, turning it slightly until it filled the screen and shook my head as I tried to make the connection, raising my brows as I handed it back.

"Stuff like what?"

"I don't know," she said, leaning against my shoulder chummily as she began to take down her long blonde hair, depositing one antique-looking silver pin after another onto the table in front of us. "When we met, I was just a teenager and I think part of him wants me to stay that way. He hates when I change my hair or wear a lot of make-up. You want to know something? Promise you won't tell."

"I promise," I said, turning my glitter-lined eyes in her direction as she ran her hand through the back of her hair. "I barely know him, Abbie. Who would I tell?"

"Jordan acts really kind and modern and, you know, pro women's rights and all that, but . . . if he had his way . . ."

She held her hand out in front of her stomach and laughed at my expression.

"Barefoot and pregnant, baby. And I mean like, all the time. I think he was just kind of raised to believe that was the way it was supposed to be. I think it would shock him if he knew how wild I had been in high school . . . and I mean *really* wild . . ."

"Is that what you want?"

She shook her head emphatically and then reached for her glass again, setting it down when she realized it was empty.

"No! No, no, no. I mean, maybe someday. I could see being a stay-at-home mom someday, but not anytime soon. He doesn't really get that, and I can tell he doesn't like it. It's like this position. You can't believe how much he wanted me to turn it down."

She stopped speaking suddenly, pressing her lips together as she looked at me as if just remembering who I was and then laughed a little nervously and reached for her phone, typing into it quickly as she pressed her hand against her face.

"God, I'm so wasted. Please ignore me. I get like this."

"Relax. I doubt any of us will remember much after tonight. I mean, that's the hope, right?"

Abbie muttered something to herself as she bit back a smile and then glanced up as the band began to play, scooting a little farther down the booth as she scanned the crowd quickly.

"Emma and Kayla are here already. They said that Paul and Alan already grabbed a table up front."

She brushed her wavy hair back from her shoulders and looked longingly toward the front of the crowd, every insider instinct in her body humming to the soft, unmistakable lure of a Better Table Someplace Else.

"We should go," she said, grabbing my wrist in a sudden burst of comradery. "They're right up front. They can see everything . . ."

"Go where?"

I glanced up as Jordan set down two beers in the center of the table and then placed another closer to his side of the booth, adding a shot glass next to it. He gave me a smirk as I dropped my eyes, setting a tumbler of some frothy pink drink down in front of me, and then handed one to Abbie, dropping two more shot glasses in front of us as she reached for hers with both hands. He slid the empty tray in his hand onto the unused side of the booth next to us and turned his head as Abbie pointed to the front of the crowd, following her eyes.

"Paul's here," she said, taking a drink. "Emma said they saved a table near the front. She said we should come up and join them. All of us."

Jordan glanced at me as I slid my drink closer and then scanned the crowd behind me, tilting his head in my direction.

"Where's David?"

"He just had to take a call," I said, brushing my hair behind my ear as I took a drink, his stare so intense I averted my eyes. "It's fine. You two can go ahead. We'll find you later. I promise."

I ran my eyes over his face for a moment as he frowned slightly, rolling his jaw in annoyance as Abbie's face dropped. He glanced at me out of the corner of his eyes as he took a seat and reached for the shot next to his beer, throwing his arm over the back of the booth without quite boxing her in.

"You can go, if you want," he said, without looking at her. "I'll be along in a little bit."

"I think they meant all of us . . ."

"What about you, Lea?" he asked, raising his voice to be heard over the band.

"I was just going to wait for the others to get back . . ."

Jordan rolled his eyes in Abbie's direction and then held them for a minute before shrugging, throwing his shot back in one swallow.

"I'll wait for the others too," he said mildly, placing the empty glass back down on the table as he reached for his beer. "I don't feel like carrying all this shit over."

Abbie looked down at her phone again and then glanced in my direction. "Are you sure you don't mind?"

I shook my head as she reached for her purse, and tried not to notice the way the lights from the stage lit up Jordan's crisp, perfect profile, the pulse of the music changing it from red to white and back again.

"Go ahead," I said. "I just want Madge and David to be able to find us."

Abbie leaned over Jordan on the booth, pressing her hands against his face for a moment as he raised his brows and then whispered into his ear as he looked up at her, his expression politely disengaged. I watched her face crumple as he took another drink and then followed her with his eyes as she disappeared into the crowd, rolling his jaw slightly as he turned his attention back to the band. I watched him out of the corner of my eye, separated on the booth by less than three feet and leaned toward him as he cut his eyes in my direction.

"You don't have to stay. Really. It's no big deal . . ."

Do you want me to leave?

I blinked as I heard his voice inside my head, the shock of it making me lean away from him and felt my brow furrow as he turned his eyes away again, smirking a little as he took another drink.

"I don't mind. I heard these guys were pretty good. Abbie doesn't really mean to be rude, you know. She likes you. She's just young."

"I didn't think she was being rude. A little drunk, maybe."

"Yeah. Well. She's not the only one."

"About what I said earlier . . ."

Jordan glanced at me curiously for a moment and then gestured for me to come closer as he sat up a little, every nerve ending in my body going on red alert as he pulled his arm off the back of the booth. He turned the full force of his attention in my direction as I slid closer and shook his head slightly, leaning closer as his too-blue eyes moved over my face.

"What was that?" he asked, leaning closer.

"Your band. I'm sorry I got it wrong. Madge just said you were in a band and I looked it up online. Your stuff is really good though. Your voice is . . . really beautiful. I was surprised I hadn't heard of you guys before."

Jordan searched my face for a moment, his expression softening and shook his head as he made a quick gesture with one hand, glancing back toward the stage.

"Thank you. And it's no big deal. Really. It wasn't even about that, trust me . . . "

He broke off and then looked up as the crowd broke into a scattering of applause and gave me a sudden smile as he dragged Abbie's untouched shot glass down the table, depositing it at the edge of the table as he raised his bottle slightly.

"Open waters. If you don't, I will."

I picked up the glass as he clinked his bottle against it and then finished it as he turned his head, brushing his smile away with his thumb as I set it down.

"You've had some practice," he said, as I twirled my other glass with one hand and raised my brows in his direction.

"Is that a compliment?"

"If you like."

"What can I say?" I asked, taking a long drink as I glanced over the crowd nervously for a moment. "Bad break-up."

"Recently?"

"Oh, about every two years or so. That's about how long it takes me, you know. To run them off."

"I thought you said you were a romantic."

"Ah. I really just meant tortured romances. Those are kind of my wheel-house. I'm not sure I'm cut out for the other kind."

Jordan looked at me curiously for a moment, his expression relaxing and smiled ruefully as he swiped his long hair away from his brow, something about it never quite reaching his eyes.

"It definitely takes some getting used to," he said, his voice clipped and ironic as he took another drink. "That's for sure. What about Clark Kent? The sportswriter? He seems like the nice, stable sort."

"David? No. God, no. I like him too much to do that to him. Six months with me and he'd lose all of his faith in humanity."

He laughed, looking at me with more interest and then grinned when the band launched into another song, the walls quaking slightly as I jumped.

"We're louder than these guys," he said, and I shook my head losing most of it.

"Plus," I said, reaching for the two beers in the middle of the table. "I was into the hero thing for a while, but not anymore. Eventually, we'd have to have that whole conversation . . ."

Jordan raised his brows as I slid him the other beer and then leaned closer as his eyes darted over my face.

"What was that?"

"I just got tired of explaining myself to guys like him. Too much hassle."

I shook my head as his eyes strayed to the inside of my arm, looking it over thoughtfully for minute as I took a drink.

"And now?"

"You get tired of always being the screw-up, you know? The one who needs to be fixed."

Jordan looked over my face seriously for a moment and then shifted his body a little closer, following my gaze as I glanced up at the stage.

"I admire your resolve," he said. "And I know what you mean. Believe me."

I held my hands up to my ears as my eardrums pounded and jumped as I felt his fingers brush against my opposite shoulder, my body curling in toward him as he spoke into my ear.

"Is that why you write?" he asked, his eyes running to my lips again. I pulled away slightly as the song ended, brushing my hair away from my face and felt my vision tilt for a moment before righting itself—the place where he had touched me pulsing slightly, as if I'd been burned.

"Is that why *you* write?" I asked, glancing at him out of the corner of my eyes as he looked over my face carefully for a moment.

"I don't know," he shrugged, reaching for the other beer. "It may have started there. Those demons have to live somewhere. Better there than here, you know?"

"I get that. I do. The stuff I write outside of the paper is like that. A little bit, anyway. Not like you. Not like your music."

Jordan stiffened a little and then waved the bottle in my direction as he glanced back at the stage.

"What do you mean?" he asked evenly.

"Just that in fiction, there are a lot of places to hide. If you want to express something you can't talk about, you can use any character you want to kind of play out that emotion. And only you know what's real and what isn't. That's why I liked your music so much. You're not hiding anywhere. You're just . . . I don't know. I've never heard anything like it. It's all so personal. It moved me. Made me want to write something real, you know? Less hiding places."

Jordan looked at me steadily for several moments, his entire expression changing and then leaned closer as his eyes moved over me with some emotion too quick and convoluted to place as he pressed his hand against the table.

"That's what you hope for," he said, his voice low and excited. "I mean, that's the goal, when everything goes right. You want to make people feel something real and you don't have a lot of time to do it."

"Like in poetry."

"Exactly like in poetry. You have to find a way to just communicate one honest moment with people, even if it scares you, *especially* if it scares you . . ."

"Lea."

I watched Jordan's face slam shut like an attic door, his expression becoming politely disengaged again as he shifted his body away from me. I turned my head as David walked up to the table briskly, his face uncharacteristically grim as he looked from Jordan to me and back again.

"Did you get it?" he asked evenly.

I turned over my phone, scrolling through a mountain of texts from Madge and stood up when I was halfway through them as David shoved his chair under the table.

"What is it?" Jordan asked, glancing toward my phone as David rolled his jaw at him without speaking.

"Madge's brother. He was arrested. When did this happen?"

"A couple of hours ago. Madge got the call almost as soon as we got here. I guess she didn't even know he was in town. I'm going down there with her."

I glanced at his face and he shook his head, his face softening a little as he glanced away.

"She needs money to bail him out," I said.

"She asked everyone else," he said, his voice low and apologetic. "It's no big deal. I know she's good for it."

"Her brother's in jail?" Jordan asked, looking up.

"He does things like this," I said as I grabbed my purse. "He's an actor."

Jordan stood up, glancing between us for a minute and I saw David smother a look of outright dislike as he raised his brows.

"You're both leaving?" he asked mildly.

David glanced toward the exit.

"I have to go," David said. "Madge's already outside. I honestly don't know how long we'll be."

"Abbie and I could give you a ride home later if you wanted to stay," Jordan said, his voice calm and polite as he looked down at me. "It wouldn't be any trouble."

I met his eyes—some emotion I couldn't quite place shifting in the dark pool of his eyes—and shook my head as I felt David's hand drop on my shoulder, scrambling for the safety of solid ground as the world shifted below my feet.

"Madge wants you there," he said, holding Jordan's eyes steadily for a moment. "You know how she gets."

"It's up to you," Jordan said, shrugging.

Because if it was up to me, you'd stay. So why fight it, Lea? Stay. Stay now. Stay forever. Stay, stay, stay . . .

I glanced over his shoulder as David bit back an unpleasant smile and shook my head suddenly as I took a step backward, my purse swinging against his leg as I dropped my eyes.

"I really can't. But it was nice seeing you again. Tell Abbie I'm sorry we couldn't stay."

"Nice seeing you too," he said, glancing toward the front of the floor. "You too, David. Stay safe."

I followed David through the crowd, looking over my shoulder to see if he had looked back. The last glimpse I caught was of Abbie throwing her arms around his neck. And Jordan smiling down at her before kissing her hard on the lips.

WEIRD SCENES INSIDE THE GOLD MINE (REDUX)

AKA: I love you Jim XXX (See You Soon!!!)

Open on a nondescript office. Could be anywhere. Gray walls, gray carpet, gray, gray, gray. A therapist in a long unflattering dress and a blazer walks in. Addresses the pretty, belligerent patient seated on the opposite side of the room.

Sez Me: I don't want to talk about any of this shit anymore. It's not helping, so what's the point?

Sez You: You seem to be feeling that way a lot lately.

Sez Me: That's because talking about the terrible shit that happens to you isn't actually designed to make anyone feel any better. You just get so sick of hearing yourself bitch one day you say, 'Fuck it. I guess it's time to make an effort.' And then we go back to pretending and you all go back to acting like geniuses. That's your whole profession in a nutshell.

Sez You: Is it possible that talking about Jordan and what happened with him is simply painful for you?

Sez Me: Isn't that what I just said?

Sez You: Tell me more about that.

Sez Me: I'm done writing this fucking journal. How about that?

Sez You: You don't have to keep a journal if you don't want to. But you have seemed a little more engaged since you started it. Is that fair, Lea? Do you feel that way at all? More open?

Sez Me: No. It actually makes me feel like I'm locked up in a fucking cage at the fucking zoo and you and all of your doctor friends keep wandering through, talking about how healthy I seem all of a sudden. How engaged. What do you think, Melinda? Do you think the animals at the zoo are emotionally invested in their lives? You know I could talk all day long and still not tell you a fucking thing? Haven't you figured that out yet? I mean, haven't you been paying any attention at all?

Sez You: (silence)

Sez Me: What's wrong? Nothing to say?

Sez You: (silence)

Sez Me: You know the silent treatment doesn't really work on me. My dad once ignored me for three months for sneaking out to see a concert. My mom had to tell me about it. I hadn't even noticed.

Sez You: Tell me more about that.

Sez Me: (silence)

Sez You: You don't talk about your parents that often.

Sez Me: (silence)

Sez You: Does talking about your parents hurt you more than talking about Jordan?

Sez Me: I know what you're trying to do.

Sez You: And what is that?

Sez Me: You want to turn this all into something about them. But it's not. I don't talk about them that much because they're just not that important to me. We have a nice, polite relationship. No abuse. No trauma. Nothing to get excited about. Just your average, distant, dysfunctional family.

Sez You: Did that ever bother you?

Sez Me: I'm sure you'd like it to. The truth is that some parents just don't like their children that much. There's no tragedy in it. It just happens. Your profession turned it into a tragedy. A hundred years ago when people didn't like their parents, you know what happened? They just moved out and started their own lives. No tears, no therapy. Just split the fucking scene.

Sez You: Do they not like you, or is it the other way around?

Sez Me: Does it matter? Let's just say that if I committed suicide tomorrow, everyone would act very appropriately about it. And no one would be that surprised.

Sez You: You've been bringing up that subject a lot too lately.

Sez Me: What subject?

Sez You: Suicide.

Sez Me: (silence)

Sez You: Have you been feeling suicidal recently?

Sez Me: Define recently.

Sez You: Have you often thought of suicide? Just in your day-to-day life.

Sez Me: Does anyone ever answer 'no' to that question? Anyone in here, I mean.

Sez You: Often then.

Sez Me: Often enough.

Sez You: Before you came here, did it ever occur to you to seek help?

Sez Me: No. I think the world should seek help. Before it's too late.

(End scene)

CHAPTER FOUR

"LEA, WHEN YOU GET A MINUTE."

I glanced up as Noah sailed past my desk, hooking his hand in my direction and felt my stomach drop as I realized the rest of the floor was almost empty. I switched my screen back to the latest City Council meeting story I had been butchering, unable to make my mind focus for more than five minutes at a time and gathered my notes for the week as I followed him into his office, putting my game face on as he sat down behind his desk.

"Close the door for a second, would you?"

I took a seat as he tapped at his computer importantly, holding up his finger as I started to chatter nervously and then snapped his fingers down on the keyboard hard enough to make me flinch before sitting back in his chair, scratching the back of his head lightly as he raised his brows in my direction.

"How's the festival stuff coming?"

"Pretty good. You know. It'll pick up in a few weeks. The Chili cook-off is next week. The Luckiest Dog thing—"

"Yeah," he said. "Do me a favor and make sure you're on that. Every damn year the downtown paper scoops us. Just once, I'd like to get that interview first."

The Luckiest Dog Contest was a sweepstakes contest conducted through a local pet store chain to award a year of free dog food to one customer a year. To Noah's eternal chagrin, the pet store owner, who advertised exclusively with the downtown Northville paper, invariably informed them first about who the contest winner was and where they could be contacted for comment. Getting that interview first had become a minor obsession for him. The month

I started, I had made the unforgivable error of not taking that obsession seriously and blowing the interview. He had yet to let me forget it.

"Right."

"We don't want a repeat of last year."

"No. I know, definitely not."

"Did you do something to your hair?"

I ran my hands through my shorter, blonder locks, brushing my long bangs away from my eyes and smiled a little as he looked me over like a stranger—not just unimpressed, but somehow vaguely annoyed by my sudden desire to seem less invisible.

"Just got it highlighted. That's all."

"I thought something was different. How is Abbie doing?"

I glanced up as he picked up his coffee cup, looking at me over the rim as he held it in both hands.

"She's doing really well. Everyone seems to like her."

Noah gave me one of his deep searching looks again, the one that said that he had finally figured out what a screw-up I was and held me personally responsible for duping him. Then he glanced toward the window and rocked in his chair a little, his head bobbing in rhythm of metal grinding on metal.

"Yeah. I like her too. Her stuff is good. A little rough around the edges, but you know, that tends to work itself out."

He looked up, staring at me solemnly for a moment and then shrugged and sat forward, pushing a pile of papers to one side as he set his cup back down.

"I was hoping to get her to do some of the festival stuff with you. Like that thing tonight."

"The 1899 thing? Mardi Gras at the Manor?"

I tried not to let my disappointment show as he nodded and glanced down at the notes in my hand, a small crescent of sweat beneath my thumb leaving a print dark as a watermark beneath the florescent lights.

"Right. That one. Christ. Where do they get these names? I think she might bring an interesting spin to it. What do you think?"

"I don't know if she's available. I could ask . . ."

"Do that," he said. "They're kind of doing a lot of things to bring people from her age group into the mix, get them involved in the city. I think it might be interesting to hear what a twenty-year-old thinks about a party like that.

Plus, I think the mayor will be there. Good chance for her to spread her wings a little."

"I think she's twenty-five."

"Whatever. What a young person thinks about it then."

I pulled out a pen and pretended to write something pertinent down as he tapped at his phone dismissively for a moment.

"Right. The Mardi Gras thing. Anything else?"

"Not right now. When it's closer to the Ice festival, I'll let you know."

"Should I go with her?"

Noah raised his brows at me, biting back a smirk as he tapped at his computer again.

"I think one reporter ought to cover it. Don't you?"

I stood up as he went back to ignoring me, turning my head as Kayla and Emma headed out of the IT office for the breakroom, always together, moving as a pack.

"Oh," he said, as I reached the door. "How are your classes going?"

I turned around to face him and tucked my notes into the pocket of my sweater as he looked me over, the disappointment in his face running a brave, distant second to his barely concealed contempt.

"Great," I lied. "Really good."

"You graduate this semester, right?"

"Definitely. Yes. As long as I pass everything."

"I'm sure you'll do fine," he said. "Keep me posted."

I shut the door quietly behind me, the desire to shriek at the top of my lungs making me press my hands against my temples for a moment and then walked down the hall, listening carefully as the two other sirens talked over one another quickly.

"I know," Emma said. "She was so upset."

"Why wouldn't she be?"

"I get it, but look at it from his point of view, he's not going to miss a show over it."

I stepped into the doorway as both girls turned their heads toward me at once, both true alphas, sensing the interloper. Kayla, the tallest of the three, tilted her head at me, looking over my hair as I walked to the coffee maker.

"Did you change your hair?"

I filled a Styrofoam cup, pouring in too much creamer and then turned around as Emma took a step closer, smiling a little as I set it down.

"It's lighter, isn't it?"

"I just got it highlighted."

"It looks really nice," she said, looking over me seriously for a moment as if changing one's appearance for the better was something that should never be taken lightly. Entire dynasties had been built on it. Cleopatra brought down two empires with a haughty attitude and a stick of black eyeliner.

"It does," Kayla agreed after a moment. "That color really works for you."

She gave me a smile then, stepping away from the counter a little as if opening up the circle. I took a sip of my coffee as they looked me over like a sorority pledge they were considering taking under their wing, whispering together before nodding sagely.

"I think you could even go lighter," Emma said. "Almost Abbie's shade even."

I glanced around the room as I tapped my fingers on the counter behind me, bristling under their scrutiny in spite of myself.

"Where is Abbie? Noah wanted me to ask her to do that Mardi Gras thing tonight."

"Oh," Emma said, raising her brows in Kayla's direction as she rearranged the bagels on the tray, shifting them until they were in perfect alignment with the edge of the box. "That's not going to happen. Her kitten's sick. She has to take her in."

"Kitten?"

Kayla rolled her eyes and then sliced herself off a precious third of one of the cinnamon raisin bagels, setting it down on a plate.

"They just got a kitten. One of those expensive Persian ones. I can't believe she didn't tell you. That thing is all over her Instagram. Anyway, it got sick a few nights ago and Jordan told her to take it to the vet's, but she just kept insisting it would get better on its own."

"Except that it didn't," Emma said. "So now, she has to take it in tonight. Or else they'll have to pay like four hundred dollars for a weekend visit. And Jordan is furious because he has a show tonight and then they were all going to the Manor afterward. The whole thing's a mess."

I felt my stomach flip a little as they mentioned his name and dug my nails into my cup as I glanced from one girl to the other, taking a sip of my coffee.

"Oh. He has a show? Where at?"

"This place downriver. They've actually played a couple of times there before but they're headlining tonight. He wanted her to be there."

"It's not her fault their cat got sick . . ."

"Her cat," Kayla corrected, taking a bite of her bagel. "And yes, you're absolutely right. But you know how she is, Emma. She does things like this. Paul told me that it drives Jordan fucking crazy. I mean, he told her to take her in days ago. But she just waits and waits until the everything is just five minutes away from a total crisis . . ."

"Maybe she just likes him to step in," I said, shrugging. "You know—create a crisis, get rescued. Lots of girls do it. She might not even know she's doing it."

Kayla and Emma both looked at me and then Emma laughed and reached for the rest of Kayla's bagel, ripping it in two as they both exchanged a look.

"God, you're so right," Emma said. "That is Abbie right down to the ground. I mean, we love her to death . . ."

"But it's always something with her," Kayla said, shaking her head. "Drama just follows her. And Jordan is great—I mean he's a really good guy. But even good guys have their limits."

I set my cup down and then glanced over my shoulder, my mind beginning to dance down a hundred different corridors at once.

"Is he still going?" I asked as nonchalantly as I could. "To the Mardi Gras thing?"

"We'll see," Emma said, finishing the other half of the bagel as Kayla raised her brows in her direction. "He wouldn't give me a straight answer. The rest of the band is going. Do you know that spring music thing they have downtown? The guy who books the bands is supposed to be there. I know Jordan wanted to meet him."

"Are you going?" Kayla asked, brushing her hands of in the sink. "I asked your boyfriend . . . David? He said he wasn't sure."

"If she can't cover it, I'll have to. And we're actually not dating. Just friends."

"I'm sorry. I just thought . . . because you two are always together . . ."

"It's no big deal. Lots of people make that mistake."

"Are you dressing up?" Emma asked.

"I hadn't even thought about it. Probably not. Why? Is that a thing? Is everyone doing that?"

Kayla smiled and pulled out her phone, flipping through it for a minute before showing me a photo of her and Emma looking like two perfect, nineteenth-century vampires—Kayla looking cool and distant, while Emma threw the camera a kiss.

"It's going to be a blast," she said. "You should dress up. We'll look for you there."

I muttered some appropriate response, my heart hammering so loudly in my chest I could barely hear myself think. I walked down the hall to the sales department, waiting politely in the aisle while our photographer chatted with two of his favorite ad men and did his best to ignore me. Lyle and I were not on the best of terms. I could blame that on a lot of things, but the truth was we just didn't have a whole lot in common. Lyle liked girls like the sirens—beautiful, gregarious women who went out of their way to tease and engage him so that he would show up at their events and photograph the holy hell out them.

That sort of negotiation had never really been my forte. The first week I worked there, we were in the middle of an election season and I ended up covering two important events right out of the gate, because it was an all-hands-on-deck kind of moment and the paper simply didn't have enough bodies to spread around. Because I didn't know any better, I ended up taking all the photos for both stories myself—decent shots—two of which wound up on the front page. It was only afterward that David told me, not without humor, that Lyle was used to being approached and booked for events in advance by the rest of the staff. What I had done was tantamount to open war in his universe and after that he went out of his way to book up quickly, my events sliding to the bottom of his priority list.

"Lyle?"

Lyle laughed loudly at something one of the ad men said and then rubbed his eye and broke off abruptly, his expression dropping as he glanced at me over his shoulder.

"Yeah?"

No greeting, no name, not even a hint of feigned interest. Pure hostility at its most elegant level.

"The Mardi Gras thing tonight. The one at the Manor. Did Noah mention it to you?"

Lyle looked me over slowly, lingering on my newer, lighter hair as if trying to think of some quick way to insult it and coming up empty. He then raised his brows and shrugged, clearing his throat into his fist as he stood up.

"Yeah. He mentioned it."

I felt every slacker instinct in my body cry foul as he reached for the satchel at his feet, knowing he was purposely goading me over some imagined slight I had dealt him over fifteen months ago. I refused to move when he tried to muscle past me in the aisle, raising my hand as he gave me a look of outright dislike.

"So? Are you going or not? Abbie was supposed to cover it and can't. I need to know what to plan for."

"It wasn't in my schedule."

I took a deep breath and imagined myself all alone in some pristine white wilderness, the entire city a speck on the horizon below me.

"It starts at eight, Lyle," I said glancing at my watch. "Look, I know it's short notice but if you could make it, I would really appreciate it. Even if it's only for an hour or two. The mayor is supposed to be there. It's just a lot of ground to cover alone."

He made a show of checking his phone, scratching his head as he scrolled through it slowly and then shrugged and tucked it back in his windbreaker, looking right through me as he glanced toward the door.

"I might be able to swing by for an hour or so. But I have somewhere to be by ten."

"I just need a little help, that's all," I said, giving him the politest nod I could manage as I turned around. "Like I said, it's a lot of ground to cover by myself."

"You know this would go a lot easier if you would just mark your events down in my schedule like everyone else," he called as I headed for the hall. "That's why it's there."

I tried to think of something to say that wouldn't result in some petty, waste-of-time fight where I would come up the loser and decided to keep my mouth shut instead, heading for my desk as I gathered up my things. I walked out the back way, tossing my bag and notepads into the passenger seat and reached my apartment in less than seven minutes, letting the car idle in the drive for a moment as I reached for my cigarettes. I lit one one-handed as I pulled out my phone, tapping at the screen quickly as Jordan's band website leapt to the top of my search engine and scrolled through recent events as I shook my head, grimacing a little as I glanced at my watch.

Nine o'clock, I thought, running my hand through the waves around my face as I felt a fresh rush of frustration run through me. *Can't make it. Lyle buys me some breathing room but not that much.*

I scrolled through the pics again, chewing my lip in quick agitation as I took another drag of my cigarette and then kicked the door open with my foot as I reached for my things, trudging up the back steps two at a time. I paused in front of my doorway, shoving the back door open with the heel of my hand as I clamped my cigarette between my teeth and felt my stomach drop as I tugged a red envelope off of the screen door, dropping my things into a pile on the bedroom floor as I let the screen slam shut behind me. I opened it as I paced into the bathroom, flicking on the lights and finished the rest of my cigarette as I read through the demand for rent notice slowly, scanning for a date before crushing the butt against the lip of the sink and tossing it into the toilet.

Still eight days until they file, I thought, practically feeling the slow crank of the guillotine being lifted off of the back of my neck. I paced back around the corner into my bedroom, struggling to clear my mind as I threw open my postage-stamp-sized closet and sifted through an ocean of utilitarian work clothes, tossing out one dark dress after another and rejecting them all before they hit the bedspread. *At least there's no court date yet. A stay of execution then. Small mercies or none at all.*

I kicked my apartment door closed, undressing quickly in front of the mirror behind my bedroom door and pulled out the most festive-looking work dress I had—a dark, wine-colored number with alpine-looking embroidery around the neck and hem. I turned to the side, something about the color bringing all the soft red tones out in my golden-brown hair and paced around in it restlessly for a moment before tugging it off with both hands.

No, I thought, hauling out a box of clothes as a quick, brilliant image of Jordan's face pulsed through my mind. *I can do better.* I pulled the top off of a dark plastic bin, kneeling down in front of it like a supplicant as I began to unload carefully preserved outfits from a different decade and shook out a black velvet corset top that laced up the front, holding it over my old gray bra

LIES THEY TELL YOU

as I glanced in the mirror. I roughed my hair up a little, the sight of myself as an almost blond still catching me off guard, and brushed my fingers down the floral brocade up the front before tossing it onto the bed behind me. I tore through my old goth clothes with a vengeance, pulling out a long, ruffled skirt that ended above the knee and fishtailed in the back and reached for the corset as I tugged it on in front of the mirror, turning toward the door as I zipped it up in the back. I fussed with the ties for a few minutes, lacing and unlacing them in a mindless loop of primping and then tugged on my tall lace-up boots as I stepped back from the mirror, brushing my hair down with both hands as I turned from one side to the other.

I walked closer as I titled my head to one side, the all black outfit making me feel like myself for the first time in several months and rummaged around for the long, blood red coat that I used to wear with everything, inhaling it deeply for a minute before pulling it on.

Cigarettes and patchouli, I thought, smiling at my own reflection as I pressed my fingers against my flushed skin, a rush of strange, convoluted memories bobbing to the surface briefly before going quiet. *Always cigarettes and patchouli. That smell seemed to get everywhere. They ought to bottle a fragrance like that. All of my teenage angst and dreams wrapped up in those two dark notes.*

I pulled the whole outfit back off, typing in a quick message to Madge before heading for the shower and looked over my hair for another few minutes as I gathered it at the nape of my neck, closing my eyes as I remembered the way Jordan had beckoned me over at the bar, his blue eyes dark and watchful as I slid to his side. I pressed my hand against my stomach as I tried not to let every terrified half-wish inside my mind ignite and burn at once, my reflection softening around the edges as the mirror began to fog, and shrugged off my bra as I stuck my hand under the water.

Just let him be there, I thought. *I don't care what happens. I don't care what he says. Just let him be there without her. Just that. Just this once . . .*

CHAPTER FIVE

BY THE TIME I GOT TO THE PARTY, IT WAS ALMOST NINE AND most of the back lot was packed, the long circular drive leading up to the house filled with bodies as someone in a dark uniform directed me to one of the last rows near the gates. I flipped down my visor, brushing a quick finger under my lips in the mirror as I tucked my notebook into my purse and checked for my electronic recorder as well, speaking into it quickly for a moment as I watched two girls dressed like medieval barmaids run up the lawn.

"November tenth. Mardi Gras at the Manor. It's a little before nine and there seems to be a decent turnout of people. I'm counting about thirty on the back terrace alone. Lots of sexy wenches, sexy handmaids, sexy angels—I'm not sure if people really understand the theme of this thing. I see a few Romeos, Juliets, a cardinal . . . could be the Pope. Strange vibes all around. I hope Lyle got a picture of the Pope. Going to get a quote."

I hopped out of my car, tucking my long-fringed bag down at my side, my press pass clipped to the side and flashed it at the door as I was swept inside by a wave of people, a brief rush of unreality washing over me as I stepped into the packed foyer and glanced up at the chandeliers. I ducked a little as a group of men laughed and tossed green and purple beads to some girl dressed like Marie Antoinette on the balcony of the stairwell at the end of the ballroom and pulled out my recorder as the throb of chamber music seemed to come at me from all sides, trying to turn my head in every direction at once as I wove my way through the crowd slowly. I tried to gauge the rough make-up of the partygoers as someone in a mask offered me a rose as I passed, and blinked as I tucked it into my bag, moving against the wall as another round of twenty-year-olds in velvet costumes made a beeline for the French doors at the end of the polished marble floor.

"This place is a madhouse," I said into my recorder, pacing along the stairwell as I noticed the open bar on the other side of the hall. "Looks like . . . *Eyes Wide Shut* meets the Renaissance Fair . . . meets—I don't know—a frat house Halloween party. Most of the crowd seems to be in their twenties and thirties. There's a bar and gambling tables in one room. I'm not sure how accurate any of this is. Still looking for my Pope. Loud chamber music everywhere. No escape from the sound of it. Literally. I think they're piping it in through some sort of integrated stereo system . . ."

I pulled out my phone as I saw another group of men toss beads to the women downstairs from them and snapped a couple of shots as I got turned around by the rush of the crowd, holding up my hand as someone grabbed my arm.

"I'm sorry. I'm press. Just getting a picture . . ."

"Did you just say that you're the press? God, you're pretentious."

I looked up as Tommy gave me a sudden brilliant smile, shaking his head as I tucked my phone away. I stepped forward to give Madge's brother a hug, glancing around for her as he wrapped his arms around me and took a step backward as another swarm of confused costumes sailed past us, raising my brows as we both turned to look.

"I'm so glad you're here," I said, feeling my mood lighten as Tommy brushed off the sleeves of his dark jacket ironically for a moment and then tucked his hands into his pockets. Tommy had that effect on people. He was comfortable absolutely anywhere and tended to spread that aura around with him. He drew admirers everywhere he went, pulling people into the fold as naturally as breathing—always inclusive, always amused.

"Are you seeing this place?" I sighed, glancing over his shoulder as he tipped his head toward the strange collection of gamblers trying their luck at some kind of turn-of-the-century roulette wheel. "I'm supposed to turn this into some kind of cohesive story. Were there roulette wheels in the nineteenth century?"

"I don't know. Maybe. Are you a fortune teller? I'm getting that evil gypsy vibe off of you. No judgement. It's good. It works."

He reached out his hand as someone lobbed a strand of beads in our direction and laughed at my expression as he tucked them over my neck.

"I think these are for you."

"What is this place? How am I supposed to write about this? Are you Poe?"

"Close, but wrong century. I'm Dante. You know—of the Inferno fame."

He primped a little and gave me a pose as I laughed and pulled out my phone, snapping a picture as I shook my head.

"Of course, you are. You know he wrote that in exile, right?"

"That's the only way great writers should write anything. If they can't do anything to get exiled, they should *self-exile*. Wait. Is that the Pope? Oh Christ. That's too good. Come on, Brenda Starr. I need to get a picture with the Pope."

We muscled our way through the melee as I tried to figure out who was directing the sudden glut of people pushing their way toward the gambling rooms and pulled out my recorder as Tommy tapped the Pope on the shoulder, holding out his hand as he turned around.

"Excuse me, sir?" Tommy said as the man raised his brows in his direction. "We're with the press. Would you mind if we got a picture?"

He grinned as the three women he was talking to whipped their heads in our direction and beckoned them with both hands as I took a step backward, throwing his hand over the Pope's shoulders.

"No. Come on in, ladies. Everyone is welcome. That's right. Everyone say 'mortal sin.'"

Everyone smiled, utterly confused and under his spell as I snapped a couple of shots and pulled out my recorder as Tommy dropped his arm and stuck out his hand as a pregnant angel hooked her arm through the Pope's, waving at someone over his shoulder.

"Such a fan," he said. "Really. You do such good work."

His expression dropped a little as someone tossed another string of beads in the angel's direction and he caught it as it sailed over her head, holding it up as he raised his brows in the crowd's direction.

"Really?" he asked, tucking the beads over his head as someone whistled. "I'm keeping them this time. Yeah. Exactly."

"Can I ask what your name is?" I asked, sticking my recorder in the Pope's face as he gave me a shy, half-drunk smile.

"I'm Austin Brewer," he said, bending his head forward as the angel on his arm inched a little closer.

"Just like it sounds?"

"Pretty much."

"And what do you think of the party tonight, Austin? Is it what you were expecting?"

"I don't know. It seems like everyone's having a good time . . ."

"It's great to see the city just doing something different," the angel said, leaning forward to talk into the recorder as the fuzzy tin-foil halo on her head bobbed and swayed. "I think it's a really fun idea. And for a good cause too."

"And what cause is that?"

She tilted her head in Austin's direction and then shook out her long, red curls as she adjusted her halo with one hand.

"Just for charity? That's what I heard anyway. It was for the children, wasn't it?"

I dropped my hand as she laughed and one of the other girls dragged her deeper into the crowd, and raised my brows as I spun around looking for Tommy, snapping the recorder off with my thumb as he noticed me and beckoned me toward the back of the room.

"For the children," he said, handing me a drink as he leaned against the stairwell and let another swell of people shift through. "Please tell me that's going in."

"If I can't get a better quote, it will," I said, taking a drink and then waving it in the direction of the French doors as they swung open. "Have you been outside yet? What's out there?"

"They have some firepits out on the patio. One of those big hedge mazes. Everyone keeps going outside to vape."

"How long have you been here? Is Madge coming?"

Tommy shook his head and finished his drink in one swallow, setting it down on the bannister as he corralled me toward the back patio.

"She keeps threatening to, but I doubt it. She had a date tonight. Super strait-laced guy. Brought her flowers—the whole bit."

"She must've loved that."

"Right. She got that same glittery look in her eyes that sharks get when someone drops a bucket of chum into open water. Poor guy. He'll never know what hit him."

He gave me a considering look then and lingered on my hair for a moment, smothering a smile as I paused at the doors.

"She tells me that you met someone new."

"Did she?"

"Some married guy," he said, raising his brows a little as I rolled my eyes. "Said you invited him to the bar that night . . ."

"You mean before we came to bail you out?"

"Now you know that wasn't my fault. And don't change the subject. Madge said he's in some band."

"She talks too much," I said, reaching for my cigarettes automatically before dragging my hand back, brushing my long bangs away from my face.

"Let me guess. He has a thing for blondes . . ."

I bit my lip as he gave me a sudden smile and shrugged as I finished my drink, setting it down on one of the waiter's trays as he swung past and gave me a polite nod.

"Look, I need to actually get some quotes I can use and try to track down the women who are hosting this thing. The mayor was supposed to be here. Where are you going to be?"

Tommy shrugged and pulled out his phone, tapping at it quickly as he pulled me closer.

"I think I saw some turn-of-the-century Elvis marrying people down the hall," he said, holding the phone above our heads as he wrapped his arm around my waist. "That should be fun. Try to look like you're having the time of your life. That's it. Perfect."

He dropped his phone as he snapped our picture and then made a quick gesture over his shoulder without turning.

"If I'm not there, I'll be in this general area. Near the bar. Or outside watching the drunks try to find their way out of the maze. Just text me."

I left him in front of the doors as another quake of people separated us in an instant, heading for one of the gambling rooms and hung out in the back taking quotes for a while before asking the dealer where I could find the organizer while he acted like he didn't know who I was talking about.

"Rhonda Messler?"

"Who?"

"She organized this event."

"Never heard of her. Try upstairs."

I wandered through most of the other rooms, chatting people up as politely as I could for a while and then headed upstairs when I realized that it was almost ten, the crowd becoming larger and louder in the ballroom as someone finally got the idea to change the music. I looked out over the balcony as a fresh rush of uncostumed twenty- and thirty-year-olds began to filter in— the party at that height almost indiscernible from an all-out frat house bash— and caught the arm of the first harried adult I laid eyes on, the frank look of worry stamped across her face instantly marking her as Someone in Charge.

"Hi. I'm Lea. With the *Tribune*? I was looking for Rhonda Messler."

The woman gave me a quick swipe of her eyes and then threw me a stiff, automatic smile as she took my arm, leading me toward the end of the hall like a brand-new, million-dollar racehorse she was afraid of spooking.

"Of course," she said. "It's so nice to meet you. I'm Christie. We've never actually spoken before, but Rhonda's said nothing but nice things . . ."

I allowed myself to be led, watching her face as she frowned at a group of men running past and swung open a door at the end of the hall, the gallery-sized library nice enough to startle me. I wandered into the middle of the floor, pacing toward the long bank of French windows that arched outward like a pulpit, and paused as the mayor laughed and turned his head in my direction, regarding me politely for a moment as a tall, blonde woman in an expensive-looking green dress stood up from her place by the fireplace before beckoning me over with a wave of her hand.

"Rhonda, this is Lea. She's with the *Tribune*."

"Lea," she said, extending her hand graciously as I approached. "It's nice to finally speak to you in person."

She gave me a warm smile and then turned to the mayor as I followed her gaze on cue, raising my brows as one of the city council members gave me a nod.

"Mayor Bingham, this is Lea. She one of the *Tribune*'s reporters. Lea this is . . ."

"Councilman Peters. Yes. It's nice to see you. We've actually met before."

Gregg Peters smiled in my direction without an ounce of recognition and nodded sagely for a moment.

"The *Tribune*'s a good paper. Is Noah still running things over there?"

"He is," I said, pulling out my recorder. "He does it all. Writes, edits . . ."

"I remember that. It's kind of his show, isn't it? He's a good man. A little tough, but a straight shooter."

"He really is," I said, trying not to roll my jaw in annoyance as I set the recorder down on the table next to me. "Mind if I just get your opinion on tonight's event?"

"What's your opinion of it?" He tossed back, looking at me curiously as I raised my hand and shrugged a little.

"Everyone seems to be having a good time."

"What a diplomatic answer."

"What do you think of it, Mr. Bingham? You've said you wanted to find a way to engage young people in the city. Is this party what you had in mind?"

"I think that anything that brings people out to support the city is a step in the right direction. I was impressed, frankly. Everyone really seems to be getting into the spirit of the thing."

"I especially liked the wedding chapel," Peters said, raising his glass to his lips. "And Elvis. That's not something you see every day."

"I'm not sure how accurate it is," Rhonda said with a laugh. "But you know. You just have to find a way to have fun with it."

"You'd probably know better than we would," Bingham said. "You've been out in the trenches all night. What are people saying about it?"

I gave them a charming, abbreviated version of the slowly careening party downstairs and passed around my phone full of photos as they all laughed and tolerated my presence, giving me nothing but a wall of cheerful platitudes. I thought about mentioning the wild, unchecked drinking that was going on downstairs, knowing they'd simply feign nonchalance and that it would never make it past Noah's eagle eye for trouble and snapped a few photos before excusing myself politely, feeling a little like I was leaving the captain's cabin after the *Titanic* had sailed through an iceberg.

I checked my watch as I headed downstairs, sending Tommy a quick text as I headed for the bar and relaxed a little as I ordered my first real drink of the night, snapping my press pass off before tucking it into my purse.

"Hey! Harley Quinn!"

I whipped my head around as a round table in the room behind the bar busted into laughter and froze as Jordan met my eyes across the floor, raising his brows a little as his eyes swept over my evil gypsy best. I glanced around for Tommy instinctively, sending another quick message as I dropped a five on the bar and tucked my purse over my arm as I moved through the crowd, blushing as one of his bandmates hooked his hand in my direction.

"Over here!"

I stopped in front of the table as Jordan gave me one of those strange, half-smiles of his, and cut my eyes toward the dark-haired guy on the other side of the table as he kicked out the stool between them and gave me a grin. None of them were in costume. I glanced at Jordan out of the corner of my eye as his friend whispered something to the tall lanky blond next to him, too drunk to drop his voice low enough for me to ignore it.

"She's the one from the picture," he said. "The one I was telling you about."

"I wasn't sure you were coming," I said, turning to Jordan as something dark and watchful passed through his eyes and then cleared as he shrugged, reaching for his glass.

"Neither was I," he said, taking a drink. He motioned to the chair next to him and then folded his hands over his chest, his blue eyes swirling restlessly for a moment as his face became a perfect blank. "It's nice to see you, Lea. Why don't you have a seat?"

"Yes, why don't you?" the blond said, letting out a long stream of smoke before tucking his vape into his pocket. I saw Jordan glance in his direction as he gave me a not-quite snide smile and sat down as he pointed in my direction, his eyes narrowing.

"You're with the paper, right?"

"The *Tribune*. That's right."

"Don't you want a quote?" he asked, reaching for his beer as his eyes swept around the room and then found their way back to me.

I tilted my head at him and then placed my elbows on the table without reaching for my recorder.

"What do you think about the event tonight? Is it what you were expecting?"

"Expecting? No. It's a little . . . pedestrian for my tastes. But you know. To each his own. Decent bar though."

"I liked the Elvis," the dark-haired guy next to him said as he raised his hand a little and gave me a smile.

"A lot of people did," I said, smothering a smile as I raised my drink to my lips.

"I talked to him for a little bit. He told me was actually ordained. I'm Terry, by the way."

"Lea. I had no idea. I guess I should've asked that."

"Paul," the blond said, making a quick motion to my purse. "Aren't you going to write any of this down?"

"I'm sure I'll remember."

"I could spell my name for you, if you want. Or better yet, just tell them a few guys from 'Heiress' Rising' stopped by. That should do the trick."

I felt the blood rise to my face as the rest of the table snickered, and then glanced at Jordan quickly as he gave me a sudden brilliant smile, looking over my face slowly for a moment.

"You changed your hair," he said.

"I did. Just highlighted, you know. Mixed reviews."

I brushed my hair away from my face and then back again as I tried to remember how normal human beings formed coherent sentences and tried not to stare back as Jordan searched my expression again, glancing away as he brushed his thumb under his lips thoughtfully for a moment.

"I like the blond," he said, reaching for his drink again.

I leaned my head on my hand as I glanced in his direction, his face softening a little as I looked over his body quickly for a moment, the tattoo across his chest just visible below the open neck of his dark button-down shirt. *Stop staring,* I told myself, dragging my eyes away as I held my glass with both hands, trying not to flip through the catalog of images I had pulled off of Abbie's Instagram account. *Stop staring, stop staring, stop staring . . .*

It's all right. You can stare. I don't mind.

I turned my head as he bit back another mysterious smile, watching me closely for a moment as his eyes narrowed and I opened my mouth to say something as Paul picked up his drink and tipped it in my direction.

"I actually liked it darker," Paul said, shrugging. "No offense."

"I liked it dark too," Jordan said. "The Ophelia thing."

"The what thing?" Terry asked, leaning closer.

"Ophelia," Jordan said, folding his hands in front of his mouth. "That's who she was named after. That girl in *Hamlet*."

He glanced at me as I sat back in my chair, his eyes running down the length of my throat for a moment.

"The one who dies of a broken heart."

You really should get thee to a nunnery, Lea. You have no idea what kind of monster a girl like you can make out of someone like me.

"Ophelia?" Paul scoffed. "I'm sorry. Didn't she go batshit crazy and then drown herself in a pond? I'm not sure heartbreak had anything to do with it."

"I guess it depends who's reading it," Jordan said. "Whether they're a romantic or not."

Paul glanced between us for a moment and then gave me a sudden grin, patting down the front of his jacket.

"Christ," he said taking a quick drag off his pen as Jordan regarded him mildly for a moment. "Romance. Same tricks, different girl. Why don't you give it a rest for a while, Casanova? I'll bet your wife is wondering where you're at right now."

Jordan's face changed quickly, a rush of sheer anger racing behind his polite expression before he caught it and brought it under control.

"Maybe you should skip the next round," he said, pushing his glass away as he rolled his jaw slightly.

Paul held up his hands as if he'd been wounded and then grinned.

"Don't listen to him. I've been drinking all night and look at my hand—steady as a rock. You can't cultivate a tolerance like that. That's pure genetics."

His dark eyes flashed with unpleasant amusement and Jordan sat forward at the table, trying to put some distance between us.

"You and Abbie work together, don't you? I know she mentioned something about it."

"We do. She's a good writer. I'm kind of showing her around. Noah wanted her to get a feel for the city."

"You're kidding. That's . . . interesting. I think there's a fable about that. Let me see if I can remember it."

Jordan face darkened and he looked at Paul flatly for a moment until he held up his hands, throwing me a look of amused apology.

"Paul," I said. "Right. I remember you now. Abbie told me about you."

"About me? What did Abbie say about me?"

I shook my head as Jordan turned his eyes in my direction and Paul nodded—his smile becoming thin and acid-laced.

"Oh. Let me guess. Her favorite story. Would you like to hear my side of it? I know it's not the popular version. My side kind of interferes with her whole meet-cute thing . . ."

"No, Paul," Jordan said, his voice clipped and even.

"No, it's good. How about another one then? How about I tell her the one about her bringing those two girls from her sorority to our first show in Nashville and how you were so fucking wasted that night you didn't even remember . . ."

"Shut the fuck up, Paul. I'm serious. Enough."

I pulled my hands away from the table as Jordan turned his shoulders slightly, his blue eyes suddenly hard and alert. He watched Paul's face carefully, his left hand resting on the table with a kind of deliberate restraint and saw Paul's eyes narrow before as he smiled, burying his bitterness as he glanced in my direction.

"And Abbie thinks I'm the one with a rage problem," he muttered.

"I was wondering where you went," Tommy said, pocketing his phone as he held up three tens between his fingers and dropped them in a little tent in front of my glass, giving me a wide, reckless grin. He pulled a stool out from the crowded table behind us, giving the two women that raised their brows in his direction a friendly nod and threw his arm over my shoulders as he picked up my glass, his dark eyes bright and bloodshot as he raised it to his lips.

"What is that?"

"This? My earnings. They're taking odds on how long it'll take the people inside the hedge maze to find their way out again. The funny thing is, it's not even really a maze. It's just like a long circle. Essentially, all they have to do is make the lap."

He finished what was left in my glass, shaking his head as he looked around the room for a moment. "I can't believe this is a city-sponsored event. What you should do is go Hunter S. Thompson on this shit and actually report what you saw. That's your story."

He paused as he noticed Jordan watching us closely, pulling his arm away as he looked down at me quickly and then gave him a small grin as he held out his hand, his tan face amused and ironic.

"I'm sorry. I'm being rude. Tommy."

Jordan considered him for a moment before sitting forward, shaking it as he glanced between us.

"Jordan," he said, his face polite and serious, glancing in Paul's direction as he stood up and walked away without speaking. He nodded across the table, making introductions automatically as I felt Jordan's eyes on me, chatting with Terry across the table for a moment, his drunken state only amplifying his quick, easy charm.

Ex-boyfriend? I heard, turning my head as he glanced at Tommy curiously for a moment. I had a sudden vivid image of Madge and Tommy and I laughing like idiots in some cemetery after dark over ten years ago, and felt my brow furrow as Jordan's expression relaxed—the image disappearing from my mind almost as quickly as it had appeared.

Are you actually hearing me or am I just imagining it?

Jordan smirked at me, his eyes narrowing again as Tommy shuffled the bills in the middle of the table like a magic trick, and stood up as he rolled his shoulders, gesturing to me with one hand as he reached for his phone.

"I wouldn't mind some fresh air," he said. "You said they're racing around at the back."

"'Racing' may be overstating it," Tommy said as Jordan looked down at his phone and frowned, tapping something in quickly as Terry and Alan got up from the table and headed for the door. "You should get a shot of them, Lea. The *Tribune* may not run it, but trust me, someone else will."

I glanced over my shoulder as Jordan's phone rang, following Tommy out as he stepped closer to the wall, and watched him speak sharply to someone before the crowd swallowed him whole, his face hard and irritated as he paced under the windows. Tommy raised his brows as he followed my gaze, something like grim respect entering his face and he held the door open for me as we stepped out onto the patio, the wind whipping across the lawn as the outdoor heaters sputtered.

"He's married?" Tommy asked, as he pulled out a pack of cigarettes and lit one between his cupped hands, passing it to me before lighting one for himself.

"For about five years. He's the lead singer in that band I was talking about. But he does some acting too. There's this independent film he was just amazing in . . ."

I broke off as Tommy raised his brows and then shrugged, pacing closer to the edge of the patio.

"I can see it. Did he ever model?"

"I don't really know. He's . . ."

Tommy nodded and flicked his ashes off the edge of the patio as a group of people at the other end of the terrace started cheering.

"Mysterious. Yeah. I got that too."

He looked at me curiously for a moment—all traces of his usual mocking good humor suddenly absent.

"You need to be careful, Lea."

"I told you, it's nothing . . ."

"It's not. Okay? I saw the way he was watching you. Just be careful with this one. That's all I'm saying."

I ran my tongue behind my teeth as I dragged a hand through my hair, glancing over my shoulder as Jordan stepped out onto the patio, a quick pang of wild jealousy running through me as I saw a group of girls near the wall turn around to watch him, following him with their eyes as he caught sight of us and moved through the crowd. He took a step forward as the crowd jostled us closer, smiling at my fluster as I dropped my hand onto his arm and pulled it back quickly and looked out toward the hedges as he held his hands up to the heater closest to us, his dark blue eyes shifting over the lawn restlessly as it began to drizzle.

"Is that them?"

Tommy held a hand up to his eyes and then tucked his cigarette into his mouth, applauding with the crowd as two girls dressed like barmaids stumbled out of the maze and collapsed into laughter.

"That's them. Wait. It looks like we have some more contestants. Three of them. Safety in numbers folks."

I stepped closer to the heater as I saw a group of people throw their hands up in the rain and then race across the lawn and swayed a little on my feet as Jordan shrugged his jacket off and placed it around my shoulders without asking, his face barely changing as he rubbed his hands in front of the heater again.

"I didn't know that you smoked," he said as his phone went off in his pocket again and he snapped it off without looking, folding his arms across his chest.

"I know. I'm trying to quit. You don't have to . . . it's really cold out here."

Jordan gave me another one of those deep searching looks again and then looked at my cigarette as I held it out to him, raising his brows as he took it out of my hand. I pulled the jacket around my shoulders as he let out a long stream of smoke, glancing at me out of the corner of his eye, and passed it back as the crowd began to move again, some of the partygoers heading back inside.

"You too?"

"I quit years ago," he said, tilting his head at me until I looked away. "Lots of bad habits."

Tommy glanced at his watch as the rain began to pick up and stamped out his cigarette as he glanced over our shoulders, looking from one end of the patio to the other.

"I think the party may be over," he said, nodding to the bar behind us as the bartenders started turning people away. "Midnight may be the cut off. Looks like they're closing up shop."

"That's too bad," Jordan said. "I'm not really in the mood to go home."

"Me either," I said. "Another bar?"

Tommy glanced between us for a moment and then lit another cigarette, shrugging a little as he glanced toward the parking lot.

"Maybe not. I actually have to meet with some lawyer tomorrow. Madge's thing. I'd rather not get into it."

"Oh, right," Jordan said, smiling. "You were the one who got arrested that night, weren't you?"

"Detained," he said, letting out a quick stream of smoke. "I was detained. Madge changed the locks on me since my last visit and one of her fucking neighbors called the cops when I was crawling in the window. Total bullshit."

Jordan laughed, the expression inching his face into a beauty so bright and vital he almost seemed immortal, and I stared as he raked his long hair away from his face with one hand, shaking his head as he glanced down at me.

"Seriously?"

"Yeah. I kept trying to convince this security dick to call my sister up and verify my identity, but he was just such an asshole. There was literally no reasoning with him. That's why I'm staying at a motel down here. Her whole condo association was scandalized."

"Down here? Which one?"

"The Timber Lodge. On Telegraph. It's a shithole, but what can I say? Drinking helps."

I looked him over as Tommy swayed on his feet for a moment, rallying like a champ as he took another drag of his cigarette and glanced at Jordan as I shook my head, tugging the sleeves of his jacket tighter around my shoulders.

"We'll drop you off first, Tommy," I said. "Where's your car?"

"Thank you. No. That's really not necessary . . ."

"It's not a problem," I said. "It's barely out of the way."

Tommy looked down at me and then sighed, tucking his cigarette into his mouth as he fished his keys out of his pocket.

"You know I'm absolutely fine, right?" he said holding them out to me. "It's just one road. I could get there with my eyes closed."

I turned my head as Jordan reached out to take them.

"Really," he said, holding my eyes for a moment. "It's no trouble."

CHAPTER SIX

I ACTUALLY ENDED UP DRIVING TOMMY'S CAR WHILE JORDAN trailed us in his Mustang, the deep red paint so pristine and glossy it looked as if he'd just driven it off of the lot. I watched Tommy doze off and bring himself back around a couple of times, waiting for him to launch back into conversation mid-sentence each time his eyes opened, and pulled into the lot as he pulled his cigarettes out again, glancing in the rearview mirror as Jordan pulled up beside us.

"You should come inside," he said, lighting his cigarette in one try and let out a quick stream of smoke. I raised my brows in his direction, still astounded at how quickly he could bring himself back from hours of hard drinking with a shrug and a grin, ever the professional—as if his drinking was the only job in the world he cared about enough to take seriously.

I'd only actually seen Tommy truly drunk once, years ago, back when Madge and I were both servers at the sleaziest bar in town and bonded over our mutual hatred of the place and practically every other waitress who crossed our path. Madge was the maid of honor in her cousin's wedding at the time and because she was too young to know what she was getting into, she had allowed herself to be corralled into planning the reception seating arrangements—a party of at least two hundred people, most of which she knew personally.

In a fit of angry desperation, she had enlisted my help one Friday night and I had gone over to help her sort through about a hundred and fifty miniature flags, blue for his side, red for hers. She had the whole seating arrangement laid out in front of her, smoking like a chimney as she stuck them into a long sheet of construction paper while I called out names and family associations from a list she had been compiling for over a week. The thing was a fiasco from the word go. To complicate matters, Tommy was colossally drunk and was laying on the couch in the living room, shouting out hilarious family anecdotes and suggestions while refusing to take part in the work himself—something that enraged Madge into an exhausted, self-righteous frenzy, which only seemed to delight Tommy more.

Eventually Madge stormed off in disgust, peeling out of the driveway in a fit of rage and I stayed with Tommy, matching him beer for beer while we both sat cross-legged on the living room floor and watched some old Paul Newman film with the volume turned way down. After a while, he simply stopped speaking and I began to get worried when I realized that his dark eyes were flat and glazed over while he drank, lifting one beer after another to his lips on total auto-pilot, oblivious to everything around him. I remember saying his name a few times, snapping my fingers in front of his face when his chin sank into his chest and felt a rush of absolute fear when I realized he was crying, his eyes seeking mine out like a stranger when I pulled the bottle out of his hand.

"Tommy?" I said, brushing my hand against his cheek as his dark blond hair fell into his face and felt a rush of absolute pain for him when he reached for me with both hands, holding me around the waist as he wept into my lap. I kept asking him what was wrong, but I couldn't understand anything he said. He talked quickly and incoherently like a man caught in some kind of confessional nightmare and I rocked him like that for a long time until he slept, telling me he was sorry, sorry, sorry.

The next morning, I woke up and Tommy was already awake, chatting with Madge in the kitchen—his old self again, as if nothing had ever happened. I stumbled into the room as he gave me an easy smile and poured me a cup of coffee, pointing out a large area of the reception hall that he and Madge had managed to arrange before I woke. I walked him out when he left, still reeling from the dramatic change in his demeanor, like some kind of cheerful mask he was determined to keep on at all times and looked up at him as he turned around at the last minute and kissed me hard on the forehead, his eyes as close to vulnerable as I had ever seen them.

"Thank you," he said against my cheek, cupping it lightly for a moment before he turned to go. And I never even knew what it was about. But after that he treated me differently, more gently, the way he treated Madge, as if his universe had permanently expanded to include me—important to him now, part of his orbit.

"I don't need a chaperone, Tommy," I said, feeling my heart stop in spite of myself as Jordan raised his brows in the window next to us and raised his hand.

Tommy smirked around his cigarette, tapping the ashes out onto the floor and reached for his door handle.

"Just come inside. A few minutes. Keep me company."

I chewed my lip as he got out, reaching for my purse as I stepped out of the car and tucked my hair behind my ear as Jordan got out after a minute or so, glancing up at the long row of apartment style motel rooms with raised brows.

"You pay by the night here?" I asked as Jordan followed us up to the door and Tommy patted down his shirt, pulling out an old-fashioned room key on a plastic keyring.

"As opposed to the hour?" Tommy said, wrestling with the lock for a moment before pushing the door wide open. He flicked the lights on as the entire layout came into focus—the bed front and center—in what was essentially a really run-down-looking studio apartment and tossed the key on the TV stand as we stepped inside, shrugging off his jacket slowly as if he was in pain.

"Actually, it's by the week," he said, sighing. "My penance for disrupting the sanctity of middle America."

Jordan glanced at me as Tommy walked to the kitchenette at the back of the room, pulling out three beers as I took off Jordan's coat and raised his hand as Tommy tossed him a beer without asking, looking over me slowly for a moment as he took a seat next to the bed.

"Mind if I use the bathroom?" I asked, as Jordan cracked his can open and Tommy pointed to the hall next to the fridge, passing me on the way as he sank into the bed.

"There's no water pressure," he said, as he reached for the remote. "Just warning you."

I stepped into the bathroom, flicking on the lights as I shut the door behind me and immediately regretted it as I got my first good look at the place—the dark, all-tile room feeling vaguely asylum-like as I leaned over the sink. I checked my make-up in the mirror, touching up my lip gloss as I heard

Tommy and Jordan talking in the next room and adjusted my bra slightly as I leaned over toward the mirror, roughing up my almost-blond curls for a minute before smoothing them down over the low square front of my top.

I sat with my back against the sink for a moment, rapping my long nails on the porcelain basin as I tried to get myself under some reasonable approximation of adult control and then smiled a little as I heard Tommy and Jordan laughing, turning off the lights as I headed back out into the room. Jordan looked up as I entered, his face becoming a little more serious as he held a beer out to me and I shook my head and sat down at the edge of the bed primly for a moment as I pulled my legs beneath me, glancing at Tommy as he played with the TV.

"You had a show tonight, didn't you?" I asked and Jordan nodded, resting his hand behind his head as he leaned back in his chair.

"Yeah. At this bar downriver. McGregor's."

He reached for his jacket on the edge of the bed and pulled a hash pipe out of one of the inner pockets, raising it toward me with a grin as he lit it with a casual wave of his hand.

"How'd it go?"

"Good," he said, taking a quick hit before offering it to me. "Really good. We had a big crowd. Some of that was the other acts, but it was mostly us."

I shook my head and Jordan offered it to Tommy who waved him off politely, unloading small bottles from the bedside table as he lined them up in a neat row, labels in.

"You were headlining, weren't you?"

"Yeah. Which was nice. These little places, you know. They kind of dick you around for a while. They have their favorite acts and if you're the outsider, sometimes you can wait months to headline. But like I said, our crowd is pretty good. Loyal. They come out to see us, which we always appreciate."

"Do you get any part of that?" Tommy asked, taking another drink.

"We split with the house—fifty-fifty. And then they pay you to play. It's pretty good money. This area has been good to us so far. We've been lucky."

"I've been meaning to come out," I said, lying on my side as I propped myself up with one elbow and watched his eyes run down the length of my body slowly, finding his way back up to my eyes—relaxed, considering.

"Yeah," he said raising his brows, his dark blue eyes so bright and intense they barely seemed like part of the same expression at all. "I've been wondering when you would."

He smiled at my expression and then pulled out his phone, tapping at it quickly for a minute as my cell let out a low chime.

"You're on our mailing list," he said, laughing a little as I blushed and scrolled through the upcoming events slowly for a minute, lingering on the black and white of him and his band long enough for him to notice.

"Nice picture."

"Think so?"

I turned my phone around to Tommy who took it out of my hand, nodding over it as he held it up.

"Intense."

"Yeah. That's what we were going for. Intensity."

"I saw your movie too."

Jordan's smile broadened for a moment and then he ran his hand over his face as I leaned over to take my phone back.

"Ah fuck. Who told you about that? Abbie? I swear to god, she tells fucking everyone."

"She should tell people. I would. You were really good in it."

"Thank you. Really. But it just wasn't even anything. A couple of my friends were doing it and they needed someone to play this kid's brother for almost no money . . ."

"His younger brother was an addict in the film," I explained as Tommy cracked one of the bottles open next to the bed, glancing in Jordan's direction. "He was the only one in his life who was trying to save him."

I looked back at him as he pressed his knuckles against his lips for a moment, some emotion too quick and convoluted for me to catch passing through his eyes briefly before vanishing.

"I didn't really understand the ending though. When he got up. I couldn't . . . I didn't know if he was dead or not. You just looked so shattered."

"Yeah," he said closing his eyes briefly, before staring at the ceiling. "That scene was tough. And other people have said that, you know. That they didn't understand that part of it. Honestly, it was pretty straightforward. I was just supposed to be this guy trying to save my younger brother. But I've heard all sorts of things online."

"Like what?" Tommy asked, passing one of the bottles in front of his nose as he closed his eyes.

"That I was a ghost. That I was already dead. That Aiden was just kind of imagining me. That I was some kind of guardian spirit . . ."

He took another hit of his pipe as he kept his eyes closed, the smoke wafting around his head in a thin cloud of white and cracked his eyes open as he looked me over again, holding my eyes as I rolled onto my stomach.

"Ever do that?"

"Ever do what?"

"Try to save someone that didn't want to be saved?"

I opened my mouth to speak and then closed it again quickly, my eyes running to Tommy in spite of myself and glanced at him as he raised the bottle again, shaking his head lightly as a low tremor ran beneath his calm expression—equal parts bliss and pain.

"No," Tommy said. "I don't think so."

Jordan rolled his eyes toward me again and then closed them as he folded his hands across his chest, letting out a deep sigh as rested his head against the wall.

"I have," he said flatly. "Trust me. It's not worth it."

I watched his face become calm and faraway, the sensation that I was some kind of intruder watching him sleep forcing me to tear my eyes away as Tommy held up the remote in my direction, clicking through the channels quickly as he shook his head.

"Twenty-two channels on this thing and half of them are porn," he said as I turned my head, blinking a little as he flipped from one blocked screen to the next. "Pay per view porn. Look at this. I Fucked my Hot Stepdad. Sexy Cum Sluts. Amateur Anal Nymphos. Amateur Anal Nymphos Part Two. This place is like the motel that time forgot."

I glanced over my shoulder as I saw the bathroom door shut out of the corner of my eye, meeting Tommy's eyes as he glanced over his shoulder and slid down to his side of the bed as he tossed the remote onto the bedspread in disgust, picking up his beer as I grabbed the pillow next to him, curling up next to his legs. I followed his gaze as the shower began to run, my eyes widening a little as Tommy raised his brows and then grinned at my expression as he took a sip and passed his beer to me.

"I'll give you fifty dollars right now if you go in and join him."

I choked a little as he laughed, shaking my head as I dragged my hand up the side of my boots and he shrugged and took the beer back, glancing back toward the TV again as the water slapped against the tile.

"No," I said. "No. I would die. No."

"Ah," he said, taking another drink. "You like him, don't you?"

He tilted his head at me as I turned my head, unzipping the side of my lace-up boots with one hand and watched me take them off and toss them to the floor, resting his hand on his chest as he grinned.

"No," he said, raising his brows. "I get it. Really."

He glanced back toward the closed door again and then rolled his eyes to me slowly.

"How much would you pay me to do it?" he asked, his eyes narrowing and then mocked my look of surprise as I sat up, pulling my pillow into my lap.

"What?"

Tommy raised his brows, his expression softening as he rested his hand on his chest, raising a hand as he shook his head.

"Come on, Lea. It can't be that much of a surprise."

"Madge never said anything . . ."

Tommy rolled his jaw a little and then set his beer down on the bedside table, reaching for one of the bottles next to it.

"Believe it or not, Madge doesn't actually know everything there is to know about me."

"You've had girlfriends. I've met them."

"Christ, you're adorable," he said as he laughed softly for a moment. "I'm going to give you a few seconds to reason it out. Let me know when you get there."

I watched him close his eyes as he inhaled deeply, his hand dropping automatically before he snapped it to attention near his knee.

"Oh . . ."

"Yeah. Oh . . ."

I brushed my hair away from my face and scooted closer as he set the bottle back on the table, looking over his smooth, angular face as if seeing it for the first time.

"Do you . . . have a preference?"

Tommy raised his brows, rubbing his fingers against the side of his head as if something was amusing him deeply and then shrugged and reached for his beer again.

"It doesn't really work that way," he said, his voice amused and ironic. "It's more about the person. For me, anyway."

He leaned a little closer and I watched his dark blond hair fall into his eyes as he looked at me seriously for a minute, his fingers so close to my knees I could feel them brush against my skin when he spoke.

"And I don't want Madge to know about it either. All right?"

"You know she wouldn't care. Your mom . . ."

"Not either of them. It's just not something I'm ready to do. Both of them are already integrated into every aspect of my life as it is. The last thing I need is for them to turn my sex life into some kind of social enrichment project."

He brushed my hair away from my face and looked me over carefully for a minute, his eyes lingering on my lips as I blinked up at him.

"Okay?"

"I'd never say anything, Tommy. You know that."

He smiled at me gently for a moment and then sat back against the headboard, beckoning me closer as the showerhead squealed loudly and then went silent.

"I know you wouldn't. Hey, let's order some porn before he gets out. Just for kicks."

I laughed as I reached over him for his beer and he pushed my hand away and held up the colorful bottle next to him, shaking it lightly as he held my eyes.

"Ever try this before?"

"Um . . . no?"

"Lea, Lea, Lea," he said, wrapping his arm around my shoulder as he unscrewed the bottle in front of me. "You're such an innocent. It's really no big deal. The high only lasts for about two minutes. Just inhale deeply. Not that close. Just like breathing."

I hesitated as he put the bottle under my nose and glanced at him as he watched me closely for a moment, his dark eyes flashing oddly as I rested my hand on his knee.

"What's it like?"

"Different for everyone. For me, it's like being incredibly aware of every nerve in your body. All at the same time."

I raised my brows as he held the bottle in front of me, leaning over to inhale deeply and pulled my head away quickly as he grinned, a rush of light-headedness hitting me instantly before crawling lower.

"See what I mean?" he asked, brushing his fingers down the length of my bare arm and I shivered as my skin seemed to come to life under his touch, suddenly aware of every inch of skin on my body as I closed my eyes. I felt a sudden sensation of floating as he shifted behind me, wrapping his arm around my shoulder as he brushed his fingers down my face and I turned to him as I felt his hand slide lower, inching my skirt up slowly as he ran his fingers against the bare skin of my thigh.

"Are these thigh highs?" he asked, his face gently amused as he spoke against my ear and I felt him slide his finger inside the tight lace at the top as my eyes popped open, sitting forward quickly as Jordan stood in the hall, watching us in the shadows as we both turned our heads. He glanced between us for a minute, meeting my eyes in the darkness as I bit my lip and curled my fingers into my lap as he walked in and sat back down in his chair against the wall, his damp hair spilling across his bare chest as he picked up his hash pipe again.

"What are you two doing?" he asked as he took a quick hit, leaning his head against the wall as he looked down at me with half-lidded eyes. I looked over his body quickly as he brushed his hair away from his face, the three swords above his heart like a dark, uneven scar across his lean, muscular chest. I glanced at Tommy quickly as I realized he was doing the same thing, his dark eyes moving over his body as Jordan turned his eyes in his direction and sat up a little as he rested his foot on the edge of the bed, watching his free hand move across his hard stomach before he raised a hand impatiently.

"What's wrong?" he asked, raising his brows in my direction. "Don't want to tell me?"

"Just talking," I said. "Tommy wanted to pick out some porn . . ."

"Really?" Tommy asked, his voice light and ironic as he reached for one of the untouched bottles next to his beer bottle. "I think I was mocking the porn selection. But you know, if you really want to see the follow-up to Sexy Cum Slut Orgy, all you have to do is ask."

Jordan smiled, his mood lifting a little as Tommy cracked the bottle open and took another hit of his pipe as he swung his attention in my direction, his foot tapping restlessly against the bedframe.

"Really? You're into that?"

Tommy snickered and I raised my brows, watching his blue eyes shift over me slowly as I rolled my eyes.

"Not really. No."

"She lies," Tommy said, inhaling deeply as he closed his eyes for a moment, his hand dropping and pausing in the exact same place it had before as if he had practiced it in his sleep. "She's all about the Cum Sluts. She's just too embarrassed to admit it in polite company."

"God. Shut the fuck up, Tommy. Seriously."

Jordan burst into laughter and I stared without meaning to in spite of myself, something about the expression changing his face completely.

"Nothing wrong with that," Jordan said, giving me a sudden, reckless grin and I felt my entire body flush as he followed my gaze down his chest, raising his brows as Tommy raised his hand.

"Full disclosure," he said taking another hit off of the bottle. "I was actually in a porno once."

"You were not," I said, and he gave me a mysterious grin, handing me the bottle as he held my eyes for a moment.

"You were *not.*"

"To my immense shame—yes, I was. It was about . . . god, twelve years ago. In New York. No one knows about it."

"Get the fuck out of here," Jordan said, letting out another laugh as he rolled his eyes in my direction.

"'Seduced by my Stepmom.' She was this older woman; I was home from college. It was a whole thing."

He shrugged as I stared, plucking the bottle out of my hand as I shook my head.

"The acting thing wasn't working out. They were offering college kids like, five hundred dollars for a day's work. I was broke, misled, jaded, confused . . ."

"And they paid you to fuck some hot older woman."

Tommy pointed at him.

"Exactly. And it was actually two of them. The first scene it was just me and my stepmom and then her friend came over and they kind of . . . shared me."

He raised the bottle to his face again and took a quick hit.

"It was pretty hot," he said.

I glanced between them for a moment as Jordan watched my face, something slightly darker than humor moving through his too-blue eyes and raised my brows in Tommy's direction as he set the bottle down, shaking his head lightly.

"Okay. No more of that for now. I need to slow it down."

"How much older where they?" I asked and Tommy glanced toward the ceiling, shaking his head as if figuring out a quick sum.

"Forty? Forty-one?"

"And you were?"

"Nineteen?"

"Seriously?"

"What? I've never minded older women."

Jordan smothered a smile as he glanced at me.

"Me neither."

I laid back on the bed and rested my hand over my head, rolling my eyes as I stared at the ceiling.

"Whatever."

"Oh, come on," Tommy said laughing. "I can see you having some of your own Mrs. Robinson moments in like ten years or so. You're a bored housewife in some upscale neighborhood along the water. Your best friend's hot son comes home from college early one day . . ."

"You are so wrong."

Tommy and Jordan both burst into laughter and I shook my head and then rolled on my side as Jordan's smile softened a little, something hard and watchful moving behind his eyes.

"They actually wanted me to kind of stay on for a few days. Complete the series."

"Really?"

"What can I say? I was a natural. I guess a lot of first timers have a problem staying hard for the entire shoot but . . . no."

I glanced in Tommy's direction, my eyes running to his cock before I could stop myself and raised my brows as he caught the look, shifting my eyes to Jordan as I ran my hand through the back of my hair.

"That's never really been a problem for me," he said, grinning a little at my expression as some of the humor went out of Jordan's face.

"How nice for you."

"It is. Thank you."

"Big talker."

"The biggest."

Jordan glanced between us for a moment, sitting back in his chair and held my eyes for a moment as he picked up his pipe, waving it in Tommy's direction.

"Show her," he said, raising his brows, his voice flat and relaxed. I whipped my head in his direction as Tommy laughed, his brow furrowing a little as Jordan took a quick hit, nodding as the smoke swirled around his head.

"Sure," Tommy said, leaning back against the headboard as he reached for his beer.

"Why not?"

Jordan shifted his eyes back to me and I felt my pulse take a quick, erratic spike as he grinned in Tommy's direction, the expression never quite reaching his eyes.

"I'm serious," he said, staring at him steadily as some of the amusement drained from Tommy's face. He glanced toward me quickly as he took a drink, setting the beer back down as he reached for a pillow.

"You're fucking stoned," he said, tucking it behind his head as he closed his eyes.

Jordan dragged his eyes away from him slowly, smirking a little in my direction and then nodded at Tommy as he picked up his pipe.

"Go ahead," he said, his voice low and relaxed. "He won't stop you. Believe me."

I tore my eyes away from his, something about his tone goading me on and crawled forward on the bed as Tommy opened his eyes, his entire body stiffening as I sat up on my knees in front of him. His dark eyes shifted over my face as I placed my hands on his thighs and I glanced in Jordan's direction quickly as he leaned forward and rested his elbows on his knees, brushing his thumb across his lips as he raised his brows.

"Go ahead, Lea," he said, a cruel note of amusement entering his voice as he egged me on. "He wants you to."

I leaned closer, running my hands down the front of his pants as Tommy inhaled quickly and unzipped them slowly as he closed his eyes—something hungry and painful moving behind his expression as I pulled his cock out with one hand. I tugged his pants down a little as I ran my fingers up it slowly, coiling them around it as I stroked him gently for a moment, and felt a strange, ferocious sense of longing and power as Tommy opened his eyes to watch, his entire body stiffening with hunger as his cock bucked against my palm.

I glanced up at him as I tightened my grip, stroking him more quickly as he let out a light moan and reached for his balls with my other hand and tugged at them lightly, watching his entire body shudder as he reached for my face with one hand. I leaned closer to the head of his cock, his expression so gentle and urgent I closed my eyes, and felt him drag his thumb from my lips to my chin, opening them slowly as I heard Jordan clear his throat.

"Don't touch her," he said, his voice low and clipped.

Tommy looked over my shoulder, pulling his hand away from my hair as his expression changed and I watched him flatten it out on the bed as I wrapped my lips around his cock, sucking at the tip until I felt his body jump beneath me. I coiled my thumb and forefinger under the head, rubbing it up and down the length of his cock quickly as I ran my tongue around it and let go all at once as I leaned forward, pulling him into my mouth as I felt his fingers brush through the ends of my hair. I ran my mouth over him quickly for a moment, teasing him gently as I pushed his legs wider and opened my eyes as I held the head of his cock with one hand, running my tongue up and down the length as I watched his lips sigh open.

I closed my lips around him as Tommy gasped, stroking him with one hand as I slid my mouth over him quickly and felt my entire body flush as he said my name, feeling Jordan's hands on my waist as I opened my eyes. I felt him run his hand against the front of my throat, pulling me away from Tommy as he unzipped my corset in the back and then yanked it off with a rough tug as he dragged me backward, turning me around to face him as he ran his hands through the back of my hair. I felt that strange sensation of shifting sand again as Jordan kissed me deeply, his tongue moving inside my mouth quickly as he tipped my head up with a push of his thumb and opened my eyes as I felt him press his hands against my face, his eyes like an ocean—dark and bottomless.

"Nothing's going to happen tonight that you don't want, Lea," he said, holding my gaze urgently for a moment as I sat forward to kiss him. He smiled a little, holding me a hand's width away as he brushed his fingers against my lips. "Understand?"

I blinked up at him and nodded as I closed my eyes, wrapping my hands behind his neck.

"I understand."

"Do you trust me?"

"I trust you."

"Good," he said, as he kissed me gently on the mouth. "Now open your eyes."

I opened my eyes as he slid my skirt off with both hands, reaching into his pocket as he glanced over his shoulder. I followed his gaze as he pulled out a pack of matches, watching Tommy stroke himself quickly for a moment before Jordan tipped my head back in his direction.

"Tell him to wait for you," he said, placing something hard and plastic in my palm, and then brushed his hands against my cheeks as his blue eyes dipped and twirled. "Use those."

I felt my stomach flip as I closed my fist around the zip ties, turning around on the bed as Tommy opened his eyes and crawled up to meet him as I straddled him at the waist, reaching for his face with both hands as I pulled him closer.

"Tell me to stop," I whispered against his cheek and Tommy looked up at me and closed his eyes, shaking his head slightly as I reached for his wrist.

"Don't stop," he said as I zip-tied his wrist to the metal headboard, brushing my breasts over his lips as I reached for his other hand. "Don't stop, don't stop . . ."

I unbuttoned his shirt quickly as I sat on his chest, unhooking my bra with both hands and ran my hand over his face as I slid my body against him, running my hand behind his head. I kissed him deeply as he leaned up to meet me, pressing my hand against his face as I pulled away and brushed my lips against his muscular chest as I slid my body backward, sliding them down the hard line of his stomach until I reached the edge of the bed. Jordan kissed me hard again as my body slid against him, releasing me gently as I yanked Tommy's pants and boxers off before tossing them to the floor and then reached for the book of matches at the end of the bed, palming them lightly as he met my eyes.

Jordan looked Tommy over from the edge of the bed, meeting his gaze as he walked to his side and stood over him as Tommy ran his eyes over his hard cock, his face captivated and terrified as Jordan raised his brows. He pulled three matches out of the pack as Tommy watched, setting them down on the edge of the nightstand before reconsidering and adding a fourth, and I sat down between his legs as Jordan sat beside him, watching Tommy close his eyes as he ran a hand through his dark blond hair. Jordan leaned over to speak against his ear quietly as he reached for the matchbook, turning his head toward him as Tommy nodded without speaking, and then smiled as his blue eyes shifted violently for a moment, putting the book of matches in his mouth.

Jordan opened the drawer next to the bed, rummaging through it casually before pulling out a small bottle of lube and poured some out in the palm of his hands before rubbing them together lightly, grabbing Tommy's cock in one hand as he closed his eyes. He stroked him in quick, hard strokes, watching his face closely as Tommy's entire body went still and I inhaled quickly as I crawled closer, watching something hard and violent move behind Jordan's too-perfect face as he tipped his chin up to watch him.

I shifted my body between his legs, placing my hand over the top of his cock as Jordan stroked him quickly and watched Tommy's back arch slightly as he took the matchbook out of his mouth, running his hand around the back of his neck as he leaned over and kissed him deeply. I held my breath as Tommy opened his eyes, wincing a little as Jordan squeezed his cock hard with one fist and then pulled away slowly as he turned to look at me, his expression softening a little as I wrapped my lips around the head of his cock. Jordan brushed his thumb over my lips, touching them gently for a moment as I opened my mouth wider and then held my eyes as he coiled his hand in my hair, pulling me closer as Tommy let out a low, strangled moan.

I sucked on his cock deeply for a moment, holding him in one hand as I ran my lips down the length in light, teasing strokes and felt Jordan slide his body behind me as he ran his hands over my breasts, cupping them lightly as he kissed the back of my neck.

You like doing that, don't you? You care about him. I can tell.

I turned as I heard his voice inside my head, gasping as I felt his hand run around the front of my throat and bowed my head as he kissed the side of my neck—his lips running against my cheek, my shoulder, the top of my spine. I felt a lightheaded thrill of hunger for him as I felt Jordan drag my body backward, my feet sliding on the floor behind me and felt a sudden quake of fear as he wrapped his hand around Tommy's ankles and yanked him toward the edge of the bed, the zip ties around his wrists going taut as he brushed his hand up the back of my spine.

I felt my elbows hit the bedspread as Jordan forced my body forward, sliding my underwear off impatiently as he knocked my knees apart and I leaned forward until my lips brushed against Tommy's hard cock, closing my eyes as Jordan wrapped his hands around my hips.

Don't be afraid, I heard. *I'm with you. I'm here. Trust me, Lea. Trust me, trust me, trust me . . .*

His eyes were an ocean. I wavered. I fell.

I woke to the sound of thunder. I cracked my eyes open slowly, the flash of lightning from the windows stuttering across the ceiling until I couldn't quite tell if I was still dreaming or not, and felt my heart stop as Jordan brushed his fingers from my temple to my cheek, his blue eyes almost vulnerable as he watched me sleep. I swallowed hard as I turned my head, his lips pulling up into something that was not quite a smile and followed his hand as he brushed my hair away from my skin, reaching up to touch him in the darkness. He watched my eyes as I touched his palm, letting our fingertips dance together and apart in the quick half-stutter of light and blinked up at him as he caught my hand, pulling it toward him as he kissed my fingertips gently, one at a time. I glanced around his body as he followed my eyes, giving me that strange half-smile again as I realized Tommy was gone and cupped my face in one hand as he looked at me seriously for a moment, something hungry and searching moving behind his teasing expression.

"Scared?" he asked, raising his brows and I pressed my hand against the tattoo over his heart and shook my head, curling my body toward him, feeding off of his heat.

"What is this? This tattoo. What does it mean?"

Jordan glanced down at the three swords on his chest, the middle one a little higher than the others and shrugged as he pulled my hand closer, covering it completely as he leaned on one arm.

"Good question. I really don't remember. I got it when I was like eighteen."

He held up his heavily inked forearm before curling his body closer, reaching over to kiss the front of my throat.

"And there have been a lot since then."

I brushed my hand over his face as he grinned down at me, kissing my lips lightly as I pulled away and ran a nail down the sword in the middle as his expression darkened, blinking up at him as I brushed my hair behind my ear.

"You don't have to lie to me, you know. I was just curious."

Jordan looked down at my hand, picking my finger up lightly as he used it to trace over each sword and then closed his eyes as he shook his head, that other look back—hunted, searching.

"It was just something I did. To remind myself."

"Remind you of what?"

"The first girl who broke my heart," he said, pulling my hand away from him as he raked his long hair away from his face.

I looked over it more carefully as his brow furrowed for a moment, and leaned up on my elbow as he rolled over onto his back, watching him tap his fingers against his chest restlessly for a minute as the rain hit the window in a hard slap.

"You were eighteen?"

"Ah . . . a little younger. It was just some stupid thing. The kind of thing a kid does. Trust me, she never felt the same way. Later on, I just felt like a fool. I had all these emotions wrapped up in this fantasy about some woman who never even really existed."

He rubbed his fingers over his forehead for a moment, his entire body tensing and relaxing as he opened his eyes.

"But I learned," he said, his voice low and clipped as his dark blue eyes shifted across the ceiling. "I learned."

I watched a low tremor of pain move behind his relaxed expression and brushed my fingers against his lips before I could stop myself, so desperate to make the look go away I felt hot tears rise in the back of my throat, utterly helpless, caught completely. He looked up at me, his eyes darting over my face quickly for a moment and then held his arm out as he rolled toward me, pulling me toward him as he leaned over me on the bed.

"You can tell me about it if you want," I said. "I've been there. I have."

"I used to be really fucked up, you know," he said, his voice coming out low and fast as if he had been holding his breath. "I mean really. And you're not the only one, either. I used to be an addict too. A long time ago."

I felt my brow furrow as he ran his fingers over my face, my mind reeling as I searched for a reason as to why he thought I had ever been an addict and held my breath as he kissed the palm of my hand, his eyes dark and frantic as he pulled me closer.

"That's why I know," he whispered against my cheek. "That's why when you said what you did, about heroin, about always being the one that fucks everything up, I understood it. I did."

I felt my throat tighten as he brushed his hands against my face, holding my eyes as the world shifted beneath me.

"Normal people never know, do they? It's like you spend your entire life translating how you really feel about things into some sort of acceptable foreign language. Some version of yourself that won't scare people. If they knew, if they ever once really saw you, what you were capable of in that place …"

I felt him wrap his hand around the back of my neck, the storm rattling the window pane behind us and reached for his face with both hands as he crawled on top of me, his long hair falling into my face as he ran his thumb under my chin.

"Don't be afraid of me, Lea," he said, kissing me gently as his entire body shifted over me, easing my legs apart with one knee as he coiled his hand in the back of my hair. "Don't be. I'd never judge you. Never. You can be anything you want with me. Confess everything. Or nothing. I don't fucking care."

I wrapped my hands behind his neck as he pulled me closer, coiling my legs around him until I could feel every inch of his body as he moved against me and kissed him deeply as he brushed his hand over my skin, closing my eyes as I felt him slide his body lower.

"Just stay with me," he said, his voice low and urgent as he brushed his lips beneath the deep curve of my breast. "Stay, stay, stay . . ."

I was into the hero thing for a while, but not anymore. Eventually, we'd have to have that whole conversation. You get tired of always being the screw-up, you know? The one who needs to be fixed.

What I said that night. And what he heard:

I was into heroin for a while, but not anymore. Eventually, we'd have to have that whole conversation. You get tired of always being the screw-up, you know? The one who needs to be fixed.

We met across that chasm—between who we actually were and what we seemed to be to the world. Oh, my love, my love, my love. We all hear what we want to hear. Has it ever really been any other way?

OTHER THINGS. SOON TO BE REDACTED:

You've been trying to get in my head. And you think you're beginning to understand. I can see it in your face. You're relaxed now, more confident when you speak to me. I am not exactly With the Program, but you think you have a diagnosis—a name for what's wrong for me. You've run the numbers, you've interpreted the data, you've played the percentages. You are the meteorologist of emotional trauma, and after a lot of hard consideration you feel confident to go back to your bosses and tell them that All Signs Point to Rain. How relieved they'll all be. And what's more, I'll never contradict you. Because the truth is, it doesn't matter anyway. I've already decided not to stay. And frankly, the less you know about that decision the better.

He was brilliant, you know. And right about almost everything in the way only true outsiders ever can be right. Because normal people really never will understand what it's like to spend your whole life living in that place—that thin, thin sliver of sanity between what the world wants you to be and everything you secretly know you could become if you'd only let the pendulum slip just a little more to the left, knock you off balance, seal your fate.

There were little things. Things I should've have seen but didn't. That night I fell asleep in his arms—I was on the left side of the bed, Tommy was on Jordan's right. I only intended to close my eyes for a few minutes but when I opened them, it was a few hours later and Tommy was speaking quietly, asking Jordan to let him up. When Jordan didn't respond, I cracked my eyes open a little wider and saw Jordan just flipping through random television stations, drinking a beer and ignoring him. When he asked again, I saw Jordan glance at him out of the corner of his eye and then simply went back to watching TV again, raising his beer to his lips as something hard and dangerous danced behind his relaxed expression.

I dug my nails into the sheets as Tommy asked again, almost a plea and felt my stomach clench as Jordan finally looked at him, turning to run his hands over the burn marks on his stomach thoughtfully for a moment before reaching over to the opposite bedstand and picking up his knife. I watched him cut Tommy loose one wrist at a time, reaching for the back of his neck as he pulled himself free and kissed him hard on the mouth as Tommy looked up at him, frightened and aroused as Jordan snapped his knife closed. I watched him set it back down on the table as Tommy got out of bed and headed for the bathroom, picking up his beer as he reached for the remote and went back to flipping through the TV as if nothing had happened, his blue eyes hard and restless—watching, waiting.

And where should an image like that go? How would that image even make sense to someone like you? Someone who has probably spent her entire life on the other side of that razor-thin catwalk that separates your world from all the people you treat. The one you need to believe in, for your life to go on making sense.

You asked me why I loved him and no matter how many reasons I give you, you never seem convinced—so let me explain it to you this way, in one of the pages you'll never get a chance to see. I loved him because he knew what it was like to exist in that place between those things that keep us sane and everything that pushes us to the edge of the abyss—both sides cheering us on, telling us to go over, over, over. He could live there and pull back and keep from going over, so naturally it seemed like a dance, and when I was with him I could dance with him and I felt safe because I knew that no matter what, he'd never let me go over the edge alone.

I tried to explain this to you once, tried to explain to you why Joker and Harley's romance appealed to me so much, but you never really understood. All you saw was the abuse. You missed the dance completely. What people like you will never understand about people like me is that we're not motivated by normal things—they hold no mystery for us, they fail to inspire. And what the Joker knew about her that no one else seemed to get was that the only thing that truly could control Harley was love. That's it. Nothing else.

Take love out of the equation for someone like that and essentially all you're left with is a violent, cheerful, ticking time bomb. A girl with nothing to lose and a hit list with a million names on it. Because at the bottom of it all, it's not the ones that hurt you that harden you the most in this world, it's the ones who knew all along and didn't do anything to stop it. The sins of good men damn us all. And here's something else that you'll never understand until life has taken so much from you that you will stand at the edge of precipice and dare fate to knock you over—at that point, any one person is the same as the next. Because they all deserve it. Even you. Even me.

I know I'm not supposed to speak in comic metaphors anymore. They seem to upset everyone. As if you honestly needed one more glaring bad habit to point to and make the case for my tragic arrested development. So, I'll close with this. At some point, you will find yourself out on that catwalk between this world and that. Not a threat. Simply fate. One side will be rooting for you. One side will be rooting against you. And instead of going over, you will do a twirling, Olympic-level triple backflip from a running start and flip over, over, over, hands up on point, stick the landing and wave to the fucking crowd. Because not everyone can stick the landing. But you will find a way to do it. And it will be amazing.

AND IN CASE YOU WEREN'T PAYING ATTENTION BITCH, I STUCK THE FUCKING LANDING. I'M STILL ME AND I'M STILL SANE. SO, WHERE'S MY FUCKING MEDAL?

CHAPTER SEVEN

THERE WAS A PART OF ME THAT DIDN'T EXPECT TO SEE HIM again after that, so I lived in that moment as long as I could, ran it over and over in my mind, allowed myself the rare thrill of total happiness for that day and the next—hearing his voice in my mind, feeling his touch, listening to his songs. I sat on the balcony outside my window, too excited and frightened to sleep, afraid I'd miss a single moment of joy without fear and drank coffee in my nightgown and long sweater as I watched the gray mist over the neighborhood behind the alley rise like smoke in the orange-red dawn—there for over an hour and then dissipating like a wave of surf.

On Monday I went to work in a fog, filing my articles like a sleepwalker, my skin hot and feverish. I began to come down a little when the hard reality of what I'd done began to sink in and filter through, the cool pang of paranoia beginning to eat away at my happiness in fits and starts. I worried about Thomas, who hadn't called, my mind replaying a vivid image of Jordan leaning over him on the bed and putting the book of matches in his mouth on some thrilling, terrifying endless loop, and avoided Madge as deftly as I could, certain she would read the panic on my face and force me to confess everything. *What had we done?* I wondered, watching Abbie out of the corner of my eye as she typed out her features as cheerfully as she always did—ever professional, ever polite. *What had we done, what had we done, what had we done?*

I sent a text to Thomas on the way to my city council meeting, shredding the nails on my right hand as I waited for a response, and picked up the phone automatically as it chimed in the middle of the budget report, heading for the door as all five members shot one collective look of disapproval in my direction. I picked up my phone as I jostled my cigarettes out of my pocket, already planning to head for my car and fumble my way through the bullet points with a lot of loose copy and quotes and paused with my lighter in the air as I heard Jordan on the other line, the flame singeing my fingers as I shook it out with one hand.

"Hello? Lea?"

"I'm here," I said, pacing down the dark sidewalk quickly as I tucked my untouched cigarette in my pocket, and smiled in spite of myself as my heart raced, pulling my long sweater around me as I watched the well-lit bar downtown bustle with bodies. "Hi. Sorry. I was in a council meeting."

"Yeah," he said. "Abbie mentioned something about that. Are you out now?"

I glanced back at the building, reaching for my cigarette again as I bit my lip and lit it with a wave of my hand as I shoved the minutes from the meeting a little lower in my purse, glancing in both directions as I crossed the street to the parking lot.

"Yeah. It was just some boring budget stuff. I can make something up. It's not that big of a deal."

"Do you do that a lot?"

"What's that?"

"Just bail on meetings and make it up as you go along?"

"Once or twice maybe. I try not to . . ."

"Afraid of getting caught?"

I pressed my lips together as I heard him smile and shook my head as I reached my car, slid inside and tossed my purse on the opposite seat.

"Haven't been yet. Noah would have to want to catch me. You know, unless I really pissed someone off or misquoted them or something . . ."

I trailed off as he went silent, cracking the window as my brow furrowed and checked my make-up in the mirror quickly as I waited for him to speak. *Calm down*, I thought. *He called you. Don't act crazy. Let him tell you want he wants.*

What if I like crazy?

"What?"

"I asked where you were headed now."

"Just home. Why? Where are you at?"

"Close by," he said, his voice low and relaxed. "You live above that little dive bar near the paper, don't you? End of the block?"

"I do. How did you . . ."

Know that? I know a lot of things about you, Lea. More than you would believe.

"Mind if I stop by?"

I felt my pulse skyrocket as I did a quick rundown of every mundane chore I had been letting go for the better part of a month and took another drag of my cigarette as I glanced at the clock, the screen on the dash flashing 8:47 as I stamped it out in the ashtray.

"Like I said, I'm not there. If you gave me like an hour, I could meet you."

"Around ten?"

I brushed my hand through my long bangs and then adjusted the rearview mirror, sticking my keys in the ignition as I flicked on my lights.

"Ten-thirty?"

"Ten-thirty's good," he said, as I heard him smile again—something about the challenge in his voice giving me a cool rush of fear. "See you then, Lea."

I threw the car into reverse as he hung up, too rattled to care that I had missed over half the meeting and there was only so much filler I could whip up on short notice, and shook if off as my excitement began to outrun my panic in leaps and bounds. I started to text Madge, the reaction so immediate I was halfway through it before I froze and deleted it all in one shot and tossed my phone aside as I headed for the highway thinking of the way his voice had sounded when he told me to trust him, trust him, trust him.

I reached my apartment a little before nine-thirty, straightening up in a hot panic as I realized what a mess the place was and shoved a week's worth of old laundry in the closet before running into the bathroom, taking a quick shower that I barely felt before I was moving again. I tore back my rumpled sheets, wrestling them into some semblance of order as I stacked books on my desk and pulled out a tight white sweater-dress as I held it up to the mirror, tossing it toward the bed as I did my make-up standing up, braiding the top of my hair into a quick double plait before pulling my long bangs out around my face.

I ran to my computer, hiding all his photo files before shutting the whole thing down and blow dried the back of my hair as I searched for a pair of pearl and brass earrings, putting them on without looking as I reached for my dress. I shrugged it on without a bra, considering myself in the mirror for a moment before pulling on a pair of black lace underwear, and reached for a pair of slightly fancier black thigh highs as I saw the lot light up below me, pulling them on quickly before arranging the long waves around my face.

I went to put my boots on, pausing half-way across the floor as I realized I had no idea if we were going to make it any farther than the bedroom, and felt every nerve in my body leap to life as I ran into the kitchen and pulled out a half-empty bottle of wine, setting two glasses down on the counter as I heard a knock at the backdoor. I was halfway across the floor when the door swung open and bit my lip as Jordan looked down at my bed and raised his brows, pausing in the doorway as he looked over my tight dress slowly for a moment before closing the door behind him.

"I'm sorry," I said, suddenly feeling about fifteen years old as Jordan looked around at my messy, makeshift bedroom, something amused and disapproving moving behind his polite expression. "It does that. It doesn't really lock . . ."

"Your door?"

I bit my lip as he glanced down at me, his face becoming a little concerned, and paused as he glanced back at the door again, brushing his thumb across his chin as he looked over the lock.

"It never has. Not really. I must've told the landlord about it five different times."

Some of the polite good humor went out of his face and he opened the door with one hand before shutting it soundly, sticking his hands in his dark jacket's pockets as he rolled his jaw slightly.

"That's kind of dangerous, isn't it?"

"I guess. I don't really have anything worth stealing."

Jordan looked me over oddly for a moment as he followed me into the living room, glancing around at the dark papered walls and low ceiling without speaking. I told him to take a seat as I grabbed the wine off the counter, bringing back both glasses as he glanced at me from the middle of the room.

"How long have you lived here?"

"A few months," I said sitting down, as Jordan walked around the open space and tipped the curtains back with one hand, flipping through the stack of old records next to my player curiously for a moment before walking back over. He held out his hand without sitting as I poured out two glasses, looking down at me for a moment before turning slightly, and took a drink as I tried not to stare—the dark blue and black of his shirt emphasizing the bright, ocean blue of his eyes. He took a seat, tilting his head at me as I glanced at the layered leather and hemp bands around his neck, and then smirking slightly as he raked his long dark hair away from his face, raising his brows as he tipped his glass toward the room around him.

"Is this supposed to be Bavarian?"

"I don't know. Maybe what people in the seventies thought was Bavarian?"

He glanced at me again as I looked away, still so unnerved by his beauty I could feel my wine glass quaking slightly as I raised it to my lips.

"You're scared of me again," he said, his voice clipped and amused as he sat back against the armrest and gave me a slow once over from head to toe.

"What?"

"Scared of me. Like you were the first day we met."

"I wasn't scared of you."

"You looked like you wanted to run out of the room."

I blushed as he looked at me steadily for a moment, raising his glass to his lips again as he finished it in one swallow.

"Would it help if I treated you like shit for a while?" he asked, setting the glass down on the table as he glanced around. I turned to look at him and he smirked, his blue eyes flashing with something a little darker than humor.

"Because this apartment is a fucking pigsty, you know."

"Thanks," I said curtly.

"I'm serious. It looks like the kind of place you'd pick after being in prison for five years."

I raised my brows at him as I set my glass down, my jaw setting slightly as I leaned away from him and Jordan smiled and ran his finger down my cheek, holding onto my chin lightly for a moment.

"That's better," he said, running his hand behind my neck. I looked up at him as he pulled me closer, his expression becoming a little more gentle as I leaned forward to kiss him and held me tightly for a moment as I ran my hands up his chest, kissing him as I felt him twist his hand into the back of my hair. I pulled away slightly as my legs slid across his lap, a quick submissive quake of hunger running through me as he dragged me back, and felt my body curl into his as he kissed me deeply, pressing his forehead against me for a moment as he coiled his hand around mine.

"Stop worshipping me, Lea," he said, his voice low and teasing as he tapped my fingers against his chest. "It's irritating."

My eyes narrowed slightly as he gave me a sudden brilliant smile, glancing around my apartment quickly, and then lowered his head as he kissed the front of my hand, his dark eyes swirling with reckless good humor.

"Come on," he said, standing up. "Let's get out of here."

I looked up at him, biting my lip as he waited for me to join him, perfectly confident and a little impatient and bit back a smile as I caught some of his mood, letting go of his hand at the door as I reached for my long black peacoat and slipped on my boots.

"Where are we going?" I asked as he pulled me toward the front door I never used and then slammed it behind me, waiting for me to lock it before shaking his head.

"Don't you like being surprised?" he asked, grabbing my hand as we trotted down the steps. We passed in front of the bar, cutting across the lawn as a crowd of people stomping their feet near the door turned to watch us and I laughed a little as he broke into a jog, pulling me across the dark lot as a soft, sugar thin shift of snow blew toward us from the west. He opened the door for me as he glanced at his watch, waiting for me to slide inside as he jogged to the other side. I brushed my hair away from my face as he sat down beside me, giving me another grin as he threw the car into reverse.

"You're seriously not going to tell me?"

"It's more fun this way," he said, flipping on the windshield wipers as the headlights lit up the dark street like a snow globe—the neighborhoods around us silent and pastel bright.

"Am I dressed all right?"

Jordan gave me a quick look out of the corner of his eye and smiled a little as he glanced away.

"You could go anywhere in that dress."

I blushed and looked down at his watch, brushing my fingers over the face of it as he made the turn onto the highway and watched one sign after another whip past us as Jordan reached for the radio, turning it up with his fingertips as the music swelled just above the motor.

"Eighteen minutes," he said. "We should make it."

"Little late for dinner," I said, playing with the stations as he flew through two more exits.

"Not if you're hungry."

"And the bars don't close for another three hours. At least. A movie?"

He shrugged at me as I rolled my jaw and looked out the window.

"Whatever," I muttered.

"Adventure, Ophelia," he said. "Think of it as an adventure. And put on anything you want. I listen to everything."

I raised my brows, scrolling through a few of his presets and then stopped when I heard an old Doors tune, turning it up a little as he glanced in my direction.

"Good song. Not what I would've expected . . ."

"What? You don't like the Doors?"

"They're a good band. Is that what all those old records are in your apartment? Are you some sort of a rock and roll purist or something?"

"They're from my dad's collection. He's gives me one on every birthday."

"Oh. You and your dad are close?"

"Close. No, I wouldn't say we're close. I just grew up listening to vinyl and I like the sound of it, I guess. Why? Are you and your dad close?"

Jordan shook his head, his face a perfect blank as he stared at the road.

"Never met him. My mom dated him after her first husband died and I guess he split pretty soon after."

"Never?"

"Nope. Trust me, she wasn't that broken up about it, so it never really seemed that strange."

He glanced in my direction as he hit the turn signal and then swerved into the exit lane at the last minute, smirking a little as I jumped.

"I'm not really that close to her either, to be honest," he said, brushing his hair away from his face until I could make out the dark outline of his neck tattoo behind his ear. "I haven't spoken to her in years."

I reached for my cigarettes as we turned onto Michigan Avenue, glancing over my shoulder as I tucked it between my lips and blinked at him as he plucked it out of my mouth and pocketed it with a smile.

"You won't have time," he said, glancing away. "We're almost there."

"I guess my family's kind of the same."

"How's that?"

"Just . . . absent. I mean we spend a lot of time together and me and my brothers are close, but . . . I've always felt like an outsider there. Isn't that funny? Like I go to all these gatherings and they always look so surprised to see me. Like I'm some foster kid they kind of adopted for a few years and expected me to just disappear after I aged out of the system."

My brow furrowed as he glanced at me quickly, letting my long bangs swing over my face as we stopped at a spotlight and laughed a little as I reached for another cigarette, cracking the window with one hand.

"I don't know why I told you that. I don't think I've ever said that to anyone out loud."

He grabbed my wrist as I started to pull another cigarette out of my pack and pulled it away from me, kissing the back of my hand lightly as he tucked them into his jacket.

"You told me for the same reason I told you," he said, squeezing my hand tightly for a moment as the light shifted from red to green. "And it's their loss, Lea, believe me. When something like that happens, it's always their loss. And sooner or later, they all regret it."

I looked up at him as his expression darkened, a river of dark shadows running over his face as we sped down the street and pulled my hand away from him slowly as my eyes ran to his pocket, turning toward him in my seat as he raised his brows in my direction.

"Are you going to give me those back?"

"We'll see," he said, biting back one of his slow, million-dollar smiles as he glanced over my shoulder and then turned at the end of the street. "It's a bad habit, Lea. And like I said, we don't have time."

I looked out the window as Jordan pulled into the half-full lot behind the train station and felt my eyes widen as he glanced at his watch again, backing the car into one of the parking spaces up front with a quick turn of the wheel.

"The train station?"

Jordan cracked open his door as he pocketed his keys.

"Yeah. And we need to hurry. The last train boards in like five minutes."

"Last train to where?"

I reached for my purse as he walked around the front of the car, pulling my door open as he caught my hand and then shut as I jogged with him up to the sidewalk, a quick rush of excitement running through me as I heard the roar of a train horn less than a mile away.

"Where are we going?" I asked again as he smiled down at me, pulling me to the ticket station as he slid his hand over the counter. He held up two fingers as the cashier looked up, glancing at me out of the corner of his eye.

"Two for Chicago," he said. "One way."

"Are you serious?" I asked, glancing over my shoulder as the cashier rolled his eyes and Jordan blocked his view with a casual turn of his shoulders, twirling one of the loose waves around my face with his fingers before brushing it behind my ear.

"Surprised?"

"Kind of," I said, as he pulled me closer and tucked the collar of my coat down a little, his expression gently amused as he brushed his hand against my face. "Jordan, I have a meeting tomorrow. At like eleven . . ."

"So?" he asked, tapping his credit card against the counter impatiently as he passed it through the glass. "Skip it. There's this band that I've been meaning to catch and they're only in town for a couple of nights."

"We'll never make it," I said, running my fingers through my hair as the train pulled up to the stop, the airbrakes echoing under the outer awning as I glanced down the long row of cabin lights winking yellow-white in the darkness. "They'll be closed before we get there."

"Not this place," Jordan said, grabbing the tickets over my head as he took my hand. "Trust me, Lea. You'll like it. Cool people, cheap wine, the bands play all night . . ."

I looked up at him as he held the tickets up to his chest, splaying them out with one hand as I shook my head, and then laughed and pulled me toward the door, leading me to the other side of the train as a group of people waited to exit on the other side. Jordan held the tickets out to one of the conductors, giving him a nod as he handed them back and I followed him up the steps into the back carriage as he glanced around it quickly for a moment, looking over his shoulder as he tipped his head toward the next car.

"Come on," he said. "We'll find our seats later."

I looked around at the sleepy college students huddled under their jackets as they talked to each other quietly and watched us pass, and felt a strange sense of unreality sweep over me as we sat down in the café car, the first real howl of snowflakes sweeping past our window in a hard gust. I looked at him over the table as he reached for my hands, holding them tightly for a moment as he brought them together and kissed them lightly and then motioned to the counter behind us, his face so bright and beautiful it almost burned.

"Coffee?" he suggested as he let go.

I raised my brows at the snowstorm around us.

"Hot chocolate?"

"Hot chocolate," he agreed, standing up sliding the tickets over to my side. "If they ask. Which they probably won't."

I turned to watch him go, shaking out my coat a little as I noticed the soft spatter of snowflakes running up and down my arms and shrugged it off as I watched a couple in the next car shift in their sleep, their bodies moving together in the cramped space as naturally as breathing. I looked out the window as the horn sounded again, brushing away a smile with my fingertips as I reached out to touch the window and drew a heart in the light film of condensation with my fingertip, scrawling Jordan's name in it quickly before whipping it away with my hand.

"Hot chocolate," Jordan said, handing me my cup as he sat down across from me. He glanced over his shoulder as the train rolled slightly on its tracks, rubbing his hands together lightly as I laughed.

"You are such a bad influence," I said, shaking my head as I lifted my cup to my lips.

"Being productive members of society is overrated. Deeply overrated."

"Think so?"

He glanced at me out of the corner of his eyes and smiled a little at my expression, that strange searching look back in his eyes as he relaxed back in his chair.

"Oh, I know it," he said, his eyes running over my tight white dress thoughtfully for a moment as he picked up his cup. "Tried it both ways, you know. The things they tell you to do, the things you *want* to do . . ."

"I know what you mean. I've tried my whole life to be someone that just wants normal things. Who gets a rush out of—I don't know—reality shows and babies and acquiring things. I think the proudest my dad ever was of me was when I got this job and then leased a new car. It was like he could finally relax, you know? I was going to make it. I had made the final ascent into adulthood instead of just circling the runway over and over."

"No shit. I get that from people too sometimes. Like, 'Really? Still the music thing?' As if all those dreams are supposed to die the moment you turn thirty."

He took a sip of his hot chocolate as he glanced out the window, nodding to the sleepy countryside of houses rushing past the window in a soft, dark blur.

"Then, you know, it's time to put down roots—get married, start a family, grind it out one day at a time like everybody else. And anything else is just seen as . . . arrogance. Why do you get to do it differently? Who gave you permission to live your life any way you want to?"

"Is that what you'd do?" I asked. "I mean wildest dreams—money's no object. Would you just tour forever? Become a huge rock star? Live in like some, I don't know, old castle that you fill up with artwork and statues and tapestries or something?"

"Tapestries?"

"Definitely tapestries. If it were a castle. What else would you do?"

"I don't know. Suit of armor, maybe?"

"A suit of armor would be good. I can see that. Maybe some cloaks . . ."

"So . . . in this fantasy of spectacular wealth, I've gone pretty much completely insane?"

"Pretty much. I mean, why not? If you're rich."

"Who can stop you?"

"Exactly."

Jordan pressed his fingers against his brow as if something was amusing him deeply and leaned back in his seat, pointing to me lightly as he picked up his cup.

"You haven't been around a lot of rich people, have you?"

"What makes you say that?"

"Your ideas about wealth are a little . . . antiquated."

I shrugged, glancing out the window as I drummed my fingers around my cup.

"I guess money's never really been that important to me."

"Ah. Which means you've always had enough to get by."

"Are you trying to figure me out, Jordan?"

"It's funny you should say that."

"Oh yeah? Why's that?"

Jordan leaned forward and brushed his fingers across the table, tapping the first three like a veteran gambler on a winning streak.

"Because I have three questions I could ask you, that would tell me everything there is to know about you. Everything important, anyway."

"Three questions."

"That's right."

"Just three."

"That's it."

"What if I lied?"

"That would be against the rules. But in the end, it wouldn't matter. The things people lie about tell you just as much about them as anything else."

"And you think you'd know if I were lying or not?"

Jordan smiled, his dark blue eyes swirling oddly for a moment as he brushed his thumb across his lips.

"I could pretty much guarantee it."

I sat back in my chair, looking over his too-handsome face slowly for a moment and then pushed my cup aside as I rested my elbow on the table, giving him my best poker face as I waved a hand in his direction.

"Fine. I'm game if you are."

"You want me to answer them too?"

"Only seems fair, doesn't it?"

"All right. But you've already asked me the first one."

"What question?"

"Who would you be and what would you do if you could do absolutely anything?"

"You never really answered me. You just went along with whatever I said."

Jordan shrugged, his expression shifting with a moment of amused respect as he raised his hands in acquiescence.

"I will answer you. I will. But I want your answer first. It sounds easy, I know, but think about it for a minute. I want a real answer."

"Doesn't matter if it makes sense or not?"

"It's actually better if it doesn't," he said, raising his cup. "Go ahead. First instincts matter here. Just tell me the first thing that pops into your head."

I dragged my eyes away from him, still absolutely unmoored by the way they seemed to blot out all rational thought, like some kind of incantation that was designed to encourage complete compliance and watched the snow shift past the window for a moment, closing my eyes as an image of driving down an empty road in Las Vegas came to my mind without warning or context. I watched the lights come up in the darkness, like some sort of garish funeral for every secret, desperate dream that had gone wrong in a billion people's lives and saw myself pop out of the moonroof of some apocalyptic vehicle in my Harley Quinn best, waving at no one in particular as I pulled out a rocket launcher and leveled it at the first casino I saw. I grinned a little as I rested my head in my hand, watching the building go up like a pack of matches and watched Harley me laugh as the Joker and I flew past the blast at over a hundred miles an hour, the whole block going up in cinders around us—as if our passage had ignited the entire world, destroying everything it touched beneath the shadow of its wings.

I opened my eyes as the image faded, brushing my hand behind my hair as I tried to turn the smile on my face into something less sinister and pressed my lips together as I noticed how Jordan was watching me, his eyes wide and interested as he watched me glance away.

"Well?"

"I don't know," I said, reaching for my hot chocolate as I finished what was left in the glass. "If money were no object? I guess I'd buy one of those tiny homes, a nice one, and just kind of drive it all over, photographing every-thing. I think I'd eventually end up near the ocean. Spend my days kind putting images together in the morning and then, I don't know, surf in the afternoon? Drink and dance until dawn."

Jordan looked over my face slowly for a moment, something quick and convoluted moving behind his searching expression and raised his brows as I dropped my hands into my lap, biting my lip as I had a sudden vivid image of the Harley me listening to my answer and laughing hysterically as she blew me a kiss.

"You surf?"

"No. But isn't that what people do when they live by the ocean? Just kind of hang out and clink bottles over a barbecue and surf? Celebrate all of their outrageous good fortune?"

"That might be a beer commercial. You know. Just saying."

"Life imitates art."

"All right," he said, laughing a little as he rubbed the tattoo behind his ear, glancing up at me oddly for a moment as his eyes narrowed. "What was the other thing you thought of?"

"What other thing?"

"The real answer that you sanitized because you were afraid it would scare the shit out of me."

I pressed my lips together as my eyes widened and turned my eyes in his direction as he held up his hands, grinning a little as he glanced over his shoulder, watching the conductor make his slow rounds away from us.

"I warned you," he said, his voice low and amused.

"I didn't lie. I really want to do that."

And I saw you too. Blowing someone a kiss as the world burned around you. Who was it? Was it me?

I blinked at him as he tilted his head at me—the magnetic drag of his attention knocking me off-kilter, and shook my head a little as I rested my elbow on the table, raising my brows in his direction.

"So what's your answer? Since you don't seem to like mine."

"I didn't say I didn't like it. It's a nice dream. News places, new things. You ... don't really like other people that much, do you?"

I dragged my hand through my hair as he brushed a thumb under his lips, smirking a little at my expression as he glanced away.

"But you value your freedom. And the world around you. I can respect that. Freedom is important."

"Is that what these questions are designed to do? Tell you what my core values are?"

Jordan glanced over his shoulder again and then reached across the table, taking my hand lightly for a moment as he held my eyes.

"Let's just say I now know the value you're most committed to."

"And you?"

"Ah . . . pretty much the same thing. I know I could make more money working for my father-in-law at his insurance firm or something. Trust me, he tells me all the time. But for what? I like music. I like acting. I like . . . creating things. I think you either decide to live free early on or you get very, very comfortable living in a cage. I live exactly the life I want to every single day. Maybe I couldn't live any other way. I honestly don't know. Other people don't seem to mind it as much. I was just never one of them."

Jordan reached across the table as he threw another glance over his shoulder and picked up the tickets, pocketing them lightly as he tipped his chin toward my coat.

"There. Get your coat."

I looked up at him as his voice became clipped and impatient and grabbed my coat as he glanced over his shoulder again, his jaw rolling slightly as he put his hand on my shoulder, blocking the conductor's view of me down the hall. He caught my expression and grinned as he urged me forward, his blue eyes shifting with a violent sort of amusement as he nudged me in the opposite direction.

"Go now. Hurry."

I bit my lip as we scurried down the hall, walking through the snack car quickly as Jordan glanced over his shoulder again and laughed a little as his eyes ran down the row of sleeping rooms in the next car, dragging me to the end of the row as I shook my head.

"They'll catch us . . ."

"No, no, no," he said blocking me in against the door as he reached behind me and opened it, holding my eyes as he pointed to the white sign above the knob. "Not occupied. They never check. I must've slept in these cars a dozen times . . ."

I bit back a laugh as I backed inside, Jordan dogging my steps as he glanced over his shoulder one last time and then locked the door behind us as he gave me a sudden, brilliant smile, catching me with both hands as I leapt into his arms. He kissed me deeply as I wrapped my hands behind his neck and coiled my legs around him as he turned his body slightly, taking a step backward as his leg hit the back of the dark blue couch facing the window. I threw my arm out as he stumbled slightly, laughing as my hand hit the cramped wall behind us and kissed him again as he caught himself with a smile, sitting down on the couch behind us as he pulled me into his lap.

I felt him tug at the back of my dress as I spread my legs around him, kissing the front of my throat and raised my arms as I slid it up my body, yanking it over my head as I held his eyes. I tossed it toward the window, pressing my hands against his face as his eyes flew over my body and leaned forward as he kissed me again, his fingers cutting into the deep curve of my waist as he held onto me tightly for a moment. I shifted in his lap, biting back a low moan as I slid against his hard cock and looked down at him as he rested his head against the low back of the couch, running his hands over my breasts as I arched over him.

I felt a strange rush of power as I brushed my hand through the back of his hair, kneeling forward as I danced my fingers over his lips for a moment and brushed my breasts over his mouth while I watched his expression, his hand sliding up the back of my spine as I arched away from him. I grinded my hips against him, closing my eyes as I slid against his cock and pressed my fingers against his neck as I leaned forward to kiss him, holding him away from me with my fingertips as he cupped my breasts in both hands. I felt him drag me closer, his hand twisting into the back of my hair as I tried to shift my body backward, and stopped fighting him as he kissed me hard on the mouth and yanked me closer, his expression becoming hungry and urgent as I teased him lightly with my tongue.

I pulled away from him suddenly as his hand tightened around the back of my neck, my pulse taking a smooth upward spike as he rolled my body away from him like a ragdoll and blinked up at him as he jostled me off of his lap, my back sliding against the rough fabric of the couch. He sat forward quickly, his eyes darting over my open legs as I slid my knee off of his lap and shrugged off his jacket as I leaned forward to unbutton his shirt, smiling down at me as he knelt between my open legs and shrugged both off impatiently—his skin warm and feverish as I ran my hands up his chest.

I ran my fingers over the mosaic of tattoos on his chest and his arms as he unzipped his jeans, closing my eyes as he reached for my hand and bit my lip as he dragged my fingers into his mouth, sucking on them lightly for a moment before lowering them to his cock. I gasped as he held onto my wrist, rubbing against my hand quickly for a moment as a low noise escaped the back of his throat and felt my eyes flutter shut as a sudden image of Jordan twirling a lit match between his fingers filled my mind, his eyes dark and bottomless as he watched me stroke Tommy's cock. I opened my eyes as Jordan reached for my face, shaking his head slightly as he tipped my chin up to meet him.

No. Not him. Not then. Stay with me.

I gasped as his voice hit me with the force of a whip—hunger and desire mixed with a quick, unchecked quake of rage, and blinked up at him submissively as he took off his jeans and then kissed my palm lightly, closing his eyes as he placed it on his cock. I started to stroke him quickly, the desire to please him pushing my hunger for him into a mindless quake of want and moaned slightly as he leaned closer and circled his fingers over my wrist, his expression becoming a little gentler as he turned my hand slightly, slowing me down.

Better, I heard. *Better, better, better . . .*

I looked up at him as I felt his fingers touch my lips, his long hair whispering over my collarbone so lightly I shivered and felt every nerve in my body go electric white with hunger as he looked over me gently for a moment, coiling his hand behind the back of my neck as he kissed me, moving against the smooth steady stroke of my hand as I felt his thumb dig into the front of my throat. I felt my hand go still as he pressed his body against me, his fingers cutting into my throat so deeply I gasped and then opened my eyes as he released me suddenly, his fingers clawing at my thin lace thong as he dragged it down around my knees.

I felt a strange sense of euphoria as he sat back slightly, his face hard and urgent as he pulled my thong off of my ankles and then shoved my legs apart with both hands as he slid his body on top of me, forcing himself inside me with one quick, violent thrust. I gasped as I felt a sudden burst of pain, my nails biting into his skin as he pressed his head against my neck and he moved inside me quickly for a moment as I buried my hand in his hair and he touched the side of my face, his blue eyes so bright and urgent they seemed to fill the sky. I bit my lip as he forced himself deeper, my eyes fluttering slightly as he rocked inside me with quick, thoughtless urgency and had a sudden violent image of Jordan holding my bound hands behind me as he shoved me face first to the floor, his expression relaxed and merciless as he snapped an inch-thick crop across my back.

I leaned forward to kiss him as the image shuddered and burned, spreading my legs a little wider as Jordan pressed his fingers against my neck and looked down at me as he held me away from him for a moment, his brow furrowing slightly as he searched my expression.

"Kiss me," I said, leaning forward. "Kiss me, kiss me, kiss me . . ."

Jordan pressed his fingers against my lips, a moment of surprised pain running through his face as he leaned forward and kissed me gently before pressing his forehead against mine as he slid down my body slowly, kissing my lips, my neck, my breasts.

No. Not like that. I'll be gentle. Stay with me, Lea. Don't go somewhere else. There are other ways. I'll show you, I promise.

I felt him slide his body lower, pushing my knees apart with both hands as he ran his tongue inside me and held me open as I shifted my body beneath him, the roll of the train bringing us together, quaking us apart. I cracked my eyes open as he pressed his mouth against me, wasting no time, eager for me to climax, and bit back a low cry as he sucked on my clit urgently for a moment, my fingers sliding over his lips as he looked up at me, pulling them inside his mouth before pushing them away.

I stopped thinking, he was everywhere—in my body, in my mind and I slid my legs over his shoulders as he pulled me toward him impatiently, burying his face inside me as my hips pressed against the couch. He brought me close to climax in a quick, fevered pitch, pulling away at the last second as he rolled his fingers over my clit and watched me arch toward him as he pressed his hand against my stomach, holding me down gently as he brought me to a sudden, frantic orgasm. I bit back a strangled cry as he pressed his lips against me, running his tongue inside of me as I brushed my hand against his face and I whispered his name as I felt him kiss my palm—the idea that we could be caught at any moment moving through my mind like a wild, panicked brushfire.

I felt the weight of his body against me as he slid on top of me, reaching for my wrists above my head as he wrapped his hands around them and felt him force himself inside me roughly as he watched my expression, biting back a low moan as he saw me wince. Jordan tightened his grip as I shifted beneath him, the warm smell of his skin everywhere as he moved inside me and I met his eyes as he forced himself deeper—my hands splaying open as I let out a quick gasp. I reached for his face as he let me go all at once, pressing his forehead against me as his lips slid over mine and I leaned up to kiss him as I felt him bury his hand in the back of my hair, pulling at it sharply for a moment before his mouth was on mine.

Just me, I heard, a quick pulsing image of Jordan running his hands over me in the motel as I woke, his blue eyes wide and urgent as he kissed the side of my neck. *Just me, Lea. I'll be anything you want, anything you need. Just stay with me. Stay, stay, stay.*

I opened my eyes wide as he pulled away from me slightly, brushing his thumb under my chin as his eyes searched my face and nodded as he pulled my body closer, his expression becoming soft with want as he rocked inside me quickly.

"I'll stay with you," I said, pressing my lips against his ear as he bit back a low moan. "I'm here, I'm yours . . ."

I cried out softly as he held my body tighter, moving inside me with smooth, thoughtless violence as I pressed my head against his chest and clawed his back gently as he came inside me, listening to his heartbeat as his body went still.

I heard him shudder a low sigh against my neck as he planted his hand behind my head and looked up at him as he pulled away from me, kissing me lightly on the lips as he jostled his body against the cushions of the couch. I shifted away from him, turning to lay in the crook of his arm as I felt him run his fingers over my skin and closed my eyes as I listened to the soft quake of the windows behind us, the howl of the wind rising above the clatter of the train softly for a minute before dissipating.

I felt him brush my hair away from my ear, every nerve in my neck responding to his whisper light touch and bit my lip as I turned toward him— the pure, uncomplicated rush of love I felt for him in that moment so unnerving I dropped my hand and glanced up at him as he caught it, looking over my chewed and broken fingernails as he watched my face.

"Tommy hasn't called me back," I said, swallowing hard as my voice came out in a strained whisper. Jordan raised his brows at me and turned my hand over, searching my expression curiously for a moment as his eyes ran down the length of my body.

"Does that surprise you?"

"A little," I said, relaxing back against him as I touched the swords scrolled across his chest, tracing them absently for a moment as he sat up, pulling his arm away from me. "He's never done that before. We've always been close. I mean, he lives in California so he's away a lot, but we keep in touch. I've known him almost as long as I've known Madge."

I watched him reach for his discarded jacket, pulling my pack of cigarettes out of the pocket and felt a rush of greedy hunger for them as he pulled one out of the pack, lighting it between his lips in the darkness as he tucked his jacket around us.

"Do you regret it?" he asked as he took a long drag, resting on his elbow beside me as he held the cigarette up to my lips and I took a drag as I closed my eyes, shaking my head as he pulled his hand back.

"No," I said as I turned my head and Jordan raised his brows, considering me seriously for a moment before relaxing back next to me. "Not at all. I just didn't want *him* to regret it . . ."

"People have all sorts of reasons for keeping that side of their lives private," he said, holding it up to my lips again as it became a slow dance between us—one unhealthy habit shared like some kind of strange, desperate prayer. "I wouldn't take it personally if I were you. If you're close, I'm sure he'll come around. Just give him some time."

I looked up at him as his face lost a little of its candor, his eyes going dark for a moment as he stared at the ceiling and glanced at me out of the corner of his eyes as I touched the scroll of artwork around his forearm, smiling as I raised my brows.

"How many tattoos do you have?"

"What do you mean? Like all together?"

"Don't you know?"

Jordan shrugged, his eyes shifting with amusement again and took the cigarette out of my hand as he tucked it between his lips, stretching his arms out in front of him as he turned them over slowly.

"Maybe twenty? I lost count a few years ago."

His smile broadened at my expression and he tilted his head as he looked over my body thoughtfully for a moment, finishing what was left of the cigarette before stomping it out on the metal frame of the couch behind us.

"I didn't notice any on you though," he said, using his hand to raise my shoulder up as I laughed and rolled back toward him, my heart constricting painfully for a moment as he brushed his knuckle down the hollow of my throat.

"I always wanted one," I said curling toward him as I tugged his jacket higher. "I'm just not that big on pain."

"Depends where you get it," he said carelessly, smiling a little as he ran his fingers down my side. "Anything close to the ribs will hurt. At least the first time. Shoulder's better for your first one. After a few though, you won't even mind."

He touched the area behind my ear and brought his face close to mine, looking over me oddly for a moment as my eyes darted over his face.

"I want to put my name right here," he said, turning my head up to meet him as he kissed me gently on the lips. "That's a good place to start. Just one word, not too painful . . ."

I felt my eyes widen as he kissed me a little deeper and pulled away from him slightly as he tilted his head at me, holding onto my chin with his fingertips as my stomach flipped and steadied.

"Are you serious?" I asked, blinking up at him.

Very.

"Are you saying you wouldn't do it?" he asked pulling me closer. He kissed my closed lids lightly, running his thumb across my lips as he leaned back to watch my expression. "Even if I asked nicely?"

I looked up at him without speaking, a sudden image of him scrawling his name along my neck and my hip and my lower back ran through my mind without warning and felt my fingers curl on his chest as he grinned suddenly, laughing at my expression as he laid his head back on the couch, glancing at me out of the corner of his eye.

"I'm joking, Lea. Stop looking so concerned. I'm not actually going to take you out tonight and brand you."

Not yet.

I felt my brow furrow as he gave me a sudden reckless grin and then turned toward me as his blue eyes flashed for a moment, touching my forehead playfully as he raised his brows.

"I have been wondering when you're actually going to come and see me play, though. You keep telling me what a fan you are."

I pressed my lips together, the honest note of hurt below his words sending a quick shudder of pain up the corridor of my spine and reached for my pack of cigarettes as he caught my hand, pressing it against his chest lightly as he met my eyes.

"I've been wanting to," I said, brushing my hair behind one ear. "I've been meaning to .."

"Except . . ."

I inhaled quickly as I thought about Abbie, chatting in the breakroom with the other sirens and dropped my head as his face became a little more serious and he looked down at my hand before rolling his eyes back up to meet me.

"Oh," he said, as I laid back down in the crook of his arm and he looked over my face, kissing the back of my shoulder as I closed my eyes, his skin warm everywhere it met mine as I glanced around the small utilitarian-looking space. "You know she doesn't always come to every show. Not anymore."

I felt him coil his hand around my waist as he spoke into my ear, pulling my body against his as I pressed my hand against his thigh.

"I could let you know," he said. "I just want to see you there, Lea. You don't have to come backstage. Just be in the crowd and I'll meet you after my set . . ."

"At my apartment?"

I reached for my cigarettes again as he caught my hand again, curling it against my chest as he shifted his body against me and kissed the back of my neck as I had that strange image of his name appearing wherever he touched me—the thin red outline of a heart appearing around the one on my neck as if by magic. I felt his hand slide around the deep curve of my hip, his lips moving down my spine as I glanced at him over my shoulder.

"Can't exactly keep me out, can you?" he said, something too quick and convoluted to catch moving behind his expression as I felt his hand slide between my legs. "Not with that lock. You really shouldn't have told me about that, Lea. Pretty soon you won't be able to get rid of me. And what will you do then?"

I exhaled quickly as I felt his hard cock press against me, reaching my hand up to run my fingers into his hair as I pressed my body against him and didn't remember until it was almost too late that the reason the heart had looked so familiar was because I had seen it before. It was the same one I had scrolled on the café window while Jordan was at the counter. The one I had wiped away before he could return.

CHAPTER EIGHT

I WOKE UP WITH A START, MY EYES FLYING OPEN AS JORDAN leaned over me, and realized he was shaking me awake as I heard the train horn sound, the car slowing down to a crawl as he sat up quickly.

"Shit."

I glanced out the window as I saw the train depot come into view, the frost on the glass turning it into a blurry pastel image of light and fog, and blinked quickly as he stepped over me from the couch to the floor, moving his tongue over the back of his teeth as he leaned his head toward the door. I felt my eyes widen as I heard someone banging on a door a few rows down from us and grabbed my dress as Jordan waved a hand in my direction, his face suddenly alert and efficient as he put on his pants quickly, buttoning them up as he shook his head in my direction.

"They never do this," he said quietly, pulling his shirt on as I scrambled to find my boots. "I swear they don't . . ."

I snapped my head toward the door as I heard the conductor move up the row, banging on doors soundly before opening and shutting them quickly and buttoned up my coat as Jordan shrugged on his, something hard and amused moving behind his expression as he beckoned me closer.

"This is so fucked up," I whispered, and Jordan laughed a little as he gave me a sudden brilliant grin, shaking his head as he became serious again and then raised his hand. He listened as the conductor knocked at another door, glancing at me as someone spoke in the hallway and cracked the door open as he glanced around the corner, catching my hand as I felt the train pull to a stop.

"Come on," he said, raising his finger to his lips. "And don't stop. No matter what they say."

I felt my hand slide against his as he threw the door open, dragging me down the hall as he broke into a run and felt my heart pound as I heard someone yelling after us, trying to keep up with him as he darted through a crowd of people stirring from their seats.

"Hey! You there! Stop!"

Jordan glanced back at me as we shoved our way through the crowd, laughing as they whipped their heads around to watch us before scattering and held my hand tighter as he pulled me toward the exit.

"Hurry," he said as the doors swung open. "Don't stop."

I ran down the steps after him as the elderly conductor at the front gaped at us in amazement and laughed with him as we burst through the crowd, pounding up the steps two at a time as I caught up with him at the top of the stairs. I looked around the cathedral-like depot quickly for a moment as Jordan let me catch my breath and then smiled down at me as he caught my hand again, weaving his way through the late-night crowd effortlessly as we jogged toward the doors. He let go of my hand as we reached one of the street exits, pushing it open as he waited for me to pass and wrapped his arm around my waist as we stepped out into the night, the soft swirl of snow around us turning the landscape into a pristine, glowing version of itself as he looked down at me.

"You all right?"

"I'm fine," I said, leaning against him in the wind as we headed toward the street, biting back laughter as I glanced over my shoulder. "I can't believe that. Why would they check?"

"That's what I want to know. One of our neighbors must've ratted us out."

He pulled out his phone, tapping at the screen quickly as the wind blew around us, and I looked around the brightly lit street as he shook his head, a long row of Thanksgiving banners and wreaths decorating the streetlights around us.

"I was going to call for a ride," he said, glancing up and down the main road and then held up his hand as a yellow cab pulled away from the curb in the opposite direction, stepping into the street as he flagged him down. I brushed my hair away from my eyes as the cab stopped suddenly, doing a slow U-turn in our direction, and shoved my hands in my pockets as Jordan stepped toward the passenger side, opening the door for me as I slid inside. He slid in beside me, slamming the door behind him as the driver raised his brows and nodded to him as he held up his hand.

"Red Door Café?"

"Never heard of it. Streets?"

"You know where the Ronin Blues Hall is at? It's right there. Literally, almost the same building."

He looked at me as the driver hit the meter, rolling onto his back as he rested his head in my lap and I laughed as he grinned up at me and tapped his fingers against his chest, whistling under his breath as he reached up to touch my face.

"I don't think we should take the train back," he said, raising his brows as I brushed his long hair away from his face.

"I'm not sure we should take a train ever again. That conductor looked pissed."

I glanced up as the driver looked at us in the rearview mirror, smiling at me as I met his eyes.

"First date?"

Jordan smiled as I bit my lip and tucked his hand behind his head, holding his ring finger up as I blinked.

"Newlyweds. We just got married. City hall."

"Today?"

"That's right."

The driver nodded at us approvingly for a moment as I searched Jordan's expression as he turned up the radio, watching the shadows pass across his face as the headlights of oncoming traffic filled the car with light.

"I thought it was something," he said. "I can always tell."

"Oh yeah?" Jordan said, his face shifting with humor as he brushed his hand against my cheek. "How's that?"

"Just hard to fake," he said, flicking on his wipers. "It's nice, you know. Rare. To see two people so in love at your age."

Jordan held my eyes for a moment, giving me a wink as I shook my head and pressed my lips together and then laughed softly as I glanced out the window, watching the traffic roll past as we entered the heart of the city. I sat in silence for several minutes—that feeling of perfect belonging so rare to me

I didn't quite know how to process it without terror and looked down at him again as he brushed his fingers against my chin, his expression gentle and serious as I shifted my hair away from my shoulder.

Don't be afraid of me, Lea. I'm here. I feel it too.

I held my breath as my brow furrowed, tapping my fingers against the side of his face as he searched my expression and leaned down to kiss his forehead as he reached for my hand, holding onto it tightly for a minute as he pulled me lower. I closed my eyes as he kissed my lips, my hair spilling around his face as he held me in place and then released me slowly as the car pulled to the side of the road, holding my gaze for a moment before glancing toward the window. He sat up as the car filled with light, reaching for his wallet as he nodded to what looked like a huge, converted warehouse, and slid the driver a twenty as he cracked open his door, stepping into the street as a line of cars swerved around us.

I slid out as the driver raised a hand, saying something pleasant I never caught and looked up as Jordan held out his hand, helping me out of the car as he guided me safely to the sidewalk. He slammed the door shut, tapping the top lightly as he looked around the well-lit street like a parolee getting his first real taste of freedom in months and smiled as he took my hand and led me toward the dark warehouse, looking over my shoulder as we blended into a thin stream of people.

"Is that it?"

"No," he said, sticking his other hand in his pocket as the snow whipped around in a soft haze. "That's the Blues Hall. Great place, but they close at two."

I followed him down a narrow sidewalk, the cement turning into steps along the way and he reached out his hand and grabbed the metal railing at the bottom as I noticed a small group of people standing in line outside of a door that was connected to another building, raising my brows as he swung us in that direction. I counted about thirty as we reached the door, the bouncer at the front shrugging and raising his hand as the people up front started to argue, and looked around as I realized that there wasn't a single window looking into the place, the glut of bodies around it the only evidence that it existed at all.

Jordan looked down at me as he noticed my expression, smirking a little as he led me to the front of the line and raised a hand to the bouncer as the guy nodded to him and stepped aside, swinging the door open as the entire crowd let out a collective moan.

"You know that guy?"

"The owner," he said as he entered a long narrow hallway heading downstairs, the wood-paneled wall lit with naked bulbs above us. "We used to play here a lot. When we lived in the area."

I heard the soft swell of music as we got closer to the bottom of the stairs, the landing packed back to the stairwell as Jordan grabbed my hand again and I followed him with a strange thrill of celebrity as he moved us through the chaos, the crowd parting for us automatically as they noticed him—an instant insider, someone who mattered. I blinked as the music broke free all at once, rising up around us in a sudden wall of sound and looked around at the small well-lit stage, in what essentially was a little more than a dive bar, my eyes turning in every direction at once.

Jordan watched the band for a few moments, nodding a little as the crowd broke into applause and looked behind us as he pointed to a tiny L-shaped booth where the hall met the opposite wall, moving toward it instantly, pulling me along. I paused as we reached it, watching him excuse himself through a group of gorgeous twenty-year-old women who turned to watch him pass and looked away from them quickly as he reached the booth first and then beckoned me over, pulling me closer for a moment as he spoke into my ear.

"Didn't I tell you?" he said, grinning down at me as his hand brushed the back of my neck. "It's like this all the time here. They don't shut down until around dawn."

He helped me take off my coat, setting it in the corner of the booth and then took his off as he glanced around, raising his hand to one of the waitresses setting drinks down on a large table.

"There's a little place around the corner, we can go for breakfast if you want," he said, coiling his hand around my waist as he took a seat against the back wall, pulling me down next to him as he placed his arm on the tiny table in front of us. "They open up right around the same time this place closes. We used to go there all the time after a set, until Paul started dating this waitress there."

I raised my brows as the waitress swung over, running her eyes over Jordan's face as she looked between us quickly.

"Anything?" he asked, raising a hand as he shrugged in my direction.

"Whatever you're having."

He smiled as if my answer had pleased him and then beckoned the wait-ress closer with one hand, speaking to her quietly for moment as she fluttered and swayed, completely under his spell, just like everyone else. She gave me a small smile as she stood up and nodded, her face becoming a professional blank again.

"You got it," she said, heading back into the crowd. Jordan brushed his thumb beneath his lips as he tapped his fingers restlessly on the table, leaning toward me as the band up front launched into a slower song.

"Paul started dating the waitress?"

"Kind of what he does. He's a fucking menace in places like this. Always dating someone—servers, shot girls, bartenders—you name it. We were on the road once and he was dating not one, but two of the hotel maids who worked in our building—both completely oblivious. Until, you know, they weren't."

"He got caught."

"Yep. Which is also par for the course. He fucks around, he drinks, and he gets caught. I swear to god, he was so stoned one night he ended up picking up a girl here—this must've been six years ago now—and actually took her to the diner around the corner where the other waitress he was dating worked. It was a goddamn mess. We couldn't go back there for like a year."

I glanced at him as he stretched his arms out on the booth behind me and felt a sharp pang of conscience as he beckoned me over with one hand, kissing the side of my head lightly as I slid against him in the booth.

"Is he married?"

"Paul?" he asked, looking down at me as he raised his brows. "No. Absolutely not. I can't even imagine what that would look like . . ."

I turned my head as he stopped speaking, glancing at me as I twitched the hem of my skirt a little lower and felt his hand on my shoulder as he pulled me closer, turning me toward himself as he spoke into my ear.

"That's not us, Lea. Don't think that it is."

I looked up as him as he brushed my long bangs away from my face, searching his expression for a moment and then glanced away, watching the crowd shift in front of us as the singer starting speaking. I turned my head as another group of model-thin girls slid past the table, giggling apologies in

Jordan's direction as they jostled the table and he raised a hand, watching my face curiously for a moment.

"I don't do this every day, Lea," he whispered, his lips pulling up into a slight smile.

"Neither do I," I said, glancing up at him. "Really. Never. This is a first for me."

He picked up my left hand, turning it over in his slowly for a moment and I had a quick, vivid image of his name tattooed around my ring finger, the image burning brightly for a moment before disappearing.

Do you trust me?

"It's not about trusting you . . ."

Jordan looked down at me as I spoke, his eyes sharp with interest as he tilted his head and I snapped my mouth shut as the waitress swung back with our drinks, putting down four shot glasses next to a bottle of beer and one swirling red mixed drink in the center of the table. He smiled as I raised my brows, thanking her off-handedly as he slid a shot glass in front of me. I shook my head as he raised his brows, his deep-blue eyes shifting with amusement as he picked it up.

"What is this? Vodka?"

"Just thought I'd go with something you liked."

"That was kind of a fire sale situation last time," I said, raising a glass as he laughed and downed his in one quick swallow, waving it in my direction as I drained it slowly.

"Here," he said, sliding the pinkish-red drink in front of me as he grabbed the neck of the beer bottle. "You'll like this one. I promise."

I took a sip of the sugar sweet drink, raising my brows as it became a little more bitter halfway through and swirled it lightly in one hand as he glanced away from me, taking a long drink.

"What is it?"

He leaned closer as he glanced up at the stage again, his eyes moving across it restlessly for a moment.

"Do you like it?"

"I do. There's something in it I can't place."

"Yeah, it's some sort of organic pomegranate juice that they mix here," he said. "But only if you ask for it."

"Mixed with what?"

"Absinthe," he said.

"What?"

He held his fingers slightly apart and then smiled at my expression.

"Tiny little bit. Don't worry. I used to have it all the time. It's harmless. Do you like the band?"

"They're good. I've never heard them before."

"Yeah," he said, leaning back against the booth as he looked at me for a moment. "They are. I actually know their singer a little. And their guitarist. He used to play in this other band around here. We worked with them a few times."

He sat up as the crowd parted, picking up another shot glass before draining it quickly and then set it down as one of the guys up front raised a hand in our direction.

"That's him," he said. "Give me a second. I'm just going to go say hello."

I brushed my hair behind my ears as he stood up, watching him move through the crowd, and nursed my drink slowly as the guitarist up front greeted him like a brother, laughing at something Jordan said as he set his Fender aside. I sat back as the crowd shifted in front of me again, swallowing my view of him as I looked around the dark, packed floor and tried to pick out one other person in the crowd I would speak to in everyday life before giving up and curling my legs up on the long bench booth, thinking about what he'd said as I closed my eyes.

That's not us, Lea. Don't think that it is.

I raised my glass to my lips, draining it all in a matter of seconds and brushed my hands through the back of my hair as I reached for my phone, taking it out of my pocket and set it down in front of me. I scrolled through my messages quickly, pausing as I came to a short one from Tommy and pulled it up as the singer began speaking again, my fingers quaking lightly as I tapped at it.

We should talk. Bar at your place? Tuesday night?

I started to respond, and then glanced up as the singer began speaking again, my eyes flying open as I saw Jordan take a seat on the stage, his face lit up by the spotlights around him as the guy he had been speaking to handed him an electric acoustic guitar and he plugged it into an amp at his feet, resting it across his knee.

"Okay, everyone. We have a little surprise for you tonight . . . I don't know . . . Is it a surprise?"

He laughed as someone called something out behind him and Jordan smiled, seeking my eyes out in the crowd as I held my breath.

"Yeah. I guess it's a surprise. This is Jordan Redd, from the band Ares Rising. They used to play here all the time. Before they got too big for this place."

He looked up as a group of people up front applauded and nodded to the crowd as Jordan raised his hand toward them.

"Yeah. But seriously, they're one of my favorite bands. And he's going to be playing a song off his new album—*Royal Blood*. You should check it out."

I rested my head in my hand, shredding my lower lip as someone lowered the microphone and he adjusted it with one hand, speaking to someone over his shoulder as the crowd applauded.

"Thank you," he said, raking his long hair back from his face as his face became soft and serious. "This song is called 'Never Knew.'"

He glanced up at me as he started playing, the melody slow and haunting, and I closed my eyes as the entire place fell silent, letting his voice move over me like some kind of a drug. It was richer in person—warmer, grittier—and I opened my eyes as he came to the refrain, watching his fingers move over his guitar carelessly as he leaned toward the microphone. I watched him through the crowd, thinking of the weeks I had spent playing the tune over and over while I laid in bed at home and felt a strange, terrifying sense of unreality sweep over me as the sand shifted beneath me again, glancing up as he met my eyes through the crowd and kept them there, holding me tight.

I'm here, Lea. Don't let go.

I felt my heart constrict painfully for a moment as he smiled slightly and then glanced away, shifting his eyes around the crowd as they swayed together near the stage. I picked up my phone before I could help myself, angling it toward the spotlight and took his picture as he ended the song in a rough, reworked flourish and the crowd went wild, his smile calm and humble as he gave them a wave. I saw one of the other guys from the band applaud behind him as he leaned toward the microphone, and dropped my phone as he glanced in my direction.

"Thank you," he said, smiling a little as the people in front of me turned to stare. He swung the guitar off of his lap with one hand, standing up as he turned his back on the crowd and handed it back as he chatted with the other guys from the band, his face bright and vital as our waitress walked back over. I blinked up at her as she set down a small bottle of champagne with two glasses and shook my head as she glanced over her shoulder.

"Newlyweds, right? Jordan said something about it. Don't worry. It's on the house. And congratulations."

I looked up as she gave me a smile and headed for another table and looked up as Jordan walked through the crowd, giving me a quick, brilliant smile as he slid in next to me, pulling me closer as he kissed the side of my head.

"God, that was funny," he said as he pulled away from me slightly, his blue eyes darting over me as I turned to face him. "You looked so surprised . . ."

"Did you plan that?"

Jordan shrugged and laughed softly at my expression.

"You did say you wanted to hear me play," he said, picking up the bottle of champagne on the table as he raised his brows. "What's this?"

I slid my legs over his lap as I moved closer and he looked over my body quickly for a moment and then curled his arm behind me, pulling me into his lap as he turned the bottle toward me.

"I love that fucking song."

"I know. That's why I chose it. Seriously, what is this?"

"It's on the house," I said, leaning close to his ear as I rested my hand on his chest. "The waitress brought it over. For the newlyweds."

"Oh, right," he said laughing, pulling my head close to him for minute as he pressed his forehead against mine. "I forgot I told her that."

"But I really, really, really love that song." I said, coiling my hands around the back of his neck.

"Oh yeah?" he said, his expression changing slightly as I brushed my fingers over his lips. "How much?"

I brushed my thumb across his cheek, leaning up to kiss him deeply as he wrapped his arms around me and then broke away when a large group of people started applauding and someone yelled congratulations. Jordan smiled down at me, his eyes wide and playful and raised the champagne bottle in their direction as I shook my head, burying it against his chest as they applauded again.

"But we're the newlyweds," he said against my lips.

"I can't believe you told her that. Don't they know you here?"

Jordan shrugged nonchalantly and then swung me around to face the table as he uncorked the champagne lightly, pouring out two glasses as he met my eyes.

"It was a joke," he said, using the bottle to point to the bar and then the waitresses gathered together near the bar. "And it's a whole new front of the house. I only know a few guys from the band."

He handed me a glass, looking down at me gently for a moment as he held it up and clinked it against mine, taking a drink as he pulled me closer. He glanced toward the stage as another band began setting up and looked around the room quickly as he finished his drink, setting it down next to the bottle as he wrapped his hand around my waist.

"Let's not go back," he whispered in my ear as he shifted me in his lap, and I looked up at him as his eyes moved over me for a moment, setting my glass down on the table.

"As in forever?"

"I'm serious," he said, something quick and searching moving behind the deep blue mask of his eyes. "Let's leave tonight. I'll take you anywhere you want to go . . ."

"Just like that?"

"Just like that."

I looked over his expression for a moment as his gaze shifted between my eyes and my lips, and glanced away as he tipped my chin back to meet him.

"What would we do for money?"

"Prostitute ourselves. Obviously."

I laughed as he smiled down at me, his face still serious below his amusement.

"Quite a life plan."

"I mean it, Lea. You and me. Total freedom. We'll live however we want, wherever we want."

He leaned his head against my cheek and I shivered as his breath whispered along my neck, his voice so calm and hypnotic I closed my eyes.

"It's what you wanted, isn't it? Isn't that what you said? All I'm doing is offering it to you. And all you have to do is say yes."

I pulled away from him slightly, looking over his too-perfect face as a sudden vivid image of driving through the desert with him at a hundred miles an hour burned through my mind like a nuclear blast, and tilted my head at him as he touched the skin below my ear again, pressing his thumb against my lips as he leaned closer.

"Say yes, Lea."

Yes, I thought. *Yes, yes, yes, yes, yes, yes, yes!*

I nodded as he pulled me closer, kissing me gently as he held onto my face and then pulled away and picked up my champagne glass, his eyes moving over the crowd slowly for a moment as he finished what was left in it.

"That's all I wanted to hear," he said.

By seven we were on the bus, headed back to the city. I was closest to the window as the dark coil of abandoned rural landscape flew past and watched the dawn creep over the horizon as I laid my head in his lap, his hand in my hair as he stared off into space. I thought of what he'd said, the entire evening spinning out like some kind of colorful, disconnected dream, with one image bleeding into the next without reason or context and listened to the road sigh beneath us as I curled onto my side, feeling his warmth beneath me as he brushed his hand over my cheek. When I finally slept, it was sudden and dreamless—not so much sleep as a deep, unplanned fall into unconsciousness and cracked my eyes open when the thread of hard sunshine began to creep through, squinting against it across the windows as I rolled toward him, pulling my coat a little farther up my cheek.

"I meant it, Lea," he said quietly, his voice low and strange as I felt his fingers touch my face, tracing the line of my lips gently as my eyes sighed shut. "Let's never go back. Let's live this way forever. I could do it. I could."

With you I could.

I'll go, I thought, so tired I wasn't actually sure if I was saying it out loud. *I'll follow you. Anywhere, anywhere.*

I felt him press his lips against the side of my head, blinking slightly as a square of daylight slid across my face and tumbled lower as his voice weaved its way into my dreams—gently, quietly—changing them forever.

CHAPTER NINE

BY THE TIME I GOT INTO WORK, THE MORNING MEETING WAS already over. I walked in right about noon after a quick fifteen-minute pitstop at my apartment to change clothes and throw my hair into a loose, second-day ponytail. I chewed my nails down to the skin before I had parked in the lot—the idea of seeing Abbie at work after spending the evening with Jordan without even an hour of buffer time straining my nerves almost to the breaking point. I considered turning around and calling in about ten times before I reached the door, my morning coffee doing little to chase away the raging headache I could feel radiating from the base of my spine upward and tucked my sunglasses on a little lower as I headed for my desk, trying not to look anyone directly in the eye.

When I finally looked up, I stopped in my tracks—realizing instantly that something was wrong and glanced between Madge and David as they hovered behind my desk, beckoning me over with a quick wave of their hands.

"Where were you all night?" Madge asked as I shrugged off my coat and set down my cup, pulling my glasses off last as she gave me a long, searching once over. "I must've called you about five times."

"I was just out," I said as David glanced at me solemnly for a moment without speaking, raising his brows as Madge pulled something up on her phone. "Jacob needed to talk. Something about the lease . . ."

"You don't know," David said as Madge turned her phone in my direction, handing it over as she folded her arms across her chest, her green eyes narrowing as she glanced over my shoulder.

"Know what? What is this?"

Madge leaned over me, tapping at my computer, and then pointed to my story about the Mardi Gras event downtown, flipping through the copy quickly as she searched for a picture.

"There," she said. "That girl. The one with the pope."

I looked at the picture I had taken of the two kids from Northville, my brow furrowing as I saw her face plastered across Madge's social media pages and shook my head as I read through it quickly, my stomach knotting suddenly as I read the condolences under a bright, sunny picture of her.

"She died last night," she said, glancing toward Noah's empty office as her lips thinned out into a red, disapproving line. "Look."

"Died?"

"She took a fall at that party," David said, stepping closer as Madge passed another photo to me, this one of a girl in a hospital bed next to a scrolling page of prayers. "Out in the yard."

"And she was drunk as hell," Madge said, raising her voice as the IT guys glanced in our direction before putting their heads together and scurrying away quickly. "She ended up face down in some fountain behind the garden. And her friends just left her there. By the time they found her, it was too late."

"Christ," I said, leaning over my screen quickly. "I talked to this girl. I took a quote."

"We know," David said. "Noah was all over it this morning. He pulled the quote. And the picture."

I looked at him quickly, my hand freezing in mid-air as I reached for my coffee.

"He did what?"

"They're not going to run it today," Madge said. "He's putting this shit all on you, because you didn't show up . . ."

"But really he just wants to kill it," David said, his jaw grim and set. "I offered to follow up on it. But he doesn't want a story about some 22-year-old girl who died at a party the city sponsored, running side by side next to all the copy about how fantastic all these new initiatives are. He said we'd run it next week."

"Which won't mean shit, because by then the story will be everywhere," Madge said. "That way he won't have to be the one who ran the first goddamn story asking the mayor how something like this could happen."

"When was this?" I asked sitting down at my desk. "What time did this happen?"

"A little after midnight Friday night. Tommy said you gave him a ride back to his motel right before."

I tried not to flinch as Madge mentioned his name and glanced up as I realized that she wasn't paying attention to me at all, her eyes running over the floor like a die-hard social crusader who had just discovered she was setting up camp with the enemy.

"That's right," I said, flipping to my story about the party quickly as I glanced at the clock. "But people were too drunk then. That place was like a frat house. I kept waiting for someone to walk in and take control. Shelly Tozier?"

"That's her. She was a junior at U of M."

"What campus?"

"Dearborn," David offered, glancing at his watch and then pulled up a chair next to mine, his eyes darting across the screen.

"And we go to print when?"

"Everything has to be into layout by two."

I muttered to myself and then scrawled a name and number down a sheet of paper, pausing with my pen in mid-air before adding another.

"What are you going to do?"

"What Noah should've done," I said. "I'm going to write the fucking story. Madge, you've been talking to the girl's family?"

"Just messages, but yeah, I've been in contact."

"Do you mind asking them to send over a photo? Tell them someone will be calling them in a few minutes if they wouldn't mind giving a quote."

"They may not give one."

"All we need is the photo," I said, looking up the mayor's number in a sudden flurry of typing. "I should be able to get enough of a bio somewhere else. What hospital did they take her to?"

"Northridge," David said.

"Give me a few minutes," Madge said.

He looked over my scraped-together appearance as I started typing, shaking my head as he pressed his folded hands against his lips and met my eyes as I scribbled down another number.

"This wasn't your fault, Lea."

"I never said it was."

"They should've been all over this."

"And I should've at least mentioned how much drinking was going on. I should've at least asked the question. And the reason I didn't, is because that's what we do here. We smile and we shake hands and we write cheerful little stories that make everyone feel better."

"That's Noah, Lea. Not you."

"Because if we don't, no one will talk to you. The whole city just closes its doors. No more ads, no more stories. You saw what happened with those classes downtown."

"Yeah," he said sighing. "I did."

"So, we run the story we should run, and some woman who was just trying to do her job gets fired and then the whole city basically tells us to go to hell. I should've known then. I honestly should've."

"You know no matter what you do, Noah's not going to run it."

"Then let him say it to my face," I said. "I'm going to at least ask the question."

David looked at me steadily for a moment and then picked up the sheet of paper I had scrawled four different names on, ripping it in half.

"Rhonda Messler. Is that the woman who organized it?"

"You don't have to do that . . ."

"You can't do it all alone in an hour. Focus on the girl's family—what she was like, who she was. And try to get through to Bingham."

"If he's smart, he won't talk to me."

"He's still pretty new. You may get lucky."

I pulled up Madge's Facebook account, scrolling through it quickly until I found Shelly Tozier's post and scoured her pages until I found a raw, heartfelt account of what had happened on her brother's page, typing up all the relevant information about it in a quick second-hand account as I looked for some way to contact him directly. I switched gears when I came up with nothing, knowing that it might be hours before he returned a message and picked up my phone as I headed for the front door, grabbing my coat as I shrugged it on. I lit a cigarette on the way out, cringing over the cavalier way Tommy and I had just dismissed her as some drunk college girl eager for her fifteen minutes of fame, and dialed the mayor's office, my eyes running across the snowy road in quick, frantic leaps.

"Mayor Bingham's office," his secretary said in the bored upbeat way she seemed to address every caller—from the president on down. "How can I assist you?"

"Hi Janet," I said, letting out a quick stream of smoke as I turned back toward the building. "This is Lea from the *Tribune*. Is the mayor in?"

"He's been in and out all day today, Lea. I could put you through to his voicemail if you'd like."

"I actually needed to get in touch with him as soon as possible. Does he have a direct line?"

"He does . . . what is this regarding?"

"Last night, a girl by the name of Shelly Tozier died after taking a fall at the Mardi Gras party the city sponsored. We're running a story on it tomorrow morning. I just wanted him to have a chance to give a quote."

The line went dead for a handful of seconds as if I had temporarily short-circuited her polite public relations filter and she was scrambling to reboot.

"About what?" she asked, her tone suddenly clipped and annoyed.

"I thought he might want to express his condolences to the girl's family. She was twenty-two, you know. A lot people are wondering how something like this could've happened . . ."

"We're aware of the situation, Lea. And the mayor has been in direct contact with the girl's family. I'm not sure a quote at this time would be appropriate."

"Like I said, if I could just get his direct number . . ."

"Let me put you through to his voicemail," she said, the line erupting into a stream of loud classical music as I pulled it away from my ear. I left a message, glancing up as Madge stepped outside and raised my brows as she lit up next to me as I hung up, rolling her eyes at my expression.

"This isn't a backslide," she said, tucking her lighter into her coat as she handed me a small post-it note. "This is righteous indignation. I can't believe he pulled her damn quote. Here. This is her brother's number. He'll talk to you. I think he needs to talk to someone."

I thanked her and dialed him immediately, pacing over to the wooden bench at the end of the sidewalk, and brushed off a slick of snow with one hand as he picked up almost at once, me pulling a notepad out of my pocket. I talked to him for almost twenty minutes, my fingers practically freezing around my phone as he spilled out a lot of confused and painful anger directed at the party, the mayor and the city itself and thanked him for his time as I hung up, rubbing my hands together for a moment before covering my face in my hands.

Could've stopped it, I thought. *Could've at least said something. They should've closed the bar. Someone should've been paying attention.*

I paced around outside for another couple of minutes, glancing through my notes before heading back inside and set them down on my desk as David sat down next to me, shaking his head as he noticed how pink and wind-blown my face was.

"Any luck with the mayor?"

"His secretary told me to go fuck myself very politely."

"Yeah, I thought that might happen."

He pushed a number toward me as I raised my brows and then leaned over to grab his notes off of his desk, flipping to the next page dramatically as he adjusted his glasses with one hand.

"And according to Rhonda Messler, this was a tragic accident and her heart goes out to *Shelia* and her entire family in their hour of need."

"She didn't actually get her name wrong?"

"She did," he said, his dark eyes flashing with anger as he set his notepad down. "I honestly don't think she gave a damn one way of another."

"What is this?" I asked, picking up the number.

"The mayor's private cell," he said, shrugging. "He may not pick up, but it's worth a shot."

"Where did you get this?"

David smiled mysteriously for a moment and then stood up, glancing toward the two lone girls putting the layout together as his jaw hardened.

"Does it matter? I still don't think Noah will run it but fuck it. That girl was twenty-two years old. The woman who organized it can't even be bothered to remember her name. And no one here will even call them out on it because they're afraid to lose a few months' worth of ad revenue. I say we burn them to the ground."

My eyes widened as he reached for his coat and glanced down at me as he put it on, pointing to me as he stepped around the desk.

"Did Madge send you the photo?"

I scrolled through my messages quickly and then nodded, pulling it up on my computer.

"Good," he said. "Call Bingham. If you can't get a hold of him, run with what you have. I'll be back in a few minutes."

I reached for my phone, typing up the first few lines to the story as they popped into my head and then turned in my chair as he picked up on the third ring, his voice tight and harassed as he asked who it was.

"Mayor Bingham? This is Lea. With the *Tribune*. We met the other night at the Mardi Gras party downtown."

"Of course. Lea. What can I do for you?"

"I was actually calling about Shelly Tozier, Mr. Bingham," I said, barreling through as quickly as I could as I picked up my pen. "She attended the party the other night too. Last night, she died from complications resulting from a fall she took that night. Your secretary said you had been in contact with the girl's family?"

"That's not . . . that's not precisely accurate . . ."

"Her brother said that she was well over the legal drinking limit when she went into that fountain, Mr. Bingham. And then no one found her for almost twenty minutes. We're running a story on it tomorrow. I just wanted to know if you'd like to comment on that."

"What kind of a story?"

"Well, her family is extremely upset as you can imagine. Some residents are saying that it was the city's fault for not monitoring the party more closely . . ."

"I'm not sure that I have anything to do with that."

"You were at the party. Were you concerned at any time that the party, that the drinking at the party, was getting out of control?"

I scrawled across my pad quickly, notating my questions as I asked them and paused as he cleared his throat and seemed to bring himself under some semblance of control, his basic talent for spin control going into quick, fever-ish overdrive.

"What I will say about it is this, Lea. What happened to Shelly was a terri-ble, senseless accident. I have nothing but sympathy for her and her family. It's always a tragedy to lose someone that young, especially someone who had such a bright future to look forward to."

I paused as he stopped speaking and gave him a minute as I tapped my pen on my pad.

"I agree," I said. "Do you think the city should take responsibility for this in any way?"

"I'm sorry but that's all I'd like to say about it at this time, Lea."

"I just wanted you to have a chance to respond. There are a lot of angry people out there wondering how this could've happened at all . . ."

"That's all, Lea. Good luck with your story. Please don't contact this number again."

I blinked as he hung up, pulling my ponytail holder out with both hands and ran my hands through my hair as I looked through my quotes—starring the ones I intended to use before blasting through the first two paragraphs at a flat clip—and what must've been Shelly's graduation photo grinning down on me as I wrote. When I had a quick rough draft, I ran back through it—clean-ing it up in a flat, mindless flourish as I rearranged quotes into some kind of cohesive story and changed the name Shelia back to Shelly several times before leaving it alone. It would hurt her family more than it would hurt Messler's reputation, I reasoned, to know that their only daughter didn't even rate high enough on the city's radar to warrant a decent, heartfelt quote.

By the time I was finished David was standing over my shoulder, reread-ing the short four-hundred-word story as he nodded and pointed out the gaffe before raising his hands as I explained, his face as vital and angry as I had ever seen it.

"Leave it in," he said, glancing toward the layout department as he shook the snow off of his jacket. "Fuck her."

"I can't," I said, shaking my head as I printed it out. "It's just cruel. You should have heard her brother, David. He's barely holding it together."

David inhaled deeply and then let out a long sigh, his face becoming a little more reasonable as he picked the story up off the printer and read through it quickly.

"Spelling right on these names?"

"Yes. Double-checked."

"Okay," he said. "Send it over to Noah's email and then to me."

"Where is he?" I asked, glancing back at Noah's desk as David shook his head.

"Chasing it, as usual. He took a long lunch to finish up. We won't have his editorials until the last second."

I watched him follow Katie around the corner, catching up with her as she headed into the sales department and glanced up at the senior graphic designer roll her eyes in my direction, giving me a frank look of dislike before lowering her eyes to the stack of ads and articles in front of her. I took a deep breath as I pushed myself away from my desk, rereading my article for what felt like the twentieth time and closed my eyes as Madge came around the corner, leaning against David's desk as she shook her head in my direction.

"I should've said something," I said, turning in my chair as I noticed two of the sirens head into the breakroom. "That party was a disaster waiting to happen."

"That's what Tommy said," she said, glancing at me oddly for a moment as Abbie glanced in our direction, raising her hand in greeting before heading around the corner. "Did she seem drunk when you talked to her?"

"I mean—a little? Everyone was a little drunk. But it just kept getting worse. There were kids out on the back lawn in the middle of this big hedge maze..."

"And people were taking bets on how long it would take them to find their way out. Yeah, he told me."

"I was one of them. I just thought it was funny."

I pressed my lips together as Abbie came out of the breakroom laughing, heading for the IT department as I tried not to cringe and tilted her head at me as she disappeared inside, looking at me over the rim of her coffee cup.

"Come outside with me for a minute," Madge said.

"It's freezing out."

"Back lot," she said, standing up. "We can sit in my car."

I looked up at her, my eyes narrowing as I realized how polite and reasonable she suddenly sounded, and got up as I grabbed my coffee, following her down the hall as my stomach knotted. I had a quick, terrifying premonition that somewhere between lucid drunken frankness and sober next day horror, Tommy had somehow confessed everything to Madge and I was being led to a cheerful ambush. I slid into the passenger side of her cute, vintage Volkswagen as she leaned over to unlock my door and decided to simply deny everything as she cranked her engine, swearing under her breath as it turned over reluctantly and then died. She cranked it again, pumping the gas quickly as she cracked her window open and then offered me a cigarette that I took, reaching for my lighter as she turned her great big pouncing cat eyes in my direction.

"So?"

"So what?" I rebutted, lighting up.

"Are you going to tell me about it or not?"

"Tell you about what?"

Stay the course, I thought. *Deny till you die.*

Madge raised her brows, pressing her lips together to smother a knowing smile, and I felt a rush of annoyance and relief as I realized that Tommy hadn't told her everything. He had simply given her just enough truth to throw her off the scent.

"Tommy told me, all right? About Jordan."

I raised my brows at her as I blew out a long stream of smoke and remained silent, quietly congratulating myself on my good form.

"I know you left with him after you dropped Tommy off," she said, tapping her ashes out the window. "And you know I don't care, Lea. Are you really going to sit there and deny it?"

"I'm not denying anything," I said, brushing my long bangs away from my eyes as I glanced out at the snow-covered, used car lot next door. "There's nothing to tell, all right? We slept together. Big deal. We were both a little stoned and it just happened."

Madge raised her brows at me, the burning stub of her cigarette poised in mid-air as she gave me one of those deep, searching looks again and then her expression softened a little as she shook her head, stamping her cigarette out as she turned in her seat.

"I knew it. The second he told me. And then when you wouldn't call me back..."

"Look," I said, tapping my ashes out the window. "It wasn't exactly my finest hour. And since I didn't think it would happen again, I didn't see any reason to bring it up. You want to know the truth? I feel like shit about it. Okay?"

"You shouldn't," Madge said, just emphatically enough to give me a sharp pang of conscience. "Christ, Lea. We've all been there. And Jordan is... I get it. How do you say no, right? I mean, how do you say no?"

I pushed my cigarette out the window, and folded my hands in my lap, glancing at her out of the corner of my eyes as she raised her brows again.

"Was it good?" she asked, smiling mysteriously as she glanced toward the building. "I bet he's crazy good in bed, isn't he?"

She raised her hand as I gave her another look and shook her head, her face becoming a little more serious.

"Right. Doesn't matter. Did you tell him? Does he know it was a one-time thing or..."

I pressed my fingers against my eye and let the lies flow through me, constructing the bunker now, barely keeping track.

"I don't think he was even thinking like that, you know? He seemed pretty relaxed about it all. Kind of got the impression he does this sort of thing a lot."

Madge nodded, gesturing toward the building.

"Naturally. What did I tell you? Poor Abbie. I'd actually feel worse for her if she didn't seem so fucking oblivious. Trying to stay married to a guy like that is like wandering out in the middle of a tornado just to watch the sky change colors."

She tilted her head at me, her expression just short of smug as she killed the engine.

"Let's get back inside. I just didn't want to have to speak in code the whole time. I am literally so disgusted with this place today I could walk out and never look back."

I followed her back inside, letting the wind slam the back door shut as we scurried back inside and then paused as I heard screaming in the next room, wandering toward the sound as everyone in the hall glanced in our direction. Madge glanced at me as a shadow passed in front of the blinds in Noah's office window and she turned toward Patrick as he folded his arms across his chest, his eyes passing between us for a moment.

"Is that David?"

"That's him."

I stepped closer as their voices rose loud enough for the entire room to catch an angry word here and there, as David's shadow paced back and forth in front of his desk.

"What are they yelling about?" I asked.

Patrick rolled his jaw at me, his eyes shifting with a moment of contempt.

"What do you think?" he asked mildly, turning his back on the crowd as he stalked back into his office and slammed the door.

My eyes widened as I glanced in Madge's direction and held up my hand as she started to follow me, crossing the floor to Noah's office in a matter of seconds. I knocked on it once, opening it before he could answer and stepped inside as I saw David's face, shutting the door behind me.

"Just run the article, Noah," David said, glancing at me steadily for a moment before turning his head in Noah's direction.

Noah looked up at me from behind his desk, his face darkening with anger and folded his hands across his chest as he raised his brows in my direction.

"Or what?" he asked, his voice clipped and enraged.

"God, you're a prick. Because it's news, all right? Because someone died. Because we're supposed to care about shit like that. And if we don't, what are we doing here? What's the fucking point?"

"Is this yours?" Noah asked, shoving a copy of the article over the desk at me as it floated to the floor.

"I followed up on it as soon as I heard."

"A little late, don't you think? And I told you already. We don't have the space."

"Pull a couple of ads," David said.

"For what?" he asked, turning in my direction. "If you knew this was a problem why wasn't it in your original article? Hmm? Why am I just hearing about this poor college girl going into a drunken coma and dying at a party you were supposed to be covering? If you knew the drinking was a problem, where is it? Did you mention it even once?"

"I just . . ."

"Of course," Noah said, cutting me off with a bitter laugh. "Blame her. As if she's not just writing exactly what she was taught to write."

"Not really. I don't remember telling her to write this up. That was you. I told you we'd run with it in the next cycle."

"This is a front-page story, Noah," David said. "Anywhere else it would be. You know that."

Noah looked between us for a moment and then sat back in his chair, his face so angry it had practically crossed the threshold back into peaceful repose.

"Next week," he said, glancing in my direction. "Next."

David stood up suddenly and shook his head as he headed for the door.

"Run the story, Noah," he said, his voice low and clipped as he pulled it open.

"And like I said…"

"Just run it."

I turned my head as he threw back his door hard enough to crash into the outer wall and wilt it a little as Noah turned all of his rage in my direction, the crowd out front scattering like a frightened herd.

"You should've asked Bingham these questions that night," he said. "And you should've known about this girl the next day. It's not my fault you don't take your job seriously. You half-ass some story two hours before we go to print, and I'm supposed to put it on the front page? I don't think so. Frankly, I don't trust you enough to do that, Lea. Take it however you want."

I looked him over as he shoved a stack of papers away from him, swearing under his breath and felt a thin coil of rage begin to unravel inside me as I took a step forward, meeting his eyes squarely for a moment as I blinked down on him.

"David was right," I said. "You really are a prick."

I picked my article up off of the floor and crept closer, setting it down on the edge of his desk as he stared at me in astonishment.

"It's a good story, Noah. You should run it. But they don't really let you do that here, do they? No. I don't think they do."

I turned and walked out of the office as I noticed Madge standing on the other side of the wall and pocketed my phone as I shook my head at her, shutting down my computer as I reached for my purse.

"I'm going home," I said, breezing past her. "Tell Noah if he needs me, he knows how to reach me."

I headed out into the back lot, so angry I couldn't immediately remember where I was headed or why, and put my head in my hands as I let out a scream, every nerve in my body reverberating like piano wire as I breathed deeply for several seconds. I pressed my head against the steering wheel, trying not to let the hatred I felt fill me up like a poison and then sat up and threw my car into reverse as I tore out of the lot, driving in the opposite direction of my apartment as I picked up my phone.

I hit Tommy's number as I dialed, slowing down as I realized I was doing forty in a twenty-miles-an-hour zone and pulled into the first restaurant I noticed as he picked up, parking in the nearby empty lot as I glanced at the clock.

"Lea?"

"Did you tell Madge I was fucking Jordan?"

"Did I what? What time is it?"

"I can't believe you told her anything. You know, the next time you want to save yourself, do me a favor and send her in someone else's direction. Do you have any idea how many lies I had to tell today? I would never have done that to you, Tommy. Fucking never."

"Okay, for starters I didn't tell her shit, all right? All I said . . ."

"Right. I know what you said. I was the one who had to say it, right? So, nothing's on you. I was the one who had to lie and say that I wouldn't see him again, when you didn't have to mention him at all . . ."

"Wait. What? Are you still seeing him?"

I fell silent as I heard him switch the phone from one ear to the other, his voice suddenly losing all undercurrent of amused annoyance as he cleared his throat.

"Answer me, Lea."

"It's none of your fucking business, Tommy. Just like it was none of your sister's business. You want your privacy? Guess what? So do I."

"Where are you at?"

"I don't know. Some shitty Chinese restaurant on the other side of town. Lim something. I can't see the sign."

"In Wayne?"

"Where else?"

"Okay," he said, his voice suddenly calm and alert. "Give me half an hour. I'll meet you there."

He hung up before I could get out more than one or two half-hearted protests and I realized that I wanted to see him as I got out of the car, slamming the door behind me as I headed inside. I waited for a table at the front, even though there was only one other couple in the main dining room and followed the hostess to a booth in the back, something about the dark interior and tacky red carpet suiting my mood right down to the ground. I ordered a pot of tea, running my hands through my hair as I realized for the first time in hours, how bone-weary I was and made a point of heading into the bathroom to wash my face, redoing my make-up in the plastic mirror over the hand dryer.

I headed back into the dining room, pausing across the floor as the waitress spoke with Tommy on the other side of the booth and felt my mood lift a little as he raised his brows at my appearance, handing her back the menu with a gracious smile.

"Just the steamed vegetables and rice for us," he said. "Three eggrolls. No. Four."

I took a seat as she smiled in my direction, sliding into the booth across from him and he looked me over as he reached for the tea, pouring himself a cup as he refilled my glass.

"Late night?"

"Don't start, Tommy. I barely slept last night. Did you hear about that girl from the party?"

"I did. Madge told me."

"It's just so hard to believe. And then Noah wouldn't run my article about it. It was this whole thing . . ."

"And last night?"

I rolled my eyes at the way he said it and rubbed my fingers against the back of my neck.

"You're going to be as bad as Madge, aren't you?"

"Not at all. You want to keep your privacy, keep it."

"Thank you."

"You're welcome. But just so we understand each other, you are still seeing him."

"I don't know. What difference does it make?"

"There's a big difference. There's a huge difference between fucking a guy like that and trying to have a relationship with him."

He glanced up as the waitress set down four plates and a bowl of rice, brushing his fingers through his dark blond hair.

"I know you, all right? You don't understand guys like this, Lea."

"And what? You do?"

"Yeah, actually. I do."

"I'm too tired to have this argument, Tommy. The other night . . ."

"The other night what? Isn't what he's really like? Let me tell you something. The other night is as close as you're going to get to figuring out what he's actually about, all right? It's like a test. And because you didn't run . . . now he knows. Get me?"

"Knows what?"

Tommy rubbed his hand across his brow and then held up his hand, his expression once more becoming patient.

"Let's try this from another tack. Logan. That guy you met in college. The first time you went to college. Remember him?"

I set down my cup as my emotions closed up like a steel trap and shrugged.

"What about him?"

"You *know* what about him. I just want you to remember how you felt with him. How he made you feel at first. And then later. Once he knew he had you."

"Jordan isn't Logan. He's nothing like him."

"Jordan is Logan with about ten years' worth of experience under his belt. He's dangerous, Lea. Don't tell me you don't see it."

I opened my mouth to speak and then closed it as an image of Jordan patiently ignoring Tommy when he asked to be let up burst through my mind in a brilliant wrap around technicolor. The way his eyes had slid to him and then away again—watching, waiting.

"He isn't always like that," I said. "He's not, Tommy. Last night . . ."

I stopped speaking as Tommy tilted his head at me, something like pity flashing through his eyes and brushed my hair away from my face as he held up his hands.

"Last night what?" he asked, his voice kind.

"Nothing," I said. "Forget it."

I sat back as the waitress delivered the rest of our food with a cheerful lack of interest, and closed my eyes as I thought of the way Jordan had kissed my head on the bus, telling me he could live that way with me forever. *I could,* he'd said. *With you I could.*

I glanced up as Tommy reached out and took my hand across the table, his dark eyes gently searching my face as he squeezed it tightly for a moment.

"I don't regret it, Lea. Not anything. Not at all. So stop thinking that, all right? I love you. Nothing's going to change that."

He let it go as I let out my breath all in one sigh, unaware that I'd been holding it and shrugged a little as I leaned my elbows on the table pushing my hair away from my face.

"You're wrong about him."

"I'm not. I wish I was, but I'm not. So talk to me about it, or don't talk to me about it. Just know that I'm here for you, okay? Whatever you need."

I got home a little before six—so exhausted, the setting sun seemed like one long red shadow over the snowy white landscape, as if the world itself were on fire. I pulled into the back lot, taking my time up the icy steps and paused as I noticed a shiny new deadbolt lock above my doorknob, my brow furrowing slightly as I pushed the door open. I stepped into my bedroom, leaving the back door open as I heard music coming from the next room, and walked through the hall like a sleepwalker as I saw Jordan sitting at the dining room table, refilling his glass of wine as he shifted through a stack of records restlessly for a moment. He stopped when he saw me, smiling a little at my expression and pressed his folded hands against his lips for a moment as I glanced over my shoulder.

"The door . . ."

"You said your locks didn't work," he said, picking up his glass as he waved it toward the couch. "I replaced them. The key's on the table."

I picked up the lone key on the keyring, holding it up as I raised my brows. "Just one?"

Jordan's blue eyes swirled with something a little darker than amusement and he pulled a set of keys out of his jacket pocket, giving me a sudden brilliant grin as he held onto the spare. He let the ring dangle for a moment before catching it in his palm and then set them down on the table as he beckoned me over with one hand.

"Come over here, Lea," he said, his eyes moving over my body slowly for a moment as I walked across the floor. I reached for him with both hands as he wrapped his arms around my waist and felt him slide his hand up the back of my neck as I leaned over to kiss him, my entire body sighing forward as he coiled his hand in the back of my hair. He kissed me deeply as his hand ran from the back of my neck to my cheek, resting there gently as I tried to pull away and then dragged me lower as I closed my eyes, sliding to my knees in front of him.

Jordan cupped my face in both hands as he smiled down at me, kissing me gently on the lips as I rested my hands on his thighs and traced my features slowly for a moment as he brushed my hair away from my face, looking me over as I rested my head against his palm.

"Long day?"

"Very long," I said. "It was a very long, strange day."

Jordan ran his hand around the back of my neck, moving his thumb across my lips thoughtfully as he pulled me closer, his blue eyes so wide and searching they seemed to fill the entire sky.

"Why don't you get undressed and tell me all about it?" he asked, his voice low and teasing. I smiled, coiling my hands around his neck as he spoke against my cheek and crawled into his lap. And home was never home until I was his and his and his.

CHAPTER TEN

THERE ARE THINGS YOU DON'T NEED TO KNOW. THINGS THAT are important only to me. The way he looked in the morning when he was sound asleep and perfectly at peace. The way I would hear him playing some chorus from a song he was working on in the next room—once, then twice, then louder, then changing it. I never really got over that, you know? The way he just stepped into my life and took it over, blowing everything apart without an apology or an invitation—calling me at night when he couldn't be with me, appearing at dawn as if we'd never been apart.

Those first few weeks were spent in a happy little cocoon—completely absorbed in one another, oblivious to the world around us. I'd find him at my apartment when I least expected it—after work, when I had been out with friends. He complained about my apartment, which seemed to violate all of his innate desire for simple, unencumbered order, but also seemed to relax into it after a while, like some cramped and loathsome summer cabin that time always softened with age—not so much for what it was, but for what it represented. He also didn't seem to mind the mess like he once had, although I would occasionally find him doing the dishes in a restless fury while the record player howled old blues classics, a compulsion I found strangely and endearingly attractive.

Most of the time though, I simply came home to him waiting for me restlessly in bed, reading poetry at the edge with one hand dangling over while he chain-smoked one cigarette after another, his whole body tense—waiting, waiting. When it wasn't that, I came home to him sleeping deeply—as if he had been up for days on end and his entire body had just given out to simple exhaustion, his eyelids twitching slightly on the mountain of pillows he'd shoved behind his head, captured by dreams he never admitted to remembering. Sometimes I would find him there in the middle of the afternoon, the sun falling across the sheets in one shifting butterfly nest of sunlight and I would curl into bed next to him as he slept, his body curling around mine instantly, hand around my waist, one leg wrapped around my calves. No matter what I did, or how hard I tried, he always, always woke first and I would startle awake all at once to the noise of him cooking in the kitchen, or sitting out on the balcony at dusk, the sound of his guitar drifting back to me through the open window.

Like I said, little things. The kind everyone seems to forget. The only difference with Jordan was that he seemed to understand it too–the fragility of our happiness, how every moment we shared together was essentially borrowed time. I would sometimes wake to him like I did that first night in the motel, his too-blue eyes moving over my face as if cataloging it for some future he could barely face and we made love like that too, like thieves in the dark, nothing held back and nothing saved—gambling everything, desperate and sweet.

One morning after days of urging, Jordan convinced me to meet him at his place, when Abbie was out. I hedged, he countered. I demurred, he argued. What I couldn't tell him was that I was trapped in some strange alternative reality, somewhere between heaven and hell, and although I lived for the moments when we were together, I couldn't shake the conditioning of a thousand breathless movies about adultery—each one with a great big puritanical claymore waiting around every corner. Every day I came into work after spending the night with Jordan, I couldn't shake the superstitious certainty that Abbie was going to somehow figure it out and I was going to be walking into some violent, computer-smashing scream fest, one where the jilted wife finally stands up for herself and the other woman Gets What She Deserves. I had no desire to get what I deserved. I just wanted to live that way forever—in that enchanted lovers' blindspot she had somehow forgotten to check.

"Come over," Jordan said his voice rough with sleep, and I could see him on the other end sprawled across his bed in his boxers, his fingers tapping his chest restlessly as he cradled the phone between his ear and the bed.

"I can't. I have about a million things to follow up on. I haven't been making these phone calls. There's an interview I need to nail down before Wednesday."

"I don't care. Blow it off. I'm heading to Chicago tonight. I won't be back until the weekend."

I sat up a little straighter in bed, glancing at the clock as I swiped my hair away from my face and felt a pang of juvenile panic when I heard him sigh on the other end, oblivious to my worry, utterly relaxed.

"Chicago? Tonight?"

"Hmm. Something Paul put together. There's this festival there, kind of a pub crawl thing . . ."

"When were you going to tell me this?"

"I just found out about it. Do you think I want to spend the next three days in some shitty motel room in this weather? I'd rather be with you. Come over, Lea. Come over, come over . . ."

"And Abbie?"

"She's in class all day. And it's nicer over here anyway. There's a fireplace in the bedroom. I'll leave the door unlocked for you. You can just let yourself in . . ."

I paused as a sudden vivid image of lying naked across a bed in the middle of a white, white room with Jordan standing over me while a fireplace blazed came into my mind.

See what I mean?

I paused, running my thumb across my lips quickly for a moment as the image faded and bit my lip as I felt another image uncoil before I could stop it—this one of Jordan and I in bed together—and Abbie coming home early and following the noise from the bedroom down the hall.

"This isn't a romance novel, Lea," he said, his voice curing with a touch of humor as I heard him switch the phone from one ear to the other. "And it's not medieval times either. You're not actually carrying the sins of Eve here. You want to be with me? Come be with me. I'm sick of having this fucking argument with you. I want you here. *Come over.*"

I ran my hands through my hair, my mind filling with about a hundred stories and deadlines that I had been pushing for days and then thought of Jordan lying in bed, curled up around me, the fireplace blazing.

"I'll see what I can do," I said, getting out of bed as he laughed softly on the other end.

Overnight, the weather had gone from a late autumn chill to full on winter snowfall and I arrived at Jordan's apartment in a wild gust of snowfall, my car's heater wheezing uneasily as I drove through the complex. I checked the addresses as I wove my car around the lake, his section of expensive-looking townhomes indistinguishable from the condos on the other side and parked in the back as I smoked one last cigarette with the motor running, letting the wipers swipe back and forth as I looked up at the windows that led to the balcony.

I jogged across the lot as the snow shifted across the lawn, trying the door tentatively before stepping inside and closed it behind me as I got my first good look at the place—the spotless modern layout so bright and gleaming it practically hurt to look at. I glanced up the stairs as I heard the shower running, peeking around the corner at the long plush living room and breakfast bar and then headed upstairs as I tugged my coat around me, pausing in front of the closed bathroom door for a moment before heading down the hall.

I felt a strange quake of premonition when I realized that their master bedroom was almost exactly as I had pictured it, one pale blue wall interrupting a palette of pure white and walked around the large bed slowly as I glanced up at the exposed brick that made up the headboard—a cheerful collage of photos and metal shelves running up both walls. The floor around it was scattered with books—some in piles, some laid open. I wandered closer as I saw his dark blue acoustic guitar on a stand next to the bed and paused as I noticed the picture of Jordan and Abbie from the festival—the image so perfect and loving I felt a quick, irrational desire to pull it off the wall and smash it to pieces. I took a step back, my fingers twitching in front of the photo for a moment as if driven by some biological urge that several thousand years of civilization hadn't fully stamped out and shrugged off my coat as I turned toward the fireplace, crouching down in front of it for a minute as I held up my hands to the flames.

It was real. All real. Jordan had built a life with this girl and she was off in some classroom somewhere, completely oblivious to what was happening—thinking of him maybe, longing to be home. I forced the image out of my head as I picked up another picture of them, this one from their wedding, and then turned it toward the lamp as I took my boots off in front of the fireplace, uncoiling my long red scarf from around my neck as I brushed back my hair in the mirror. I glanced toward the door again as the water kept running, my eyes darting around the room with a wild pang of curiosity. I opened the drawer beneath the lamp quickly before slamming it shut, my head tilting slightly as I noticed a stack of notebooks beneath the bed and crawled closer before I could stop myself, pulling them out as one toppled off of the top.

I flipped through it quickly in the light that seeped through the blinds, running my fingers over the pages as I realized that they were lyrics and read several songs quickly before shuffling one single black notebook from near the bottom of the pile, flipping the well-worn cover open as I laid down on the bed. I pulled a pillow under my body as I browsed through it slowly, the sketches inside it catching me completely off guard, and ran my fingernail across the image of a woman's face as I read the song next to it, the pain in it so raw and open I paused, wondering who she was as I searched for more artwork.

I turned around as Jordan cleared his throat, raising his brows in light amusement before he noticed what notebook I was browsing through and I saw his face change quickly for a moment as he turned to the dresser, pulling out a white thermal shirt as he shrugged it on with his back turned.

"Find anything interesting?" he asked, a low current of annoyance dancing just below his careless amusement and I looked over his body quickly as he raked his still-damp hair away from his face, biting my lip as I flipped to another picture of the woman inside.

"I've never heard any of these songs before," I said as he watched me closely for a moment and then laid down on the bed next to me, pulling the page I was on closer before pushing it away.

"That's because none of them were any good. Old book. I wrote that shit when I was a teenager."

I glanced up at him as he rolled onto his side, smiling a little as he pushed my long bangs away from my face and I met his eyes seriously for a moment as I came to another sketch of her—this one darker, scrawled and angry.

"Who is she?"

Jordan glanced down at the photo and pulled it away from me gently as he held my gaze, leaning over to tuck it back under the bed carelessly as he raised his brows.

"Just someone I used to know."

"Pretty personal."

Jordan's eyes narrowed for a moment and he raised his brows as he noticed the spilled pile of notebooks on the carpet in front of the fireplace, tilting his head at me.

"You'd think so, wouldn't you?"

He smiled at my expression, leaning over to give me a kiss and then dragged me on top of him with both hands as he rolled onto his back, his expression becoming more relaxed as I laughed.

"I could get used to this," he said, as my hair tumbled into his face and I pressed my hands against his chest as he hugged me tighter, resting my chin on them as I looked up at him. "I just call and you come over. No arguments, no complaints . . ."

"I really don't complain that much," I said, leaning over him as he glanced at the ceiling for a moment, his smile deepening as he brushed his hand behind my head.

"No comment."

I kissed him deeply as he pulled me closer, one of his legs wrapping around my heels as I tried to pull away and then relented as I leaned back and pressed my lips together, his eyes searching my face gently for a moment as he brushed his thumb across my cheek. I touched the tattoo on his neck as he raised his brows, watching me curiously as I sat up a little.

"A compass."

"Yep."

"Do you need direction in life?"

"Sure. That's me. All journey. No destination."

"What do the roses mean?"

Jordan tilted his head at me, his humor losing a little of its candor and then shrugged as he rolled me into the crook of his arm, pulling me closer as he brushed his fingers over my lips.

"I don't know. Just about beauty, I guess. Taking time to see it in unexpected places."

I dragged my nails across the outline of his chest tattoo, my eyes darting over his mouth quickly for a moment and then laid back as he ran his hand down the length of my side, watching his expression closely before closing my eyes.

"The one over your heart. Was that about her?"

I felt his hand freeze on my waist, opening my eyes as he dragged it away and raised my brows as he rubbed a hand over his forehead for a moment before leaning over the bed and shoving most of the notebooks back under.

"No. Not her, all right? She was just someone I tried to help out once. A long time ago."

I ran my hand through my hair as he sat up, a ferocious wave of jealously running through me as I thought of Jordan sketching her, filling up two hundred pages with all of his unchecked, adolescent desire and looked up as I felt his fingers touch my chin, turning my head to him slowly as he searched my eyes.

"Don't be jealous," he said, smiling down at me as he kissed me lightly on the lips.

"I'm not jealous. Just curious. You never talk about your past. Not ever."

"I told you everything already."

"You didn't. I don't even know where you grew up."

Jordan looked at me for a moment and then reached for his guitar, pulling it into his lap as he shrugged.

"Louisiana."

"Really? Louisiana?"

"Originally," he said, glancing down at the neck of his guitar as he strummed a few notes and then adjusted the strings and tried them again. "I moved around a lot."

I pulled my legs up beneath me as he began to play in earnest—the soft, yearning melody hanging between us in the silence. I met his eyes as he gave me a wink, turning his body away from me slightly and listened for several minutes as he played without singing, caught up in his own world as he bowed his head slightly, his damp hair falling across his cheek as I reached up to brush it away.

"Is that new?"

Jordan slapped his hands across the strings, the music stopping abruptly and reached for a red notebook that had scattered with the rest, smiling a little as he handed it to me. I opened it up, flipping through what looked like a dozen freshly penned songs and paused as I came to a sketch next to a song called "Finished Now." I brushed my finger over my face, looking up at him quickly as he smiled and glanced away as I realized that there were flowers all through my hair—something about it reminding me of Ophelia after she had drowned, beautiful in death as her long dark hair spilled out around her.

I felt a quick, painful rush of love for him as he began to sing, setting the notebook aside as his voice filled the room and realized in that moment how much I loved him and how terrifying it was to know that and not be able to tell him—fearing it would ruin it, somehow break the spell. I looked over his face as he sang, wondering if he knew, if he had any idea how hopelessly adrift I felt and had a sudden image of him reaching across an expanse and grabbing my hand tightly in the darkness, his eyes turning to meet me as he gave me a smile.

I love you too, Lea. Don't run. Don't let go. Trust me. Trust me, trust me . . .

I closed my eyes slowly for a moment, a strange chill running through me as the image sweltered and grew, and smiled a little as I saw that we were actually walking on a beach somewhere, the sun setting over a rocky stretch of ocean. I wondered where it was as Jordan tugged me closer, the sensation of sand under my feet so real I held my breath and saw the image jump again to some place along the coast, a lush green oasis of light surrounded by miles of open desert. I turned my head as the surf hit our feet, watching dozens of paper lanterns take flight in the darkness at once and opened my eyes as Jordan sang the last verse over again, his face calm and inward as the image faded.

I glanced at him out of the corner of my eye as I chased the image a little, his voice weaving its way through the darkness as I lost my way and sat up and curled my arms around his neck as he set his guitar aside, looking at me quickly as his eyes darted over my expression.

"Do you like it?" he asked as I crawled into his lap, brushing his hair away from his face as he wrapped his hands around my waist.

"I love it," I said as his eyes softened a little, his hand running up my spine as I curled my legs around him. "It sounds like it's about . . ."

The end of the world, I thought. The sensation of the ocean surf over my feet as we watched a hundred red–orange lanterns take flight in the darkness filling my mind in a sudden kaleidoscope of color and joy.

End of one world, maybe, I heard as he pulled me closer, watching my lips carefully for a moment as he smiled a little, his blue eyes bright and searching. *Beginning of another. It's what you wanted, isn't it? I could give you that, Lea. All you have to do is have a little faith.*

"It's about you," he said, his words whispering across my lips like a kiss. "They're all about you. I've been writing about you since the day we met . . ."

I ran my hands around the back of his neck as he dragged me closer, his hand running up the column of my throat and felt him coil his fist around the length of my hair as I closed my eyes, pulling me closer as he kissed me hard on the mouth. He held me against him as his lips crushed against mine and I opened my mouth as he pulled my head forward, brushing my hand against the side of his face as his tongue explored my mouth with sudden thoughtless urgency, and then broke away from him lightly as he tugged at the back of my dress. I sat forward on my knees as he yanked it up my thighs, curling toward him as he dragged it over my head and watched his face as he ran his hands over my breasts, every natural instinct for self-preservation melting in the wake of my sudden, all-consuming desire to please him. I slid my hand against his cock, pressing my forehead against his as I coiled my fist around it and opened my eyes as he broke my grip gently, touching his lips with my fingertips as he leaned up to kiss the hollow of my neck.

Stop rushing it, Lea. Stop trying not to feel anything. I'm here. I'm with you.

I dropped my hand as he ran his lips between my breasts, pulling me closer as I leaned away from him and I felt him press his hand against my spine as he jostled me to my back, laughing a little as I landed with my arms above my head.

"You're really bad for me, you know?"

Jordan smiled, dragging my body closer to the middle of the bed and crawled on top of me as he knocked my thighs apart, leaning over me as he whispered against my neck.

"I'm bad for everyone," he said, his voice low and teasing as I felt his hands slide down my body—every nerve responding beneath the trail of his touch. "Haven't you figured that out yet?"

I closed my eyes as I felt him brush his fingers above the thin black band of my thong and arched my hips slightly as I felt him kiss me gently from one hip to the other, rolling it lower with his fingertips as I felt my hands curl over the edge of the bed.

"I still can't believe you don't have even one tattoo," he said, his voice low and thoughtful as I opened my eyes. "Your skin is so perfect . . ."

"I told you, I always wanted one," I said, my voice catching a little as he rolled my thong lower and felt his lips brush against my inner thigh.

"But?"

"I don't know. Then everyone had one. And I never knew what to get . . ."

I cracked my eyes open as I felt him sit up, reaching across the bed as I rolled my head to watch him and blinked quickly as he shook a ballpoint pen loose from one of his notebooks, giving me a quick, brilliant smile as he rolled it between his fingers for a moment.

"Let's take care of that," he said rolling one side of my thong off of my hip and I jumped a little as the pen touched my skin, sitting up on my elbows as he leaned forward to kiss me. "Relax. It's not permanent."

I opened my eyes as he let go of the back of my neck, laying back down as I felt him yank my legs closer and caught my breath as he rolled my thong off of my hips, leaning over me closely for a moment as he held my skin taut. I felt the pen dig into my skin, blinking a little as he retraced it slowly, and then bit my lip as he blew on it lightly, brushing his thumb over it as he met my eyes. I sat up on my elbows as he crawled up next to me on the bed, watching my face as I brushed my fingers across a scrawled, cursive version of his name and turned to look at him as he ran his fingers along my jaw, tipping my face up to meet him as he held my eyes.

"That's what you should get, Lea," he said against my ear as he brushed his fingers down the curve of my neck, pressing me back against the bed as he turned my head to one side. "Right there. Just that."

I shivered as he kissed my throat behind the ear and froze as he pressed my jaw away from him with his thumb, holding me gently as I felt the pen scrape against my skin.

"And here. Right here."

I let out a quick sigh as he moved the pen in quick, cutting strokes, shifting beneath his touch as he held my body still and opened my eyes when he finally turned my head to face him—some emotion too violent and convoluted to place moving behind his loving expression. I pressed my fingers against it as he smiled, his eyes running to the dark imprint of his name across the lowest part of my hip and touched the tender skin gently for a moment.

"Show me," I said.

Jordan raised his brows, his dark blue eyes leaping with something like excitement and slid his legs to the floor as he stood up, pulling open a drawer that seemed to disappear into the wall. I rolled to my side as he pulled out an expensive digital camera, turning it on with a brush of his hand as he climbed into bed beside me and then got up on his knees as he leaned over me, turning the camera slightly, before glancing at me over the top.

"Tilt your head back," he said, his voice suddenly brisk and impatient.

I tilted my head back as he snapped my picture, his eyes moving over my body restlessly as he snapped a few more and I hooked my thumb through the thin lace sides of my thong as he sat backward, pulling it down below his name as he dropped the camera slightly and met my eyes.

I felt my stomach knot as he smiled at me, crawling between my legs as he passed the camera to me and kissed the side of my neck as I scrolled through them quickly, a panicked burst of excitement running through me when I saw his name scrawled across my neck, surrounded by a crisp, perfect heart.

"Like it?"

"I do," I said tilting my head back to look at him as he pulled the camera out of my hands. "They look professional. Almost like . . ."

They belong there?

I glanced at him as he smothered a smile with his fingers and then pulled me closer as my hands touched his chest, setting the camera down behind us.

"I could keep going if you want," he said, kissing the heart gently for a moment as I arched my neck toward him. "Put my name everywhere. Here, here and here . . ."

"Maybe just one . . ."

For now, I heard as he kissed my wrist and then dragged his lips lower, kissing my arm, my collarbone, my breast. *For now, for now, for now . . .*

I blinked as I felt his hand slide over my thong, his face focused and hungry as he reached for the camera over my head and I grabbed his wrist as he looked up at me sharply, his eyes becoming patient again as I pressed my lips together.

"Please stop. I really don't like having my picture taken that much."

He raised his brows as I brushed my hair away from my face, tilting his head at me curiously for a moment and then turned the camera around to face me, his blue eyes moving over my expression with something a little too dark to be humor.

"Take some of me if you want," he said. "I don't mind."

I bit my lip as he grinned down at me, blinking quickly as a sudden landslide of images from the folder on my laptop seemed to open in my mind at once and took it out of his hand, blushing a little as he bit back a grin. I sat up as he rolled next to me, reaching over the bed for a moment as I sat up on my knees and I heard him light a cigarette, letting out a quick stream of smoke before laying down on his back. I took a picture as he closed his eyes, watching his free hand drum across his chest restlessly before he tucked it behind his head and crawled closer as he opened them, looking at me steadily for a moment as he raised his cigarette to his lips. I moved to his side, zooming in on his face as his eyes wandered over my body and felt his hand brush against my waist as I got close enough to touch, crawling between his legs as he watched me closely, an image of him walking out of motel room bathroom bursting through my head without warning.

I saw him raise his brows, sticking the cigarette between his lips as he pulled his sleeves down and then set it on the floor as he sat up to take off his shirt, his eyes shifting with hard amusement as I dropped the camera slightly.

Want to write your name across my heart, Lea? Go ahead. I won't mind. Not at all.

I crawled closer, watching his expression change through the viewfinder as I moved my body over him slowly and then straddled his waist as he closed his eyes for a moment, his hand drifting down the side of my body. I snapped his picture as he opened them again, the image so perfect I pulled the camera away from my face and ran my fingers over the swords on his chest as he handed me what was left of his cigarette, taking the camera out of my hands as he aimed it up toward my face.

"You never told me the second question," I said, turning my head as I let out a quick stream of smoke and he tipped the camera a little lower, taking another picture.

"What question?"

"Your formula. For figuring out everything there is to know about someone."

"Oh," he said, smiling a little as he set the camera aside and then took his cigarette back when I offered it to him, his face becoming thoughtful for a moment as his blue eyes narrowed. "The second question. That's right."

He crushed the cigarette out on the lip below the edge of the bed, running his hand over his face for a moment. I leaned over him as he looked up at me and ran his fingers up the column of my spine, twirling the ends of my hair lightly for a moment where they brushed against his chest.

"So what is it?"

"Like I said, these questions sound easy . . ."

I rolled my eyes as he ran his hand around the back of my neck and pushed back as he tried to drag me closer, laughing softly at my expression.

"Just tell me."

"All right," he said, brushing my hair away from my face as he ran his knuckles over my cheek for a moment, his smile fading a little as he held my eyes. "Second question. What's the first thing you ever lied about?"

"Lied about?"

"That's right."

I pressed my lips together, my eyes darting over the headboard for a moment and then tilted my head at him as I sat up slightly.

"Okay. When I was about four, I had an imaginary friend. I can't even remember her name. I think it was some name I didn't like. Like Beatrice or Darla or something. And I blamed her for everything, you know? She was always screwing everything up. I kind of hated that bitch."

"Okay . . . so, Darla the screw-up."

"Yeah. And I kind of knew she was imaginary, but everyone around me just played along. Like they thought it was funny. Until this one day, when my dad came home and caught me writing all over my bedroom walls. And I just told him that Darla did it. He didn't seem to find it so funny then."

"He caught you afterward?"

"Nope. Crayon in hand. You should've seen the look on his face. After that, my parents sat me down and had a very grown-up discussion with me about how I was getting too old for imaginary friends. And I knew then that the gig was up."

Jordan smiled broadly for a moment and then pulled me toward him as he wrapped his hands around my back, kissing me gently as I watched his face.

"That sounds about right," he said. "God. I can just see you. Poor Darla . . ."

"Yeah. After that she wasn't any fun. I gave that useless bitch her walking papers pretty soon after that."

I leaned away from him as he tried to pull me closer and touched his chin as he leaned up to kiss me.

"So, what about you?"

"Me?"

"Fair's fair, Mr. Pop Psychologist."

Jordan tilted his head at me and then relaxed back against the mattress, raising his brows as his face became a little bit more reserved.

"Easy. When I was about six, my mom had this friend. He'd come over, they'd drink, and she would bitch until they had an argument. This happened at least once a week. Like clockwork. So one night, when I knew he was coming over, I took my blankets and my pillow, this little lunchbox that I had, and spent the night in the woods behind our house. Deep inside the woods. And when I came home the next day, I just told her that I was spending the night at a friend's house."

"You were six?"

"About that, yeah."

"Didn't they wonder where you were? God. My parents would've been scouring the neighborhood."

Jordan shook his head, his eyes calm and half-lidded as he ran his hand up my arm.

"I don't know. She didn't seem that worried. She kind of just accepted it. And that was that."

My brow furrowed as Jordan lifted my hand from his chest, kissing the palm lightly as he let it go and I felt a sudden rush of pain for him as he ran his hands down the sides of my body, looking me over slowly for a moment before rolling his eyes back up to meet me.

"That's really kind of fucked up," I said, pressing my hand against his cheek as he shrugged and pulled me closer. "Anything could've happened to you. You could've just disappeared."

"I would've been okay. I was pretty tough. I brought along this little arrow set I had. You know, in case I had to defend myself."

He turned his head to kiss my other hand, and smiled a little as I had a sudden image of him hiding below a stairwell as the two adults in his life had a violent screaming match, his face grim and set as he pulled his arrow set closer.

"Don't pity me, Lea. I can't tell you how much I hate that shit."

"I'm not pitying you. It's just sad, that's all."

"Everyone lives through something. We learn to lie the second we realize that the world is a pretty terrible place. And then you either find a way to make it through, or you don't. I'm not sad about my past. I feel lucky I made it out alive. My mother wasn't really cut out for the whole selfless thing. Once I figured that out, I did all right."

Tell me what you want, Lea. Tell me, tell me, tell me . . .

"You don't like to talk about it."

"No. It's not that. I don't mind talking about it. I just don't like the aftermath. Some girls get to know you a little and they see a big black hole where your heart should be and think, 'Well, I'll just throw myself in. That should help.'"

"Maybe you let them."

Jordan shook his head, his eyes widening a little and I saw something quick and desperate move behind his hungry expression as he ran his hand up my back, running it behind my neck as he pulled me closer.

"I don't. I swear to god I don't. I warn them. I fucking warn them all the time . . ."

I closed my eyes as he touched my lips and felt him slide his hands around my face as he dragged me toward him, kissing me lightly as I wrapped my hands behind his head.

"So don't do that," he whispered. "Please don't try to make me make sense in your life. I don't even make sense in my own life. You're so sweet, Lea. So sweet. You have no idea what that means to someone like me . . ."

I felt my entire body sigh toward him as he kissed me deeply, his hands running over my breasts as I tightened my arms around the back of his head. I broke away lightly as I felt him slide his hand between my legs, pushing my thin lace thong aside as he shifted his body at the same time. I closed my eyes as I felt him spread me open gently, holding my eyes as he brushed his fingers over my clit and I leaned over him as I felt his free hand coil around the back of my neck, his mouth sliding over my nipple as I dragged my breasts over his face.

Anything you want, Lea. Just tell me, tell me, tell me . . .

I let out a quick gasp as I felt him slide his fingers inside me, holding me against him as he moved his mouth from one breast to the other and had a sudden vivid image of watching him from above as he pulled away from me quickly, looking up at my face as he slid his hands around my waist. I felt a quick, thoughtless rush of want as he urged me forward, sliding his head back on the mattress as I knelt above him and closed my eyes as he shoved my thong aside and dug his fingers into my hips, moving me over his open mouth for a moment before burying his tongue inside me.

I gasped as Jordan held onto me tightly for a moment, barely letting me move as I felt his tongue move inside me and dropped my fingers into his hair as his hands slid to my thighs, leaning up slightly as I forced my eyes open. I looked down at him as I felt his hand shift beneath me, moving me gently as I spread my knees wider and let out a low moan as I rocked above him without thinking, closing my eyes as I coiled my hand into his hair. I felt him pull away as he shifted again, holding onto his hair tightly for a moment as I held his mouth against me and had a sudden image of Jordan laying bound and naked in some dark motel room, turning his eyes to watch me as I paced around the bed.

I blinked quickly as I watched the fantasy me brush a long, thin whip down his chest and gasped as I brought it down hard across his thighs—watching his cock quake as I sat down at the edge of the bed.

Don't come until I tell you to, I said, taking his cock in one hand as Jordan closed his eyes. I set the whip down on his chest, running my other hand up the length of his cock as I began to stroke him quickly, rolling my tongue around the tip as I watched his whole body shudder. *Not yet,* I said, stroking him more quickly. *Not yet, not yet, not yet . . .*

I opened my eyes as my body quaked toward orgasm, looking down to meet Jordan's eyes as he slid me forward by the back of my thighs and felt my hands hit the mattress above his head as he pulled my thong down with both hands, urging me to turn around as I pulled them off in a soft haze of compliance. My eyes shot open as he pulled his cock out with one hand, stroking himself quickly as I leaned over to watch him and reached for him before I could stop myself, my knees pressing against his shoulders as he let go and pulled me closer. I held his cock with one fist as I felt him spread me open, rubbing my clit urgently for a moment as I began to stroke him and watched his cock buck against my hand with a thoughtless rush of hunger as he pulled me closer, running his tongue inside me as I wrapped my lips around him. I pressed my body against his as the fantasy of tying him up began to burn brightly again, sliding my mouth over his cock quickly as I felt his body quake beneath me, and rolled my tongue around the tip as he let out a low moan, squeezing him gently as his fingers dug into my skin.

I pulled my mouth away from him as he dragged me backward, holding me in place as he ran his tongue over my clit and felt my hand freeze on his cock as an image of Jordan as a late teen filled my mind, watching him walk into a sunny kitchen from the backyard of someone's house. I blinked quickly as he stepped up behind an older woman in a bikini and a thin cover-up at the counter and held my breath as he wrapped his arm around her waist, watching her close her eyes as she bent her head forward.

Not now, she whispered. *He's upstairs.*

I began to stroke him quickly again as I watched Jordan kiss the back of her neck, his hands sliding over her body as he brushed her long hair away with his head. *Okay*, she said, turning around. *But be quick.* I gasped as she lifted the cover-up and he dropped to his knees in front of her, clawing her bikini bottoms down with both hands as he shoved her back against the counter. I bit my lip as I watched him bury his face between her thighs, my entire body quaking as Jordan ran his tongue inside me and came to a quick frantic orgasm as his lips brushed against my clit, squeezing his cock tightly for a moment as I let out a low cry.

I swallowed hard as I felt Jordan push me forward, looking back at him vacantly for a moment as I moved to his side and started to turn toward him as he got to his knees behind me, shoving me back toward the mattress as I felt his hand coil around the back of my neck.

You weren't supposed to see that.

I felt him force my head down toward the mattress as his hands slid down my body, tensing as I heard the soft coil of rage below his annoyance and cried out as he forced himself inside me in one rough shove, wrapping his hands around my hips as he thrust inside me quickly. I shifted my body slightly, my fingers coiling around the sheets as I felt him lean forward and caught my breath as his hand found the back of my head and pushed it back down, forcing himself deeper as he slid his hand up my back. I felt my lips sigh open as I pressed my hips back against him, trying to meet his quick frantic rhythm as I heard him moan behind me and had a sudden vivid image of him binding my hands to my ankles in the middle of the floor as his fingers dug into my hips, the image burning to a bright fevered peak as I felt him come inside me.

I watched the image snap to black as Jordan bent his head forward, holding onto me tightly for a moment as I felt a quick, confused rush of anguish and let me go as I leaned forward, shifting his body to my side as he gathered me into his arms. I let my head slide over his arm, turning to my side as he turned to face me, and felt a quick, desperate burst of love for him as he searched my expression quickly for a moment, his eyes wide and worried as I leaned forward to kiss his chest. I pressed my head against him as my entire body shivered, feeling him pull me closer as his fingers brushed down my back and felt a sudden desire to take his cock in my mouth as I felt it press against me, my entire body going electric with urgency as I thought of him forcing it down my throat.

Don't, Lea, I heard, something violent and unwell stirring behind his gentle expression as he tipped my chin back up to face him and pulled me tighter. *Don't, don't, don't . . .*

I brushed my hair back from my face as he pulled me closer, the soft smell of cigarettes and sweat making me sigh deeply and smiled a little as he pressed his lips against my forehead, leaning down to kiss me as I coiled my leg around his. I drowsed against him for several minutes, the heat from the fireplace making me feel warm and light-headed and turned my head up to meet his eyes as I brushed his long hair away from his lips, his face so gentle and beautiful it practically burned.

"What was the other question? The last one?"

Jordan raised his brows at me and I felt him tighten his arms around me, looking down at me seriously for a moment as he smiled a little and shook his head.

"What? Don't you want to tell me?"

"No. It's not that . . ."

"Then what? Come on. How will you know what I'm really like unless you ask the question?"

I already know what you're like, Lea. You're perfect. If only you knew how I saw you. If only you believed me . . .

"Okay. But fair warning. You may not want to answer me."

"Try me."

His smile deepened for a moment before fading quickly and he let me roll away from him a little as he leaned back to look at me, something bright and intense moving behind his too-blue eyes.

"What's the worst thing you ever did to someone you loved?"

HIS ANSWER: I FELL OUT OF LOVE AND DIDN'T TELL HER. SHE knew and it destroyed her.

My answer: I disappeared when he needed me the most. And then he destroyed himself.

Who's worse? Does it matter? Oh, my love, my love, my love. Who pays for all these terrible things we do to one another in order to save ourselves? Who pays?

Who pays, Who pays, Who pays, Who pays, Who pays, Who pays, Who pays, Who pays, Who pays . . .

CHAPTER ELEVEN

I WENT INTO WORK THE NEXT DAY LIKE A SUCCESSFUL THIEF—A little on edge, a little too smug. I dressed nicely—black on black in a brand-new white coat like some homicidal heiress out of a Hitchcock film, prepared for anything, pistol in purse. I glanced around for Abbie when I entered, secure enough in my love for Jordan to feel almost sorry for her and paused as Madge raised a hand at me from the hall, shaking her head slightly as I saw the owner of the paper speaking with Noah quietly outside his office. She lowered it when Margaret turned her eyes in our direction, looking me over like a traitor as Noah beckoned me over and I glanced around for David so quickly I almost didn't notice it, my stomach taking a smooth unpleasant dip when I didn't find him.

"Lea, you have a minute?"

I pulled off my sunglasses as Margaret stepped into the office, fumbling them into my purse as I followed them inside and glanced in her direction as she looked at Noah pointedly for a moment, her steel blue eyes grim and set.

"Get the door please."

I closed the door behind me, noticing that the blinds over both of the large windows in his office were drawn and set my purse on a chair as Noah picked a paper up off of his desk, tossing it to the edge as I leaned over to read the headline.

"Have you seen this?"

I picked the paper up, freezing as a large color photo of Shelly Tozier and the boy who had been dressed like the Pope at the Mardi Gras party greeted me on page one, my face flushed and intense as I raised a recorder toward her face. I blinked quickly, scanning the caption and felt my insides backflip into a bed on pine needles as I gleaned the slant of the story.

"*How Could This Happen? Drinking Death at Mardi Gras party*"

I dropped the paper as I scanned the first few lines quickly, shaking my head as I realized Margaret was staring a hole into my chest and set it down on his desk as Noah cleared his throat, his expression a sad, practiced blank.

"I've read," I said, glancing between Noah and Margaret for a moment. "Not this story, but..."

"That's you in the photo, isn't it?" Margaret asked, her voice hard and calm.

"Someone must've shot it when I was interviewing them. The *Gazette* has been running stories on this for a few weeks now. It was the story we wanted to run, the one I gave you..."

"Did you know that the girl's family is suing the city over this?"

I pulled my white peacoat a little tighter as she turned the full force of her attention in my direction, momentarily staggered by the look of open dislike she gave me.

"I assumed... I hadn't heard..."

"And you were drinking too."

"I might've had a drink. Just one. Afterward..."

"After what?"

"Look," Noah said, holding up his hand to Margaret as he tuned in my direction, and I realized then that I was in real trouble, that the only reason he would have to feign diplomacy would be if I was already finished.

"I think we can all agree that this was a tragic situation all around. I guess our concern is that their reporter mentioned you by name..."

"She did what?"

"She said that several witnesses mentioned the drinking game that led to this poor girl's death. She said that two of them mentioned seeing you there."

"I was in a lot of places that night," I said, a cold trickle of sweat rolling down the column of my spine as Noah raised his brows in my direction. "I couldn't begin to tell you where some anonymous witness might remember *seeing* me..."

"Are you saying she's lying?" Margaret asked, her voice cool and furious.

"I'm saying that I had one drink. One. After I was through interviewing. And beyond that interview, I never saw that girl again. The end."

"Well," Noah said. "It's not exactly that simple."

I brushed my hair behind my ear as he rubbed his thumb below his lips, one of his proverbial tells. I folded my hands in front of my waist, dropping them again as I saw the emotional combine in his eyes begin to sputter and spin, and shook my head as a deep thread of rage began to uncoil and take hold, turning in Margaret's direction as she folded her arms across her chest.

"This is bullshit, Margaret. I brought this story to Noah the day I found out about it. We could've been the first on this. David told him to run it. He refused."

"And then we'd be digging ourselves out of that hole too," Noah said mildly. "Once someone mentioned that you were part of the crowd that egged her on."

I opened my mouth quickly and then closed it again as Margaret looked me over, shaking her head as Noah folded his hands in front of him and glanced toward his door.

"Would you mind if I spoke to Lea alone, Margaret?"

She gave me one last withering look and then stepped behind me, letting the door slam as she left.

"You know you're wrong about this, Noah. You should've listened to us. If we had run this story first—"

"David's out, Lea. He quit this morning."

"What? Why? Over *this*?"

"Look," he began again—ever the captain, easing his vessel to shore. "Things a few weeks ago may have gotten a little out of hand. The truth is, I honestly believe you are a talented writer—maybe exceptionally so—"

"Are you firing me, Noah?"

"I think, after December, we may decide to go another way."

"What does that mean?"

"I just think you may find a better fit somewhere else, that's all. Like I said, I've always enjoyed your work. It's part of the reason I kept you on this long."

"But never actually hired me."

"Lea, you've gotten a lot of good experience here and I'm happy to write a letter of recommendation to anyone you want. But let's be honest. This place was never going to be a perfect fit for you. You should focus on graduating. And then finding something you would be happier doing."

He picked up the *Gazette* off the edge of his desk and then tipped it toward me slightly before setting it down in a pile to his right.

"And honestly? We need someone who gets this kind of stuff without being told. Like I said, it's about trust. Feel free to submit any intern paperwork to me you still need. I still value you as a team member, Lea. I hope that goes without saying."

I headed into the bookstore on campus, my eyes glazed and bloodshot and fished my still-new syllabus out of my pocket as I read through the list of coursework for two of my three classes. I found all but one book, wincing a little as I read the prices and carried them up front, checking my watch as the cashier rang them up slowly. I tucked my sunglasses back on the moment I left the building, braving a flurry of snowflakes as I trudged across campus to the liberal arts building and headed upstairs to the French class I had visited all of three times, cracking the door open as the teacher's back was turned.

I glanced around quickly when I saw the room was packed, making a face of apology as I held up my hands to a few kids at the back who let me pass and slid into the last desk against the wall as I took off my sunglasses, pausing with my hand in mid-air as I noticed the professor staring.

"Who are you?"

I raised my brows as he looked me over like an interloper, running my hand through my snow-damp hair as I set my sunglasses down on the desk, and slid my pile of books in front of me importantly for a moment, blushing as the entire class turned in my direction.

"I'm Ophelia. I'm in this class."

"Ophelia?"

"Yes."

The professor looked me over, his eyes lingering on my dark blonde hair for a moment.

"Didn't you used to be a brunette?"

I bit my lip as the class snickered, and nodded as his annoyed expression shifted into a more genial kind of boredom before he gave me a dismissive shrug.

"Oh, right," he said, turning his back on me as he added another phrase to the blackboard. "I remember you now, Ophelia. Nice of you to join us. We'll try to hold your attention for the next forty minutes or so."

I was not With the Program. And the Powers That Be had finally decided that they'd had enough.

I came awake slowly, the soft sound of music above a windstorm weaving an uneasy path through my dreams. I stood at the edge of a precipice, a ribbon of some urban street I didn't recognize, a narrow white river in the ocean of dark below me, and then turned as I heard the low creak of someone in the chair by the window, my eyes opening wider as I saw Jordan flick his ashes out through a sliver of the open window. I stretched my arms above my head, curling toward him under the comforter as he looked down at me and felt that strange thrill of excitement and worry when I realized he had been watching me sleep, his expression caught somewhere between resentment and a kind of fleeting, half-hidden hope. I raised my brows as the record in the next room went silent for a moment before launching into another song and smiled a little as I pointed to the next room, closing my eyes.

"Ziggy Stardust," I said, clearing my throat a little as I curled my feet deeper into the blanket. "Good choice."

"From your dad's collection?"

"Hmm. Most of them are. It took me months to pry this one away, though. Such a perfect album. I used to listen to 'Soul Love' over and over when I was a kid. Drove him absolutely nuts."

I opened my eyes again when Jordan remained silent, something about the weight of it bringing me out of my pleasant cocoon of half-sleep and tucked my pillow below my head with one arm as I rolled my eyes up to meet him, watching him throw his arm over the back of my plush white armchair as he flicked another long stream of ashes onto the windowsill without looking.

"What's wrong?"

"What do you really want from me, Lea?" he asked quietly, his too-blue eyes calm and serious as he rested his elbow on the arm of my chair, raising his fingers slightly as he glanced around the room.

"What do I want from you?"

Jordan met my eyes, stamping his cigarette out behind him and then leaned forward, sliding his feet off of the edge of the bed as he folded his hands on his knees.

"What do you want from me?" he asked, enunciating the phrase in a way that I knew meant he was angry and trying hard not to show it. "I've been sitting here. Wondering."

I blinked up as he searched my face carefully for a moment, catching a little of his mood and let out a sigh as I brushed my hair away from my face and reached for my cigarettes on the floor above my head, sitting up on one elbow to light it.

"You mean like, money?" I asked, trying to keep my tone light.

"Is that what motivates you? Money?"

I raised my brows as I threw my arm in a wide arc toward the spartan room around me, glancing at him over the top of my cigarette.

"Does it look like money motivates me?"

"I don't have any idea," he said, his voice low and intense. "Does anything motivate you? I'm just trying to figure out why someone like you would choose to live like this. Would settle for living like this."

"Someone like me . . ."

"Beautiful. Talented. You're too good for the life you settled for. And you know it. It's like you've deliberately chosen to live below your potential. I can't figure it out."

"Who says it's a choice?"

Jordan made an impatient gesture and then rubbed his brow quickly as he closed a book at his feet, reaching for another cigarette.

"Everything's a choice, Lea," he said, lighting it with a quick snap of his wrist. "Don't pretend it's not. I mean, what would you be doing if I hadn't come along? Sitting around in this shitty apartment alone? Grinding away at that sad excuse for a paper until you could, what, afford a decent condo somewhere?"

I felt my stomach clench as he shoved it aside impatiently and followed it with my eyes as I realized it was my book. One that I had never shown anyone—not even Jacob.

"Is that mine?" I asked, curling my arm across my waist as I sat up.

I turned my eyes away from him as I heard the soft edge of accusation creep into my voice, tapping my ashes over the edge of the bed as I took another quick drag of my cigarette. Jordan glanced back at me, his expression softening a little and rolled his eyes down my body slowly as I stood up, picking it up off the floor as I pulled out the drawer below my laptop.

"It was just laying out. You wrote it?"

"It's just something I do for fun," I said, trying to keep my voice low and even as I placed it carefully and then shut the drawer. I ran my hand through my messy waves again, catching Jordan's stare in the mirror behind the door and watched something smooth and hard shift behind his eyes as I walked back over to the bed, pulling a sweater on over my tight camisole and underwear as the wind squalled behind us.

"It's good," he said, something about the respect in his voice giving me a quick rush of happiness in spite of myself. "Really good. The guy in it. Someone you know?"

I rested my elbow on my knee, pushing my hair away from my face and looked over his expression closely for a moment as his gaze ran down the column of my throat, lingering on the low front of my light gray cami for a moment before finding its way back to my eyes.

"No," I said, shaking my head as I tapped the ashes off of the edge of the bed and then stamped it out next to the mattress. "No, no. Just some dumb story I write for fun."

"Who's it based on?"

"It's just an origin story. Based on the Joker."

"From the comics?"

"Yeah. You know. Pretty much. It's a combination of characters really. But mostly him. Mostly."

I waited for him to make fun of me and then glanced up as he only nodded, his expression curious.

"Ah," he said, making a quick gesture up and down my body before brushing his thumb below his lips thoughtfully for a moment, smiling a little. "Your Harley Quinn thing."

I reached over the edge of the bed, suddenly feeling exposed in a way that sent a quick pulse of dread up the corridor of my spine and pulled my jeans out of a pile of clothes as I stood up again, blushing as his too-blue eyes followed me around the room.

"It's pretty violent," he said, his voice low and reflective.

"I guess," I said, buttoning up my sweater in the mirror as I set my jeans over the back of my desk chair.

I turned around, pausing as I noticed how closely he was watching me, his eyes roaming over my body as if I was no longer precisely present. He tilted his head up to meet me, a sudden vivid image of him pacing around my bound and naked body in the middle of an empty room filling my mind, and I felt my fingers curl around the back of my desk chair as he crouched down in front of me, glancing over his shoulder as someone knocked at the door behind us.

"Are you into that sort of thing?" he asked, his voice smooth and even.

I pressed my lips together as I reached for my jeans and pulled them on quickly as I tried to think of a way to explain it but couldn't. There was simply no way to talk about it—no way that made any sense. He turned his head to follow me as I stayed silent, pulling my wallet out of my purse as I counted what was left quickly, grimacing as I glanced at him out of the corner of my eyes.

"Oh," he said, smiling a little. "You really don't know, do you?"

"I told you. It's just a story. I'm going to order something from that place down the street. Do you want something? You know they always take forever."

I turned as Jordan stubbed out his cigarette, slamming the window shut and then leaned against it for a moment, the light moving over his smooth, muscular back as he rolled his shoulders slightly.

"If it's going to be more than an hour, I'm just going to run down there..."

"Take that off."

"Excuse me?"

Jordan glanced at me over his shoulder, his eyes shifting with something a little too dark to be amusement as looked me over.

"You heard me," he said quietly, turning back around. "Take that off. Unless you want me to do it for you."

I blinked as his voice became calm and authoritative—some deep, unhealthy side of me taking a quick panicked breath as I stood rooted to the spot for a moment, quieting her down, keeping her safe. I raised my brows as he didn't move—the idea that he was watching my reflection in the window filling me with more excitement than dread, and forced myself to break the spell as I pocketed a twenty, jostling my purse to the floor as I walked around to the end of the bed.

"I'm just going to run down," I said reaching for my boots. "It'll be quicker ..."

I dropped my hand as Jordan took a quick step in front of me, his face smooth and hard as he looked down at me with half-lidded eyes.

"You heard me, Lea," he said mildly, holding my eyes as he reached up to brush my hair off of my shoulder, his gaze moving over my face with a sudden, focused intensity. "Take this off. I'm not going to ask you again."

I looked up at his face as he ran the back of his hand along my jawline, tracing a slow path down my throat before taking a step back. I unbuttoned my sweater slowly before I could stop myself, swallowing quickly as he watched my face. I closed my eyes as he ran his hand beneath the loose waist of my jeans, his hands moving to my hips as I unzipped them and inhaled quickly as he ran his fingers along the smooth line of my stomach, sliding my cami up over my breasts as I let my jeans pool at my ankles. I opened my eyes as he yanked it over my head impatiently, taking a step closer as he grabbed the back of my neck and kissed me deeply as his free hand roamed over my body, dragging me closer as I tried to break away.

I coiled my hands behind his head as I felt his fingers move through my hair, fisting it lightly as he dragged my head backward and held my breath as he ran his lips beneath my jaw, pulling me away with a snap of his wrist when I leaned forward to kiss him again. He looked me over seriously for a moment as I pressed my hands against his chest, following my gaze as I slid my hand down the hard line of his cock and I watched him close his eyes briefly, a sudden violent image of him kneeling over me on the bed and shoving it down my throat running through my mind before I could stop it. He let out a low moan as I slid my hand inside his boxers, grabbing ahold of his cock as he opened his eyes and cupped my cheek lightly as I stroked him quickly for a moment, something deep and anguished struggling against the quick fury of excitement in his eyes.

You can't help yourself, can you? I heard him say. *You can't help yourself. You can't.*

I looked up as he grabbed hold of my wrists, pushing me away from him as his face shifted with a hungry sort of anger, and then let me go all at once as he ran his hands around my face, his mouth crushing against mine with sudden urgency as he forced me backward onto the bed. He crawled over me quickly as I slid my body backward, catching my wrist as I brushed it against his face and coiled his fist around it hard enough to hurt as he met my gaze, pinning it above my head as he shifted his other hand over my face without quite touching it.

You have to stop this, Lea. You have to find a way to control it. I can if you can. But not if you don't try. Not if you don't even want to try . . .

Kiss me, I thought, raising my other hand to touch his as he passed it over my neck, the sudden pulsing need to wrap his fist around it coming off of him like a poison. *I'll try, I promise. Just kiss me, kiss me, kiss me . . .*

Jordan turned his head as I lifted my hand, splaying my fingers apart to touch his as if a razor-thin wall separated his world from mine and he watched me with quick, focused fascination before turning his head to meet my eyes, looking over my face as he coiled his fist around my wrist and raised it above my head. I closed my eyes as he shoved my thighs apart with one knee, shifting my hands in his grip as he held them together, and felt a quick jolt of excitement race through me as he leaned over to kiss me—his fingers digging into my skin as he ran his tongue inside my mouth. I tried to pull him closer as he pulled away to look at me, turning his head to kiss me gently as his skin dragged against mine in a hundred different places and felt every nerve in my body ignite under his touch as he ran his lips down the column of my neck, a warm wave of submissiveness running through me as he ran his lips down the deep curve of one breast and turned his head to look at me.

Open your eyes, Lea, I heard him say. *Don't go somewhere else. Don't disappear. Stay with me. Be with me.*

I inhaled quickly as I watched him wrap his lips around my nipple, a sudden convoluted rush of love and desperation and rage rolling through me in a quick bursts of darkness and light, and felt him release my wrists all at once as I lowered my hands to the back of his head, curling my legs around his waist as he pressed his body against me. I brushed my fingers against his face, my fingers quaking slightly as he shifted his lips from one breast to the other and closed my eyes as another image filled my mind, feeling his hands move over me as I watched him lying alone on what looked like a motel room bed, his face hard and furious as someone opened the door.

My brow furrowed as I saw a beautiful woman with long black hair and dark skin close the door behind her and he leapt out of bed as she dropped a small stack of bills on the table under the window. I saw him walk toward her quickly, her eyes moving over him defiantly as he ran his hand along her jaw and looked her over before shoving her backward, his entire body tensing with rage.

I told you not to, I heard, his voice dark with anger. *I said I would handle it. What the fuck is* wrong *with you?*

I felt Jordan shrug off his shirt as the woman turned to leave and saw him slam the door shut as he blocked her way, giving her a shove as he forced her back against the wall. I wrapped my arms around his neck as I felt him slide my underwear down my thighs, gasping as the woman in the dream went to strike him and Jordan caught her wrist and slammed it above her head, his blue eyes watching her with a love so tortured it was almost something else.

Stop hurting me, I heard as he pressed his forehead against her, bringing her chin up to meet him as he kissed her. *Stop hurting yourself. Stop this. Stop, stop, stop, stop.*

Yes, I thought. *Yes, yes, yes, yes, yes.*

I dug my nails into the back of his neck as I felt him freeze on top of me, the image careening forward in a quick shudder of images. I imagined myself as her as I leaned forward to kiss him, watching him wrap his hand around my throat and slid my fingers inside his boxers as he crushed my body against the wall, kissing me as I struggled.

Jordan jerked back slightly as my lips pressed against him, wrapping my hand around the tip of his cock, and watched his blue eyes widen and dart over me quickly before sighing shut, his entire body moving against the smooth slide of my fist urgently for a moment as I closed my eyes. I stroked him more quickly, holding onto the image of him pressing his fingers around my throat and blinked quickly as he broke my grip, looking me over like a stranger as something quick and ruthless moved behind his gentle expression.

My eyes shifted over his too-perfect face quickly for a moment as I imagined him wrapping his hands around my throat as he fucked me, wondering if he could actually see it—if he really was reading my mind—and picked up his palm and kissed it gently as I imagined him letting me slide almost to unconsciousness, his eyes shifting over my body with a calm, well-controlled fury. He closed his eyes, his expression becoming almost violent with want and I rested his hand just below my neck as I brushed my fingers up his arm, watching his eyes move over my expression like a sleepwalker as something desperate and unwell rose behind the curtain of his eyes.

No, Lea. You don't want that. Trust me. You don't.

I looked up at his face, coiling my hands behind his neck as I leaned up to kiss him and felt his hands slide over my body with sudden urgency as I slid down and kissed his chest, running my tongue over his nipple lightly as my hand crawled down the hard line of his stomach.

I do want it, I thought as vividly as I could. *I do. And I do trust you. You know I wouldn't blame you. You know I'd love you anyway. Just love me. Love me the way you loved her. I'll do anything you want, anything you need, if you love me forever just like that.*

I pressed my hand against his thigh, twitching the fabric of his boxers down with my fingertips and wrapped my mouth around him as I felt his hand move to the back of my head, his entire body going tense as I began to suck. I coiled my fingers beneath the head, shifting my fist over him slowly as I pulled the tip in and out of my mouth and rolled my tongue over it gently before dragging him into my mouth again—his hand tightening on the back of my head. I slid my mouth over him smoothly, following the soft, urgent pump of my hand and closed my eyes as I felt him hold me in place as I tried to pull back, uncoiling my grip impatiently as he forced himself deeper.

I gagged slightly as my lips slid almost to the bottom of his cock, bracing my hands against his thighs as he dragged me away by the back of my hair and then brushed his hand over my cheek as he tipped my head back to meet his gaze, pumping himself in and out of my mouth quickly for a moment as he looked down on me with half-lidded eyes. I tried not to fight him as he forced himself deeper, my entire body going electric with the desire to please him as he moved in and out of my mouth with sudden ruthless urgency, and felt him shove me back against the bed as my lips slid away from his cock, a thousand violent images suddenly entering my mind at once.

I ran my hand up his thigh as Jordan moved over me on the bed, pressing his hand on the mattress above my head as he knelt above me and I let out a low moan as he slid it behind my head, shoving his cock into my mouth as an image of him fucking some guy over the back of a motel vanity entered my mind quickly, the girl he had been arguing with earlier lying naked across the bed in the next room. I dropped my hand as he looked down at me, my eyes sighing shut as he leaned forward and felt his hand slide away from the back of my head as he pumped his cock in and out of my mouth quickly, watching two men fuck some bound and naked woman in the middle of a dark, crowded room. I inhaled sharply as I saw Jordan wander in and out of the back of the crowd- his fury and excitement filling me up like an electric charge and tried to control the quick, frantic pulse of his rhythm as he thrust himself halfway inside my mouth, sliding deeper as I pressed my palm against his thigh. I saw him look down at a girl in her late teens, holding her neck against his cock as he came into her mouth and felt my nails dig into his skin as he slid his body away from me all at once, his hand coiling around the back of my neck as he leaned forward to kiss me deeply.

I opened my eyes as Jordan pressed his forehead against me, panting slightly as he opened his eyes, and then kissed me again as he pulled my body against him and rolled away from me on the bed, pulling me on top of him as he slid his cock inside me. I felt a quick, excited rush of lightheadedness as he used his knee to push me forward, kissing me again as he ran his hands up my breasts and then pulled my arms behind my back gently as he let me arch away from him, his eyes darting over my body as I rolled my hips on top of him. He let me go as I felt his hands on my hips, leaning over him on the bed as I brushed my hand against his neck and I held his eyes as I reached for the head board behind him, pulling my body forward as I slid over his cock with sudden thoughtless want, wincing a little as he shifted my hips with one hand and forced himself deep enough to hurt.

I coiled my fingers around my headboard as I opened my eyes to look down at him, closing my eyes as he ran his hands over my breasts and felt my body quake toward orgasm as he pulled me closer, feeling his knee box me in as he forced me in and out of that strange place between pain and pleasure, letting his cock slide too deep before pulling me back, watching me wince. I opened my eyes as I felt him push me backward, his hands sliding up my breasts as my fingers brushed his face and opened my eyes quickly as I felt his hands slide around my neck, his thumbs tipping my head down to look at him for a moment before digging into my throat.

I closed my eyes as I tried to gasp and couldn't, looking down at him as Jordan shifted me over his cock and met his eyes as the first wave of panic hit me, his eyes moving over my face with sudden hungry fascination as he dug his fingers in deeper. I blinked quickly as I felt his cock pulse inside me, my blood rushing to my face as I leaned away from him and inhaled quickly as he released his grip slightly—my entire body suddenly awake and raw to the touch as he let out a low moan, snapping his hands tighter again as he jerked me forward. I rocked on top of him without thinking as I kept my eyes closed, all my movements feeling heavy and light at the same time and wrapped my hands around his wrists as he dug his thumbs in deeper, a burst of sudden bottomless want filling my mind as I felt my head sigh forward, first above water, then beneath it.

Don't, I thought, looking for him in the darkness as I sunk somewhere just at the edge of dreaming. *Don't, don't, don't, don't . . .*

I inhaled suddenly as I felt his hands pull away from my neck all at once, the sensation of coming awake half-drowned driving me toward a sudden frantic orgasm and shifted over his cock quickly as Jordan reached for me and dragged my body against him, holding onto me tightly as I felt him come inside me.

I swallowed quickly as I felt Jordan press his head into the hollow of my neck, kissing me gently as he flattened his forehead against me and I felt a sudden wave of anguished love roll through me quickly as he sat forward on the bed, pulling me with him as he gathered me in his arms. I ran my hand into the back of his hair, my brow furrowing as he flinched, and tried to catch his eyes as he ran his fingers over my neck thoughtfully for a moment, leaning down to kiss the tender part of my throat as his entire body shuddered.

Why, Lea? I heard him say. *Why, why, why, why.*

I shivered—a quick, frantic pulse of excitement running through me as I thought of the way his face had looked when he wrapped his hands around my throat and shook my head slightly as I turned his hand toward me, kissing his fingertips as I snuggled into the hollow of his throat.

I don't know, I thought. *Does it matter? I love you. And you stopped. You stopped when I asked you to. You didn't hurt me. You didn't . . .*

188

My eyes shot open as I saw an image rise into my mind that I thought I had buried a decade ago—one of Logan slapping me hard across the face as I begged him to stay. I felt my fingers curl against the back of Jordan's neck as my entire body went tense, watching myself pull a razor out of my nightstand and then sit down on the edge of my bed, my eyes vacant and bloodshot as I dragged it lightly across my skin.

I tried to pull away from him, the image so terrifying and painful I ran from it before it had fully formed and he pulled me back to look at him as he ran his hand over my face, his deep blue eyes bright and urgent as he searched my expression.

Is this really all you want from me? To finish what he started? To be someone just like him? Someone who hurt you? Someone to blame?

I felt tears rise in the back of my throat as I clung to him tightly for a moment—terrified to speak, terrified to feel. I brushed my hair away from my face as I pressed my head against his chest as he ran his hand through the back of my hair and swallowed hard as I felt his anguish and his uncertainty and his deep rush of self-blame—trying to reach me, desperate he wouldn't.

Because I can't go back to that life, Lea. Not for you. Not for anyone. Love me or don't. Understand me or don't. But I won't just sit here and watch you bleed. I won't.

"It's not all I want," I said. "It's not. I love you, Jordan. I do."

I felt him shift me forward, sliding his hands around my face and felt a wild burst of hope temper his self-hatred as he brushed his thumbs down my cheeks, kissing my forehead lightly as he pulled me closer, his words whispering over my lips like a kiss.

"I love you too," he said. "Stop running from me, Lea. Just stop."

"I'm not running. I'm here. I'm with you."

"You've been running your whole life," he said, kissing me lightly as my hand fluttered to the back of his neck, trying not to cry, hating myself for feeling so vulnerable. "I know. I've been there. And I'm telling you, you can stop. With me you can."

What if I didn't want to stop? I thought. What if I just wanted to run forever? What if I looked at this whole fucking world and couldn't find a single thing in it worth living for but you?

"Then I'd go with you," he said against the side of my head as he rocked me lightly. "I would. Anywhere you want."

But you don't have to. They're just lies, Lea. The lies people tell you to keep you scared, to keep you weak. Don't believe them. Believe me. If you need a version of yourself to cling to, let it be mine.

I curled my hand against the back of his neck as a sudden image of him turning his head as I walked into the breakroom came into my mind, the beauty in it so fragile and genuine I watched it unfold, fascinated in spite of myself. I saw it unravel into a dark ink drawing on the inside of a notebook, the flowers in my hair floating gently as I closed my eyes and blinked back tears as I saw Jordan smoking at the edge of his bed, sketching my face quickly as a thousand old wounds seemed to lift away from me at once, filling the air from darkness to light. I looked up at him as he smiled down at me gently, searching his eyes as I brushed my fingers against his throat and saw it fade a little as I traced the dark outline of the tattoo on his chest.

Who was she?

Jordan dropped his head—his face shifting with some old pain and ran his finger over my lips for a moment as I had a sudden image of him pulling his black notebook out of my hand and tucking it away forever.

"One day, Lea," he said tipping my head up to kiss him. "One day. I promise."

How could I know then that he had been right all along? We were already living on borrowed time. One day is the always the lie, my love. And those first lies, you know, they cut the deepest.

CHAPTER TWELVE

IT WAS A LITTLE MORE THAN A WEEK BEFORE CHRISTMAS WHEN I saw David again. I had been doing my part to keep the peace at work, patiently filling Abbie in on everything she would need to replace me while she did her best to pretend not to know what was happening, and hit the wall one Friday morning before a big meeting, my hands frozen on the steering wheel outside the building as I realized I could no longer force myself to stomach another day of polite disengagement. I looked up at the gray one-story building that I had been calling home for almost two years and watched a thick layer of snow clot the gutters in both directions, suddenly wondering why I bothered—what my life would look like without it.

I could always go back to waitressing, I thought, the idea of it filling me with so much anger, I ran my tongue over my teeth, reaching for a cigarette. *Talk about a backslide. And then I get to go home at Christmas and explain that once again, and just like Jacob, I could never hold onto a good thing for long . . .*

I lit up as a sudden image of Jordan and I driving past the place in the middle of the night at a hundred miles an hour, while I lobbed grenades at the front lawn, burned through my mind in a blast of candy red and then blinked quickly as someone knocked at my passenger window—my mood lifting instantly when I saw it was David. I leaned over to unlock his side, smiling in surprise as he shook snow out of his hair and then sat down in the seat next to me, his expression just as serious and amused as it always was.

"Did they fire you too?"

I shook my head as he took off his glasses, holding them up to the heater for a moment as he raised his hands and then put them back on as he kicked

some of the garbage in my front seat out of his way, glancing toward the front door as Emma and Kayla headed across the lot in lockstep.

"Not quite," I said, letting out a low stream of smoke as they reached the door at the same time and then waited for whoever was standing there to open it for them, their matching black peacoats and sunglasses making them look like something out of a magazine ad. "Stay of execution. They're getting rid of me after the holidays."

David looked at me quickly, his face dropping, and I felt a sudden burst of sad comradery with him as he patted down his jacket and pulled out his cigarettes, his eyes darkening with anger as he lit up with a shake of his wrist.

"Are you serious? I was just joking."

"I guess what Noah really said was that after the holidays, they had decided to 'go another way.' And since he figured he had never really hired me to begin with, I wouldn't take it so personally."

"Who's he going to replace you with? *Abbie?*"

"That's my best guess. He's basically had me grooming her for the Fire and Ice stuff since he told me."

"And what does she have to say about it?"

"You know Abbie," I said, cringing a little as a sudden image of Jordan rolling me on top of him in their bed blotted out every rational thought for several seconds. "Always sweet. Always polite. She knows, of course. Everyone does. But honestly, I've never seen anyone quite as consistent as she is in her ability to ignore the unpleasant. Give her two weeks. She'll have those sacred cows in Northville eating out of her hand."

"Fucking Stepford wife," David muttered, tapping his cigarette out the window. "If she'd had any backbone at all, she would've told Noah to get bent."

"It's not really her fault," I said, letting my hair tumble in front of my face to hide my expression. "I mean, what was she supposed to say? It's not like we're friends. And she's actually a pretty good writer. I'm not sure she's a reporter ..."

"No. She's just exactly what Noah wants. Next, he'll be siphoning off Madge's articles to the other two. It'll be like having a whole squad of cheer-leaders writing about their home team week after week."

"Madge will never let that happen."

"I'm not sure she's going to be able to stop it. What did I tell you, Lea? Cultural cold war. We're just the three latest casualties in a generation the world is determined to underestimate."

"Good thing we know we're great."

David tipped his cigarette in my direction, raising his brows as he tapped it out the window.

"Amen to that."

I flicked my cigarette out the window, tugging at my fingers as I turned in my seat and watched the snow drift past the window as the heater hummed, the idea that the world was shifting too quickly and all at once filling me with a strange sense of fear and destiny, as if some cosmic roulette wheel was determined to keep spinning—the whole world watching—frightened, waiting.

"I never meant for any of that to happen, David. That whole story was my fault. You shouldn't have even been involved . . ."

"What? Oh, screw that, Lea. You think what happened a few weeks ago was you? Trust me, it wasn't. That shit has been coming between Noah and me for a long time now. I just can't believe he took it this far. Firing you is just an act of spite."

His brow furrowed a little as he cleared his throat and looked at me seriously for a moment, glancing toward my apartment down the road.

"So? What are you going to do?"

I felt my stomach knot as his face shifted with concern and brushed my hair away from my face as I shrugged, smiling a little to hide my panic.

"About a job? Probably just go back to stripping. Or hook. You know, wherever the money is . . ."

"I'm serious. Have you thought about it?"

"Yeah, David. I think about it all the time. What are you going to do about it?"

"That's kind of a weird story, actually," he said, reaching into his pocket as I raised my brows in his direction. He pulled a card out of his wallet and passed it to me as he folded his hands over his lips, watching my expression as I read it.

"The Tower Press and Times. What is this?"

"My new paper. Well, not just mine. Me and a couple of guys I knew from school are putting together a little cash and we figured, you know, since we all happened to be disgruntled former reporters with no foreseeable job prospects, why not just commit to that shit and empire the hell out of it?"

"Is this for real? You're starting a paper? Here?"

"Already started canvassing for ads. You think what they're doing here is unique? Outside of what we do, it's just sales. Except that, you know, we'll actually get to tell the truth. Our truth."

I shook my head as I handed it back to him, too stunned to say anything.

"I just . . . it's so great! I thought . . ."

"That I'd hole up in my mom's house and relive the good old days at this dump until I went Norman Bates? Not really my style."

He re-pocketed the card and then nodded to the back door as a slow smile lit his face.

"I'd rather go head to head with Noah and watch his newspaper career die a slow, agonizing death. I think that would incredibly gratifying for me. Especially since he'll never see it coming. So? You in?"

"In? You mean as an investor?"

"As a reporter. We have no building so, you know, no meetings or mornings or anything. Strictly freelance. Write anything you want. I know you like doing reviews. Why not start there? We plan to release the second week of January. Roll it out right alongside Noah's Fire and Ice issue. That should piss him off."

I looked up as David looked at me intensely for a moment, the idea that he was going out of his way to throw me a life preserver so palpable I blushed, and shook my head a little as I bit back a smile.

"David. That's so nice. Really. I'm just not sure . . ."

"It's not charity, Lea. I actually want you there. You and Madge are the two best reporters in this place. And trust me, Madge will come along. If only to screw Noah over once and for all."

"Reviews, huh?"

"Free reign, Lea. I know you know what you're doing. I'm not going to condescend to tell you what's news and what isn't. You tell me what you're thinking, I'll tell you what I need and how much space I want. I'll pay you per word. As easy as that."

He glanced up as Patrick stuck his head out of the door and then slunk back inside when he saw us, quick as a groundhog. David shook his head a little and then cracked his door open as he glanced at his watch.

"I have to get inside before he decides to duck out. They've been holding my last check for over a week now. Not that it's much, it's just the point of it."

He glanced at me as I sat rooted to the spot and raised his brows as I started to light another cigarette and then thought better of it, reaching for my purse.

"Coming?"

"Might as well," I said. "I've missed most of the morning meeting anyway."

I got out of the car, tucking my purse over my shoulder as David waited for me on the other side and suddenly wondered how many times David had politely intervened between me and disaster—swooping in at the last second as if it were the most natural thing in the world, to inch me back into security. I looked up at him as he slammed the door close behind me, tugging at his sleeve, and then let him go as the backdoor slammed behind us, my entire body tensing as I heard Abbie's delicate voice break off mid-sentence. She paused on the sidewalk, speaking into her phone quietly before hanging up and then pulled the pale blue hood of her jacket on a little tighter, glancing between us quickly for a minute.

"David," she said, stepping into the lot. "It's nice to see you. Are you two going to lunch?"

"Not quite. I just need to pick up my last check."

"Oh," she said, her face darkening with embarrassment as she gave him a sympathetic nod. "Right. No one could believe it when you left. That fight was just crazy . . ."

"Actually, it was kind of Noah at his two-days-before-festival best. So, you know, good luck with that."

He glanced in my direction, raising his brows.

"Did you want to go to lunch?"

"I don't know. I really need to catch up with that guy from the Aquinas Club. We've been playing phone tag for days. And I can't get an agenda from the Chamber of Commerce . . ."

"I got it," Abbie said, giving me a nod that I felt like a slap. "Came through this morning. It's all on your desk. They were sending everything through my email for some reason. Actually, if you don't mind, I was hoping to duck out a little early. Everything is in place and we have that interview at eleven tomorrow, but Jordan has a show tonight and I have about a million things to do between now and then."

"The Christmas thing at McGregor's?"

"That's the one. You should come. Both of you. It's really pretty great. They do this cover of 'Carol of the Bells' at the end of their set . . ."

David shrugged and I shook my head quickly as she picked up her phone. "I don't think so, Abbie . . ."

She ignored me as I tried not to scream, and then tucked her phone back into her jacket as she gave David a smile.

"It's fine. Whatever. But if you change your mind, you're both on the list up front. No cover. I just told Jordan to add you. Either way, tomorrow at eleven. Nice seeing you David."

I followed David's gaze as he turned to watch her go and pressed my lips together as he reached for the door.

"Seriously. Come work for me, Lea. This place doesn't deserve you."

"I'll think about it," I said, letting the door slam shut behind me.

When I left work a few hours later, I had almost no intention of going to Jordan's show. He had invited. I had declined. I could tell it irritated him in the way he refused to bring it up again—the guilt I felt over our involvement beginning to grate on him in a thousand little ways—and I distracted myself the best I could knowing he would be back in my bed by dawn, his body too warm as he slid in next to me, whispering my name, kissing the back of my neck. I rearranged my father's record collection, something I knew would drive Jordan nuts and then cause him to put it back in the order he liked—an image of him sifting through piles of records restlessly filling every stray corner of my mind, his face calm and intense as his fingers danced next to his head, as if keeping time to some mad, ever-present symphony only he could hear.

I called him around nine, the desire to hear his voice knocking some of my long-term precautions against my karmic comeuppance right out of my mind and hung up when it rolled over into a voicemail he never checked, glancing down at my phone quickly as it chimed in my hand.

Going to the show?

I glanced down at the number, my brow furrowing as I realized I didn't recognize it and looked at it for a couple of seconds before shrugging.

Who is this?

I stood in front of my kitchen window, looking down at the phone as I waited for an answer and began to feel uneasy when one never came, scrolling through a long list of contacts before setting the phone aside. I ran my hand through my hair, chewing my lip a little as I headed for my bedroom and leaned over my desk as I pulled up Jordan's website again, rushing through a long album of last year's New Year's show as I braided the hair that grazed my collarbone into a quick, frantic knot. I pulled one up of him and Abbie, smiling for the camera as the other sirens preened behind them, and touched my stomach as I remembered the way she had invited me to the show, something a little too vital and alert moving behind her shy, whisper-sweet smile.

She knows, I thought, minimizing the screen quickly as if her eyes could somehow bore through the screen, and shook my head as I glanced at my watch, taking it off quickly as I set it on the nightstand.

She does not, the rational side of my mind insisted, rolling her eyes at me as she put her foot on the floor and sent the dark velvet chair she was lounging in into a hard spin. *You're just being paranoid. That girl is as blind as they come. He could move you into their spare bedroom and call it an act of charity, and she would just smile sweetly and roll over and die. Don't worry about her. Worry about* you.

Then what was that all about? At work. Why did she go out of her way to have Jordan put us on the list?

Because she's not completely stupid, pet, she said, her long hair dusting the floor as she popped a sucker into her mouth and watched me upside down. *She notices the way he watches you. That's just her way of telling you he's taken.*

I paused as I caught a glimpse of myself in the mirror, the blonde highlights in my hair looking almost red in the light behind me and I saw the girl in my head blink at me and then right herself in one motion, grinning from ear to ear as she clapped her hands slightly beneath her chin.

Oh, you're going, you're going, you're going! This is going to be so much fun.

I looked over my face with a quick critical eye, heading into my closet as I realized it was almost nine-thirty, and tore through a pile of new clothes before pulling out a low-cut black halter top, turning around in the small space as I shifted through a pile of skirts laying in a neat pile on the floor. I grabbed a short black sliver of a skirt before tossing it back and then held a slightly longer one up in a shiny pale green, holding it against my body quickly before heading for the bathroom.

I did my make-up standing up in the bathroom mirror, swearing to myself as a dozen tubes and pencils clattered into the sink as I moved and curled my hair in a quick, impatient blitz of motion and raked my hands through it as I ran back into the bedroom, reaching for the long black sweater hanging above my headboard. I shrugged it on as I reached for my tights, pulling them up as I heard my phone chime in the other room and walked toward it quickly, pressing my lips together as my brow furrowed.

See you there :)

I shook my head slightly as I read the other message again, pocketing my phone as I tugged on my boots and coiled a long black shawl over the top of my sweater as I noticed it was snowing, checking my purse for cash before heading out the front door.

Outside, the evening was brisk but mild, the snow gusting across the parking lot in gentle swirls of white as I made my way through the crowd heading into the bar below my apartment. I felt my heart beat quickly for a moment as I thought of watching Jordan sing on stage, the bright lights shifting over his face as I made my way through the darkness, and turned on the radio as I drove across town, the weather and Friday-night traffic turning Michigan Avenue into a slow crawl of motion. I made the turn onto I-275 right around ten o'clock, accelerating quickly as the highway opened wide and took out my phone when I was close to the last exit, biting back my annoyance when I realized Jordan still hadn't returned my call. I reached for the cigarettes in my dash as I lit up at the turn, swearing under my breath a little as I noticed how heavy traffic was and plowed through the stop sign without looking as a barrage of horns blared behind me, turning up the radio as I craned my neck in both directions, looking around for the sign.

I smiled a little as I caught sight of it at the next intersection, the huge standalone building packed with cars on all sides and took the street after the lot as I wove my way back through the clot of vehicles slowly, pulling to a stop as I waited for another driver to pull out. I checked my hair in the mirror as I parked, brushing my finger across the shiny green–gray eyeshadow around my eyes and took off my shawl quickly as I pocketed my ID and a handful of bills, shoving the door open with the tip of my boot. I folded my arms across my chest as I heard the loud echo of music around me, walking to the door quickly as I tried to make out the song and flashed my ID to one of the door-men before he swung the glass door open, the hall so dark and filled with bodies I stopped in my tracks and stepped aside for the next wave of people.

I blinked quickly as my eyes adjusted to the light, following behind a wide swath of college students as they cut through the crowd without stopping and brushed my hair behind my ear as the hall opened up on a well-lit, oval-shaped bar—the floor below it filled with bodies overlooking a long wall-to-wall stage. I stepped closer to the bar as the band launched into their next song, biting back a smile as I recognized it from their first album and felt my heart constrict painfully for a moment as Jordan started to sing from the back of the stage, his voice clear and rage-laced as he moved to the front quickly, the floor lights sweeping over the crowd.

I wandered closer to the stairs leading down onto the floor, resting my hand on the guardrail as Jordan moved across the stage, and watched his face as the crowd clamored for him at the front—the red lights moving over his face for a moment as he bit back a smile. I turned my head as a gang of sirens in training headed downstairs as a scantily clad set and followed them down as Jordan ran toward the front of the stage quickly, the crowd going wild as he held the microphone up to them and then pulled it back, stepping back as Paul took his place.

I felt the heat of the bodies around me as I reached the bottom of the stairs, the music so loud I could hear the hard thump of the amplifiers through my spine as I moved and stayed close to the back wall as I wove my way through the crowd—glancing up as two lights from opposite sides of the room skipped from one end of the floor to the other, one red, one green. I felt a dozen people move past me at once as I let the music wash over me, mouthing the words as I drifted toward the stage and paused as I saw Kayla near the front, laughing as she grabbed Emma's hand behind someone's head. I took a quick step backward as I glanced around for Abbie, the light moving over the crowd as Jordan stepped to the front quickly—his voice rich and clear as it carried over the crowd—and closed my eyes briefly as it came to its sudden, dark peak—the entire room going quiet for less than a minute before bursting into applause.

I cheered with them as Jordan held up his hand, his smile so bright and vital it seemed to fill the space around him like an electric charge and he pulled the microphone up to his face as he stayed in place, shaking his head as he noticed the sirens up front and glanced in Paul's direction.

"Thank you," he said. "Thanks, Detroit. We're going to take a quick break. Merry Christmas."

He replaced it as he stepped to the back of the stage, talking to the drummer as the crowd cheered again and I saw his face lose some of its candor as he glanced in Paul's direction, making a quick rolling motion with his hand as Paul held his hand up to his ear. I watched Jordan's face darken a little as he turned his head, crouching down to speak to someone at his feet and held my breath as he headed backstage, making my way around the amplifiers as I headed for the hall. I held up my hands as a handful of people ran past me as it bottlenecked, glancing up as the speakers filled the room with something low and bluesy, and paused as I realized there was no way through—looking around the body-filled dead end as I felt someone touch my arm.

"Lea?"

I blinked up as the drummer I had only met once raised his brows, looking over my outfit quickly before giving me a friendly smile.

"Terry?"

"Abbie said you might be coming. How come you didn't give your name up front? She put you on the list."

I shook my head and laughed a little as two girls walked behind him and greeted him at once as he raised a hand, following them with his eyes.

"Friends of yours?"

"They're all friendly back here," he said, making a quick motion to the room behind us as he tilted his head at me. "Where's your boyfriend at? Danny? David?"

"He's not actually my boyfriend . . ."

Terry laughed as two guys near the back picked up one of the girls next to them and tossed her toward the couch while she screamed, motioning to me with one hand as he headed for the doors.

"Yeah, this place is nuts. Everyone is on the other side. Come on. I'll take you around. It's quicker."

I wrapped my arms across my chest as we stepped outside, the wind making my long sweater flutter up to my knees and followed him across a narrow sidewalk as I noticed the crowd began to thin, my eyes following the windows as we headed around the back. I looked up as we entered a narrow alleyway, a handful of people stomping their feet beneath a snow-covered fire escape.

"Everyone's here?"

"They were. I think Kayla and Emma are still at the bar. But Jordan's in the back. And Paul should be—"

"I should be what?"

Terry paused as Paul glanced in my direction, his face changing suddenly as his eyes narrowed and took a quick drag of his cigarette, glancing toward the door as someone stepped inside.

"Miss Quinn. Abbie said you might be coming."

He grinned at my expression and then shrugged, motioning toward the door.

"You know," he said, "before she vanished."

I felt my brow furrow as he held out his pack of cigarettes and took one as he shook it loose, watching him fish his lighter out of his pocket before I asked.

"Abbie's gone?" I asked, leaning over to light it as I curled my arm across my waist.

"She does that," Terry said, shrugging. "She almost never stays for a whole set."

"Really? Why not?"

"You know the girls in that other room?"

"You mean the groupies?" I asked, raising my brows as I let out a quick stream of smoke.

"Yeah. Right. Well, she's sort of the opposite of that. I think that's what Jordan kind of liked about her. At first."

"And now?"

"I don't know. Sometimes I get the impression that she'd be happier if he worked in a bank or something."

I blushed as Paul looked me over for a moment, his grin darkening a little.

"Yeah," he said. "Good luck with that. Especially now."

Paul dropped his cigarette and crushed it under his heel, watching me closely as Terry raised his brows.

"Yeah. You know that movie he was in? The one about that addict?"

"Blue Dawn. I saw it. He was incredible in it."

Paul bit back a laugh and scratched his chin as Terry threw him another look, his expression darkening a little.

"I guess one of those guys he went to school with kind of went Hollywood. Some big studio bought the script. And they want Jordan to star in it."

I froze with my hand in midair, looking between them both quickly.

"What? Are you serious?"

"As a heart attack," Paul said, his voice low and mocking. "Marriage, huh? Abbie can barely handle Jordan being a rock star. How much do you think she'll like being the ex-wife of a Hollywood movie star?"

"For fuck's sake, Paul. Abbie's a nice girl. Why do you always have to be such an asshole?"

I felt my fingers flutter a little as I raised my cigarette to my lips, finishing it as I turned my head and glanced toward the door as Paul followed my eyes.

"I just call them like I see them," he said, his eyes narrowing a little as he tipped his head toward the door and then turned his head, smothering a smile. "You can head inside if you want. Jordan's in the back. We'll be along in a few minutes."

I glanced at Terry as I tossed my cigarette into the snow, curling my arms a little more tightly around my body as he stepped around me, pulling the door open as he nodded.

"You should. It's freezing out here. The girls should be back by now too. They never stay up front for long."

I ducked under his arm as I glanced over my shoulder, watching the door slam shut as Paul noticed Terry's expression and laughed under his breath. I looked around the dark corridor, walking toward the large, well-lit room at the back as I heard someone strumming a guitar idly and felt a strange, panicked sense of lightheadedness as I thought about what Paul had said—the idea of Jordan starring in some film that would make him a star almost too terrifying to approach.

I thought about his face, the natural way the camera had followed him around in his first film as if he'd never been born to do anything else and paused as I came to what looked like a basement apartment, the empty room cluttered with chairs and loveseats turned in every direction. I stepped inside as I heard laughter coming from the opposite room, turning my head quickly as I heard Jordan speaking quietly to someone and stepped over a dozen over-flowing ashtrays and empty bottles as I made my way to the back, stepping into the doorway as I heard someone laugh.

"No. It didn't hurt. Not really. This one, though. This one was awful. I almost left right in the middle of it."

I craned my head around the doorway as I realized the room had been converted into a quick, bare-bones bedroom and felt my stomach drop as I saw Jordan laying back against the headboard with his guitar across his chest, glancing toward the girl sitting next to him as she leaned closer and pulled the thin back of her dress with her fingertips, watching his expression as his deep blue eyes moved over the long coiled dragon that ran from her back to her side. I tried not to breathe as Jordan reached for his cigarette on the table next to him and took a long drag as he leaned closer to take a look, and then paused when the girl whipped her head in my direction—dropping her hand as Jordan raised his brows.

I pressed my lips together as the girl ran a hand through her long red hair, something about her fine-boned face and sharp, angular body making me think she was a model, and placed my hand on the doorframe as I saw something shift behind Jordan's calm expression—the strange blend of angry gratification in it rendering me temporarily speechless.

"Lea," Jordan said without getting up, holding the neck of his guitar in one hand as his eyes moved over my body slowly for a moment before drifting up to my face. "I didn't think you were coming."

I glanced in the younger girl's direction as she bit back a snide smile, and folded my arms over my chest as I blinked at her slowly, my jaw shifting a little as she looked away.

"Really?" I asked, turning my gaze back in his direction as a quick convoluted rush of annoyance and jealousy tried to eat through all my better judgement. "That's funny. I was on the list."

Jordan's face shifted with something a little too angry to be amusement as he raised his hand slightly and set his guitar aside, his eyes wide and watchful beneath his mask of polite disinterest.

"That's right," he said, tapping his ashes out in the ashtray next to him as he glanced over my shoulder, following my gaze with his eyes. "Abbie told me she was going to add you. Lea, this is Shelly. Shelly, Lea."

"Hi," she said raising her hand slightly as Jordan met my eyes, resting his hand on his chest for a moment as I shifted on my feet.

"Why don't you come sit down?" he asked, his voice smooth and clipped as he glanced toward the ceiling briefly and then raised his cigarette to his lips, looking at Shelly as he gave her a small smile. "Not that there are any chairs..."

Shelly laughed as if it were a private joke between them, shifting her legs closer to him on the bed as he followed the long slit of her dress right up to her thigh and then raised his brows in my direction as his anger turned on me like the crack of a whip, there for a moment and then gone.

"Thanks. I'll stand."

"I'm happy you came."

"I missed most of the first set. I only caught a few songs."

Jordan shrugged and I saw him run his eyes over the low front of my halter top again, glancing away as he stamped out his cigarette.

"So, where is David? Abbie told me she added you both."

"Nope. Just me."

I blinked quickly as he looked at me steadily for a moment, an image of David and I laughing over drinks at lunch rushing to the forefront of my mind.

"We're just friends," I said.

Jordan raised his brows as another image filled my mind, this one of David standing on the sidewalk below my apartment in the dead of night, his eyes moving over my window slowly for a moment before turning and walking away.

He's not your friend, Lea. Trust me on this one.

I glanced in Shelly's direction as she rolled next to Jordan on the head-board, the desire to drag her off the mattress by the back of her hair running through my mind so vividly I took a step backward and then gave her a small smile as she turned her great big doe-eyes in Jordan's direction, fluttering under his attention—a human butterfly.

"How do you two know each other?"

"Oh, we don't really . . ." she said, shaking her hair out slightly as Jordan's eyes darted over my face. "We kind of just met. I know Terry a little. And Paul. It's kind of funny, really. Paul and I used to date. Like over a year ago. I worked at this little waffle place around the corner and he was just always there . . ."

I watched her brush her fingers down Jordan's arm as if by accident, running my tongue across the back of my teeth as his face stiffened and nodded a little as I heard voices behind me.

"Of course, he was."

I watched Jordan pull his arm away from her as he sat up a little, the pain of seeing him lying in bed with someone else beginning to outrun my anger in a smooth, frantic arc and I bit my lip as his brow furrowed slightly, his expression becoming a little gentler as I heard one of the sirens laugh behind me.

"Jordan, Jordan. You won't believe what just happened."

I held his eyes as he ignored her and felt my nails press into my palms deep enough to sting as I heard Terry scream something back, shaking my head as he sat up suddenly.

"Lea . . ." he said.

"I heard you're going to be in some film your friend is making."

"Oh my god, really?" Shelly said, piling her hair on top of her head before letting it fall. "I didn't know you were an actor too! Paul never said anything."

"Nothing's final yet," he said, standing up. "It's all just a lot of talk."

"I'm sure you'll be great in it. Nice meeting you, Shelly."

I turned just as Emma ran up behind me, bursting into the room as Terry followed her inside and headed for the door as Kayla looked up from the couch, her face lighting up with an excited rush of drunken recognition as I sailed past them.

"Lea! I didn't know you were here . . ."

I didn't look up until I was in the hall again, walking as quickly as I could without breaking into a run. A throng of people near the door split apart as I approached, watching me pass as I slammed my hands against the door and shoved it open and felt the cold hit me like a slap, the sugar-thin fall of snowflakes coating my hair as I passed under the fire escape. I walked around the building quickly, the image of Shelly dragging her fingers up Jordan's arm while she shifted next to him on the bed running through my mind in a painful, mindless loop and cut across the lot as I avoided another wave of people heading back inside, pulling my car door open as I collapsed inside and slammed the door shut behind me.

What did you expect? I thought. *What did you expect, what did you expect!*

I turned my head quickly as I saw a shadow move in front of the glass, my heart leaping into my throat as Jordan reached for the door handle and blinked up at him as his face darkened with anger.

"Open the door, Lea," he said, meeting my eyes through the glass. I pulled my hands away from the steering wheel as he stood up suddenly and then leaned back over, pounding his fist against the window as his face twisted with impatience.

"Open the goddamn door!"

I watched him struggle to control his temper as he paced around to the passenger side of the car and got out as he opened the other door, slamming it hard enough to rattle the window as I stood up.

"What the fuck is wrong with you?" I asked, moving in the opposite direction when he tried to cut me off. I took an instinctive step backward as he swore under his breath, moving in a wide arc around the back of the car and reopened my door as he broke into a run, shoving it shut with one hand as he reached for me with the other.

"Running already?" he said, his fist closing around my wrist as I turned to run. "There's a first."

I jerked my hand backward and Jordan stepped with me as I slipped out of his grasp, shaking my head as he paced on the sidewalk in front of me.

"You're right. I should've just pretended that you planned that whole thing just for me!"

"I didn't invite her in."

"And that's supposed to what? Make it better? She practically crawled into your lap when I was standing there."

"You think I give a shit about some whore who fucks my friends in the back of our tour bus for kicks?"

"I don't think you were thinking about anything at all. And don't tell me you were trying to make me jealous. You didn't even know I was coming tonight."

"Don't give me that shit, Lea. I told you to be here. I *wanted* you here . . ."

"I can't believe you think I'm this stupid. I know who you are, Jordan, all right? You tell me all the fucking time."

"Then you should know that it's different with you. *I'm* different with you. But instead, you just left. You didn't even fight with me about it. You didn't even *question* it . . ."

"All I know is that the first time I turn my back, I find you in bed with some other girl. Big surprise, right? Considering how we started."

I flinched as Jordan's eyes widened with pain, a deep wave of anguish filling me as I realized that it was only going to get worse.

Once he makes that movie, that'll be it, I thought. *There'll be a thousand more girls like her in every city he plays in. How can I trust him? How can I trust him when I already know that I was a girl just like that once? Just like Abbie. Just like everyone.*

Jordan stopped moving, taking a quick breath as his eyes flew over my face and I took a step backward as he walked toward me—a deep gust of snow shifting between us in the darkness. I had another sudden vivid image of David and I laughing over lunch, his face calm and watchful when he thought I wouldn't notice and felt a sudden rush of remorse as Jordan shoved his hands deep in his pockets, as if he didn't quite trust himself to revisit the memory in a fit of anger.

"I could accuse you of the same thing. I could torture you about the way we met for the next ten years if I wanted to. But I'd never do that. Because I trust you. Trust is a *choice*, Lea."

Except that you did, I thought, the way he had let Shelly fawn all over him running through my mind before I could stop it. *You did. You did the exact same thing that I did. You just hid it better.*

That was about him, I heard. *Not you. I hate the way he thinks of you, Lea. If you only knew . . .*

"How long before it's me?" I asked quietly, barely able to put my worst fear into words, as if simply admitting it would become some kind of curse between us. "How long before I'm the one you don't want to go home to? Will cheating on me even be enough for you then? Tell me, Jordan. What's the worst thing you ever did to someone you loved?"

Jordan looked at me quickly, his face shifting with a moment of ugly, unchecked rage. I raised my hands in front of me as he stepped forward, closing my eyes as I felt his hand close around my cheek. I opened them as I felt him run it through my hair, his fingers digging into the back of my neck and exhaled quickly as he looked down at me, his eyes darting over my face with so much love and regret that I pressed my head against his chest, holding onto him tightly as his fingers curled around the back of my head.

Don't, Lea, I heard as he pulled me closer, my fingers curling around the fabric of his jacket as I felt him kiss the top of my head. *Don't use the things I tell you against me. You're not her. That's not us.*

I looked up as I felt him touch the sides of my face, his fingers warm and whisper light in the cold around us and leaned up to kiss him as he pulled me toward him with both hands, cradling the back of my head as his lips crushed against mine. I moved with him as he shifted me closer, feeding off of his warmth as he kissed me deeply and inhaled quickly as I felt his hands tug at the low front of my halter top, an image of him holding my head on the bus as we headed back to the city twisting my heart deep enough to bleed.

That's us, Lea, I heard, as his hands slid back up to my face and he kissed my lips gently for a moment as he held my body against him. *That's us.*

I closed my eyes as he kissed the side of my cheek, the image expanding to one of us chasing down the dawn on some empty stretch of desert highway, blotting out all of my fear in a sudden burst of reckless, unconditional love. *That's us.*

"I'm leaving her, Lea," he whispered against my cheek. "I'm telling her tonight. This film is going to happen. I can tell. I'll have to move there. To California. You want to run? Run with me. I don't want to be without you. I've lived almost half my life without you already."

I looked up as his eyes darted over my face, touching my lips gently for a moment as he held my eyes and let his image of us fill me up like a waking dream, all color and light and possibility—a journey with no destination.

A world without end.

Stay with me, Lea, I heard him say. *Stay with me forever. Even if I hurt you. Because I'll never mean it. Could you trust me enough to do that? Could you trust in us enough to do it? Would you if I asked?*

I trust you, I thought. *I trust you, I trust you, I trust you . . .*

"Say you'll follow me," he said, his words whispering across my lips like a kiss. "Like you did that night. I heard you. I did . . ."

"I'll follow you," I said. "I will. I trust you. I do . . ."

I wrapped my hands around his neck, holding onto him tightly as he kissed me and brushed my hands against his face as he gave me a sudden brilliant smile, leaning up on my toes as he wrapped his arms around my waist.

I love you, Lea. No matter what happens or what I say, remember that. That never changes. I'll love you forever . . .

I turned my head as I heard someone clear their throat behind us and pulled my hands away quickly as Paul stood in the parking lot, his eyes running between Jordan and I with some emotion too quick and convoluted to place. I saw Jordan's jaw harden with anger as Paul's eyes shifted to his face with something like amused contempt, and felt his hands tighten around my waist as Paul glanced away, stomping out his cigarette as he turned back toward the building.

"We're on in about five minutes. Just thought you should know."

"Yeah," Jordan said, looking back down at me as Paul glanced back at us and then turned away, running a hand through the back of his hair. "Thanks."

I bit my lip as Jordan pulled me closer again, pressing my hands against his chest and looked up at him as he tilted his head at me, his blue eyes sweeping over me as I looked away.

"Don't worry about Paul," he said, kissing the side of my head as I blinked up at him. "Tonight, all right? I meant it. It doesn't matter what he knows now."

I should go.

"No," he said, smiling a little at my expression as he kissed my lips lightly for a moment. "Stay. At least for the beginning."

"The beginning?"

Jordan slid his hand up to grab mine, squeezing it tightly as he let me go.

"You'll see," he said, smothering another grin as he held onto my hand tightly and tugged me briskly across the lot.

He laughed as I glanced at him out of the corner of my eyes and then pulled me close as we reached the front doors, pulling my sweater a little tighter around my shoulders as he kissed my forehead, his face becoming serious again.

"Inside, okay?" he said, pacing away from me backward as the late-night smokers along the front entrance turned to gawk. "Ten minutes. That's all I ask."

I bit back a smile as he turned around, heading back around the building as I slipped around the crowd at the front and paused as the doorman asked for my ID, pulling it out of my pocket as he raised his brows.

"Ophelia. I'm on the list."

He waved me through without glancing at his sheet as I swept down the front hall again and felt the weight of what he'd said fill me with a strange, panicked rush of euphoria—the idea that we were actually going to be a real couple so surreal I couldn't think of it without smiling. I wound my way through the dark crowd as I passed through the bar area again, looking for a place along the guardrail before giving up and heading down to the main floor, glancing around at the ocean of people vying for room as I searched for someplace near the back where I could watch the stage unencumbered. I ended up against the stairwell in the middle of the floor as dozens of people walked down from the floor above and brushed my hair away from my eyes as I saw the lights come up downstage.

I applauded with everyone else as the band took the stage, my heart leaping into my throat as Jordan stepped up to the microphone and watched the sweeping red and green lights cut across the floor as the crowd raised their hands as it passed—a thousand cell phones turning at once as he smiled and glanced in Terry's direction.

"Hey, Detroit," he said, low and relaxed as the crowd raised their hands and let out a sudden wild cheer. Jordan laughed a little and then made a quick motion to Paul as he moved closer to the front of the stage. "How's everyone doing tonight? Is everyone having a good time?"

I ran my hand along my collarbone as the lights behind the stage went from white to red to blue, and saw him sweep his eyes over the front of the crowd as the rhythm guitarist began to play something soft and mellow and Paul joined him at the bridge.

"That's good. Glad to hear it. This next song is actually kind of a new one for us. So, bear with us. Terry, especially."

Jordan laughed as Terry flipped him off and swept his eyes over the crowd again, a sudden bright smile lighting his face as he spotted me near the stairwell and I shook my head a little as he held my eyes for a moment, glancing downstage as his face became a little more serious.

"It's called 'Finished Now.'"

My eyes flew open as the band launched into a soft dark melody, the image of Jordan strumming his guitar at the edge of his bed racing through my mind, and wandered closer to the stage as he began to sing the song he had written for me—his voice so clear and soulful I paused in the middle of the crowd. I listened closely as he sang, his words burning through me like a world on fire, and watched the crowd sway as I realized suddenly that somewhere between fantasy and reality, I had wandered too deep—that there would no turning back after this, no pretending, no retreat. I listened to him pour out his feelings for me, not hiding anywhere, confident enough to stand at the edge of the precipice and invite me out to join him and realized that if I lost him there would simply be no replacing him—I would have to fall too.

Or watch the world burn.

I shivered as he sang the last few verses—the image of us standing on the beach hand in hand while a thousand paper lanterns filled the sky filling my mind, and held my breath as the lanterns changed around us, a dozen different nuclear bombs going off on the horizon beyond us.

Your choice, the girl in my head whispered. *Your choice, your choice, your choice.*

I bit back a smile as the song ended, brushing it away as he looked in my direction and then watched him kiss his fingers lightly as the crowd cheered, the lights at the back of the stage beginning to pulse quickly as he shrugged on his guitar. I smiled as I recognized the song, the crowd rushing toward the front of the stage as the first few notes of 'Carol of the Bells' began to fill the room and held my hands over my face as the lights swept over the crowd, so many people moving at once it was like watching the dark belly of the ocean break apart into a thousand shadows.

I tried to move backward as the crowd began to crush into me on either side, moving into a pocket of space near the back wall just as it closed in front of me and closed my eyes as the music pounded through my veins, feeling like a part of something larger than myself as the entire floor held up their hands. I watched Jordan's face as the red lights swept over him, his face calm and intense as his hands flew over the strings—and then blinked as I heard something that sounded like a firecracker go off behind me, turning my head toward the stairwell as it went off again. I heard the music falter slightly as a few people on the bar level started to scream and heard it stop abruptly as the back of the lower level ducked at once, running in every direction as I froze in place.

Gunshots, I thought, ducking down against the wall as three dozen people ran past me at once. *Those are gunshots.*

My eyes swept toward the stage as I saw Jordan run toward the front, ducking down with the crowd as the stampede of people in front of me cut off my view of him and ran toward the far exit as the echo resounded louder—turning in every direction at once as I tried to figure out where it was coming from. I closed my eyes as screams tore through the room, running with the crowd blindly as a hundred people got to the door before me and tried to step aside at the wall as two dozen bodies jostled me forward, running across the sidewalk as they headed for the other side of the street.

I felt an agony of panic as I ran with them, the blood in my veins pulsing so quickly I felt like my heart would burst and stopped when the crowd I was in began to fill up the parking lot of a closed salon lot and huddled together in the darkness, some people screaming when more shots rang out across the road. I closed my eyes as a sudden image of Jordan's face as he ran to the front of the stage filled my mind and ran back to the edge of the road as someone threw out their arm to stop me.

"My boyfriend's still inside!" I said as a guy who looked about my age yanked me back, his face furious.

"I'm sure he got out," he said, glancing at the dozen people talking on their cellphones as I scrambled for mine. "You can't help him now."

Oh my god, oh my god, oh my god . . .

I fumbled with the keys as I tried to keep my hands from shaking, my vision going blurry as I shook my head and dialed 911 as I heard the first sirens go off behind me, dropping my hand as the entire lot turned to look. I heard several people burst into tears as five police cars whipped around the corner and began to surround the building and pressed my hands over my face as I realized I was crying, kneeling down in the grass as my legs seemed to give out all at once.

Please god. Not him. Anyone but him . . .

I swallowed hard as I picked my phone back up, dropping it as a black and white photo of Jordan greeted me instantly and curled my hands into my lap, my entire body shrieking in panic as a police cruiser rolled into the lot. I glanced over my shoulder as a dozen people milled toward it at once, desperate for someone to take control and tell them what to do, and raised my shaking phone to my face again as I scrolled for Jordan's number, looking up as a young girl put her hand on my shoulder and sat down next to me.

"Don't," she said, pushing my wrist down. "I know what you're thinking. Just don't."

"I have to know," I said, blinking back tears as she wrapped her arm around my shoulders. "I have to make sure he's all right."

"He could be hiding somewhere," she said, her eyes wise beyond their years as she swept them over the chaos around us. "Trust me. I know. I've been through this before. Don't call him. I'm sure he'll be all right. I'm sure he will."

I covered my face in my hands as I burst into tears and felt a wave of blind comfort when she rested her head on my shoulder for a moment, holding me tightly as someone spoke out over a loud speaker.

"It'll be all right," she said. "It will. I promise."

JORDAN

I'VE NEVER BEEN A VERY GOOD PERSON. HEMINGWAY ONCE wrote a great quote about that and death and since I'm going to butcher it, here it is verbatim:

The world breaks everyone and afterward many are strong at the broken places. But those that will not break, it kills. It kills the very good and the very gentle and the very brave impartially. If you are none of these you can be sure it will kill you too, but there will be no special hurry.

Living the kind of life I have, that one always lent me a strange sort of comfort. I had never been all that good or decent or brave, so those words beat a pleasant mantra into the back of my mind as if they were some kind of running bargain between fate and the damned. One day I'd find myself on the wrong side of eternity, about that I had no doubt, but until then I relaxed into the idea that because I was damaged goods there was no particular reason for death to seek me out. Spiritually speaking, I was off the hook.

I know you think I'm talking about you here, Abbie, but I'm not. Believe me when I say that I felt your anguish that night, felt everything you had been burying for months in the hope that whatever madness possessed me to blow our lives apart would shake me loose and set me free. And would you even believe me if I said that part of me hoped for that too? Would you understand what I meant at all if I told you I had to kill part of myself forever in order to leave you?

What I didn't take away from that bargain was really the only other important thing, and the one that I forgot until it was almost too late. And that is that when your number is up, death will hunt you down like a predator and come for you on all fronts- open war, take no prisoners. In that moment, when the cosmic roulette wheel in the sky comes to its great and final shakedown and decides it's time to settle your account once and for all, fate doesn't really care who gets to you first.

Anyone will do.

Anyone at all.